MOUNTAIN BRIDE

"All those men couldn't take their eyes off you tonight, Coralee. And I didn't like the way they were looking at you. I knew what they were thinking, knew what they were wanting."

"So you're claimin' to be some kind of mind reader?" she scoffed.

"I'm no mind reader," John said harshly. "But I have no doubts about the thoughts and desires of all those men who were gawking at you tonight . . . because I was wanting and thinking the very same thing."

She regarded him warily. "Then I reckon you'd best tell me what it is that you're wantin'."

"I don't have the bloody patience to tell you," he snapped and then he pulled her against him. His kiss was hot and hungry, fueled by a raw, primitive need he could no longer deny . . .

Mountain Bride

SUSAN SAWYER

AVON BOOKS NEW YORK

This is a work of fiction. Names, characters, places, and incidents either are the product of the author's imagination or are used fictitiously. Any resemblance to actual events, locales, organizations, or persons, living or dead, is entirely coincidental and beyond the intent of either the author or the publisher.

AVON BOOKS
A division of
The Hearst Corporation
1350 Avenue of the Americas
New York, New York 10019

Copyright © 1997 by Susan Sawyer
Inside cover author photograph by Mary Schamehorn
Published by arrangement with the author
Visit our website at http://AvonBooks.com
Library of Congress Catalog Card Number: 97-93022
ISBN: 0-380-78479-3

First Avon Books Printing: October 1997

AVON TRADEMARK REG. U.S. PAT. OFF. AND IN OTHER COUNTRIES, MARCA REGISTRADA, HECHO EN U.S.A.

Printed in the U.S.A. —

WCD 10 9 8 7 6 5 4 3 2 1

Prologue

April 1880

"**I** don't know why you must insist on leaving so soon." Seated at the dressing table in her bedchamber, Mirabella Stratford pursed her lips into a sultry pout. "Wouldn't you rather stay here in London with me?"

"I would like nothing better, my love." Lord John Winslow looped a silk cravat around the winged collar of his starched shirt, then reached for the frock coat that he'd draped over the bedpost during the wee hours of the night. "Spending the morning in your bedchamber sounds much more appealing than traveling to Havenshire Manor."

"I wish your father hadn't seen us leaving the ball last night," Lady Stratford complained, absently running a brush through her dark hair. "If the duke hadn't caught sight of you, he wouldn't have had the chance to ask you to meet with him at Havenshire Manor this afternoon. And we could have spent several more hours together..." Her voice trailed off, and she cast a meaningful glance at the tangle of sheets strewn across the bed.

"Atrocious timing," John agreed, shrugging his broad shoulders into the dark, tailored coat. "Still, I believe it's best if I don't tarry any longer than necessary. I doubt your husband would be pleased to find a visitor in your bedchamber when he returns from France today."

"But he won't be returning until this evening. If you delayed your departure for another hour or so . . ." Mirabella's silk dressing gown swished about her bare legs as she rose from the bench and ambled toward John. ". . . I promise you won't have any regrets," she finished, coiling her arms around his neck.

"Ah, what an enchantress you are, Mirabella," John murmured, trying to ignore the heated rush of desire searing through him. "But I truly must be on my way."

Mirabella heaved a sigh of disappointment. "Until next time, then," she whispered, lifting her lips to his.

He bent his head and kissed her. "Until next time, love," he returned.

But even as he voiced the words, John knew he would not be visiting Lady Stratford's bedchamber again.

The pursuit of beautiful, desirable women was nothing more than a pleasurable game to Lord John Winslow, an idle pastime he'd mastered with the skill of a practiced artisan. Winning, of course, was the object of every game; one evening of unbridled passion was the ultimate goal, the decisive measure by which each victory was claimed.

Like a bona fide gentleman, John adhered to the standards of good sportsmanship in the game of seduction. But one evening of pleasure always marked the end of the game. After winning over his feminine opponent, Lord Winslow promptly withdrew himself from further rounds of play.

John quietly slipped out of the room and made his way down the stairs. Skillfully evading the watchful eyes of household servants, he exited through the rear door of the posh London town house.

A half hour later, he was galloping through the English countryside, heading for Havenshire Manor. But his thoughts lingered on the woman who had given herself to him with such eagerness throughout the previous evening.

"Bloody hell," he muttered, disconcerted by Mirabella's parting words. Obviously, Lady Stratford was presuming he would return to her bedchamber for a repeat performance of their heated romp between the sheets.

But that was more than Lord Winslow was willing to give to any woman.

Like so many of the married women he had known, Mirabella was weary of contending with an aging husband who gave little thought or consideration to her physical desires and needs. And John had been more than happy to provide the lovely Mirabella with a passion-drenched night of sinful pleasure.

But experience had taught Lord Winslow that re-stricting the number of encounters with the same woman prevented anyone from penetrating the barriers around his heart. Over the years, John had discovered that the game of seduction was much easier—and much more amusing—if he viewed the process as a form of entertainment rather than an emotional commitment. Playing to win had become the guiding philosophy behind his favorite pastime of luring desirable women into bed.

Now, plundering through the English country-side on horseback, John threw back his head and laughed. Considering half the females in London were willing to share their beds with him, why should he risk losing his heart to one woman? And with endless opportunities to sample a variety of available goods in the marketplace, why should he limit himself to the same fare every night?

All of life, he reminded himself, was simply a game. And victories were awaiting only the most skillful of players.

Two hours after departing London, John crested a hill that overlooked the site of Havenshire Manor, his family's country estate.

He paused, sweeping his gaze over the familiar setting. Rolling hillsides and greening fields were blossoming with the first signs of spring. Budding trees and flowers dotted the landscape with splashes of color, while neatly trimmed hedges and well-manicured gardens lined the various walk-ways that connected the small buildings on the estate with the magnificent manor house.

Though the imposing manor had been built of gray stone and mortar more than two centuries before, there was an ageless beauty about the place, a sense of tradition and elegance that defied the passage of time. For six generations, the estate had remained in the hands of the Winslow family. And someday, the manor and all that surrounded it would belong to ... *Alexander*.

John shrugged. Nothing he could do or say could change the inevitable. His older brother was the rightful heir to the Havenshire title and fortune. Eventually, Havenshire Manor and the bulk of the Winslow wealth would be passed down to Alexander and his descendants. Under the British rules of primogeniture, John, the second-born son of Edward Winslow, the sixth Duke of Havenshire, was entitled to little or nothing from his family's estate.

A warm breeze, fragrant with the scent of spring blossoms, billowed through the air. John shifted uneasily in the saddle, suddenly mindful of the reason behind his father's request for a meeting with him.

Each time the seasons changed, the duke summoned John to the library at Havenshire Manor for the sole purpose of discussing his future. In the four years since John had completed his studies at Cambridge, the duke had become increasingly distraught about his son's lack of interest in establishing an honorable profession for himself. Time after time, Edward Winslow had encouraged his son to utilize his skills and talents as a solicitor.

But the prospect of pleading cases in stuffy court-rooms, day after day, year after year, held no appeal to Lord Winslow. John had no intention of subjecting himself to the torture of being cooped up in an oppressive court of law for the rest of his life. As far as he was concerned, assuming the role of a solicitor would be a fate worse than death.

Steeling himself for another verbal battle with his father, John tightened his grip on the reins and headed for the manor.

Just as he stepped into the foyer, two women, chattering in animated tones, appeared at the top of the curving staircase. Both were wearing small-brimmed hats with colorful plumes that matched the hues of their fashionable gowns.

John grinned as his mother and sister descended the stairs. "Embarking on another of your shopping expeditions, I presume," he surmised aloud.

"Anytime is a good time for shopping, my dear." The Duchess of Havenshire swept across the foyer with a regal grace. "Sabrina and I have planned a short trip into the village this afternoon."

"We're hoping to find a few accessories for my spring wardrobe." Lady Winslow adjusted the tilt of her hat over her dark hair. "I desperately need some decent bonnets and gloves and slippers for the coming season."

John bit back a smile. At seventeen, Sabrina already owned more hats and gloves and slippers than most women could hope to wear in a lifetime. But she was vividly aware of the importance of her appearance in London society, and her choice of apparel reflected her status in life. Even now, she was impeccably dressed for an afternoon excursion, wearing a stunning gown in a vivid shade of blue that emphasized the beauty of her fair complexion and dark hair.

Undoubtedly, his sister would do well for herself, John thought. Sabrina knew what was expected of her, and she adhered to the unspoken rules of London society with the utmost charm and grace. For a wealthy viscount or marquess in search of a suitable bride, Lady Winslow would be the perfect candidate.

"I suppose a lady can't have too many accessories to complement her outfits," he mused with a devilish wink. "Especially when she's hoping to snare the attention of an acceptable suitor on a permanent basis."

"You heartless scoundrel." The hint of a smile appeared on Sabrina's lips. "A lady doesn't want the world to know about her intentions, brother dear. And if you utter one word about my hopes of finding a suitable husband this year, I shall cheerfully strangle you!"

John clutched his neck in mock horror. "You would strangle me . . . for telling the truth?"

"Of course I would." Sabrina laughed. "It's not becoming for a lady to appear anxious about the prospects of marriage, even if everyone knows—"

The rumble of carriage wheels and the clop of horses' hooves cut off the rest of Sabrina's thought. John bolted across the foyer and hurled open the door. A shiny carriage embellished with the Winslow crest rolled to a stop in front of the manor. The driver hopped down from his perch to help the ladies into the carriage.

Sabrina scooped up her skirts and rushed outside, obviously anxious to begin her afternoon of shopping. "I do hope the village merchants have a good selection of spring merchandise," she murmured.

The duchess turned to John. "I hope the meeting with your father goes well today, dear. He's extremely concerned about your future." She patted his cheek with a gloved hand. "You don't have all the advantages that Alexander has, you know."

John saw the concern glinting from his mother's eyes, felt the affection in the touch of her hand. Wanting to ease her worries, he bent his head and whispered into her ear. "But everyone knows I have one major advantage over Alexander," he insisted. "No one can deny that I'm much better looking than my older brother."

That brought a smile to her lips. "And you've been blessed with the Winslow sense of humor, too."

After the duchess was comfortably settled in the carriage beside Sabrina, John bid farewell to the women and retreated into the manor. He had just ripped off his hat and leather riding gloves when a stout man with a receding hairline scrambled up to greet him.

"Welcome home, my lord."

John acknowledged the valet's greeting with a

dip of his head. "Is my father waiting for me in the library?"

George nodded. "His Grace will be pleased to know you've returned from London. He has been quite anxious to see you."

"I suppose I shouldn't detain the duke any longer." John's laughter was cynical and low. "I had every intention of leaving London at the break of dawn, but the hospitality of my hostess was rather difficult to resist."

"I understand, my lord." George nervously cleared his throat. "Shall I set out a fresh change of clothes for you?"

"That won't be necessary." In a hurried attempt to make himself presentable to the duke, John raked a hand through his dark, tousled hair, then brushed off the dust that had settled on his jacket during the ride from London. "But I would like for you to prepare my golfing attire. If time permits after meeting with my father, I would enjoy traipsing across the golf links this afternoon."

"Certainly, my lord." George turned and scurried up the staircase.

John inhaled a deep, steadying breath, mentally preparing himself for a confrontation with the duke, and opened the massive library door. But he'd taken only one step into the room when he stopped cold, startled by what he saw.

He'd expected his father to greet him with a scowl or a disgruntled glare. But Edward Winslow, Duke of Havenshire, was actually *smiling*, acting as if he were genuinely glad to see his younger son.

"Come in, John," the duke invited. "I've been quite anxious to talk with you."

Disconcerted by his father's cheerful welcome, John frowned. Obviously, his future was not the subject that his father wished to discuss. The duke *never* smiled when he was contemplating the topic of John's future.

Other differences in the duke's demeanor puzzled John, as well. Instead of pacing the length of the library, wringing his hands in dismay, the duke was seated in his favorite winged chair, contentedly puffing on an aromatic cigar. Behind him, ribbons of April sunlight were streaming through the massive library window, highlighting the smoky rings that drifted above his head and wreathed him in an aura of serenity and peacefulness.

Although perplexed by his father's unexpected demeanor, John had no desire to spoil his jubilant mood. Planting a pleasant smile on his lips, John crossed the length of the room with bold, confident strides. "Splendid day, isn't it?"

"Without a doubt, it's one of the finest days I've seen in months." Edward rose from his chair and retrieved a decanter from the table beside the window. "And it's a splendid afternoon for indulging in a taste of fine brandy, as well."

As the duke poured the dark liquid into a pair of snifters, John couldn't help but notice that he and his father shared many similar features. Both of them possessed piercing blue eyes with dark, thick brows, deep clefts in their chins, and the same broad-shouldered build that had been predominant among males in the House of Winslow for generations.

But there were notable differences between them, too. Though jet-black hair crowned the young lord's head, the tides of time had streaked the duke's dark hair with gray. John stood taller than his father, stretching at least three inches above Edward's height of six feet. And while an increasing lack of physical activity had softened the duke's once-firm physique, John's muscles were toned, hard, sculpted to perfection from endless hours of rigorous sporting endeavors.

"Have a seat, son," the duke invited, offering one of the snifters to John.

"This isn't exactly what I expected," John admitted uneasily, accepting the brandy. "I assumed you wanted to discuss the matter of my future this afternoon. But I've never known you to approach the topic with such eagerness. As I recall, the subject has never been one of your favorite topics of discussion."

"True." Edward chuckled as he settled down in his favorite winged chair. "But, then, I've never known what to do with the likes of you . . . until now."

John sank into the nearest chair, preparing himself for another lecture. "Nothing has changed since our last discussion, Father. The most obvious course for my future—the profession of law—holds no appeal to me. Medicine is out of the question, as well, considering that my stomach churns at the mere mention of letting blood or purging patients.

And I'm far too much of a scoundrel to be a candidate for the priesthood."

"But there comes a time in every man's life when he must assume responsibility for his future," the duke countered in a calm, quiet tone.

"I'm certain I can procure some sort of honorable profession for myself when the opportunity presents itself." John's fingers tightened around the stem of the snifter. "After all, I am the son of a duke. It's not as if I belong to the working class."

"No one can argue that your lineage is impeccable, son." The duke sipped his brandy. "But you've always known Alexander will be the one who inherits my estate and title."

"Everyone knows a man's fortune lies in the order of his birth," John returned smoothly. "Even the ladies are acutely aware of the importance of marrying a firstborn son. Already, Sabrina is—"

"Your sister should have little trouble in procuring an acceptable title for herself. It's your destiny— not Sabrina's—that troubles me, John. If you would agree to take a suitable bride—a woman with a substantial dowry who could support your standing as a gentleman of privilege—your dilemma could be solved quite easily. Yet scores of acceptable ladies have been clamoring after you for years, and you haven't shown the slightest inclination to wed any of them."

John lifted one shoulder in a careless shrug. "I prefer the company of more mature women. Most of the acceptable young ladies are babbling fools."

"But if you intend to remain a gentleman of privilege, you must find the means for supporting your indulgences." The tip of Edward's cigar glowed with an amber hue. "Do you honestly believe you can secure a bright future for yourself in London's gaming halls?"

John bristled with irritation. Contrary to his father's opinion, he bore no resemblance to the carefree, irresponsible rogues who held little regard for anything other than the frivolities of life. In fact, he'd reaped a small fortune at the gaming tables in recent weeks, far more than he could earn in a year's time as a solicitor. And he'd even invested a portion of his winnings in several financial ventures, hoping to increase the size of his investments in the coming years.

Yet, there was no need to tell the duke about his stroke of good fortune. Edward Winslow was a staunch opponent of gambling, and he would not be pleased to learn that his son had acquired a hefty sum of money at the gaming tables.

"Actually, I've done rather well for myself," John finally offered, choosing his words with care. "In fact, I've been blessed with good fortune of late."

"But Lady Luck doesn't guarantee that she'll stand by your side all the time," the duke countered. "In the past four years, you've done nothing with your life other than enjoy the privileges reserved for gentlemen of good standing in the British aristocracy. And I'm convinced you would be more inclined to establish a sound future for yourself if you were living in America instead of England."

"America?" The notion was so preposterous that John nearly laughed aloud. Had the duke lost hold of his senses? Worse yet, had a strong dose of spirits addled his brain? "Surely you jest, Father. I saw everything America has to offer during my last trip abroad, and nothing about the bloody place appealed to me. It's far too uncivilized for someone with British blood pumping through his veins."

"But a new British colony in America is attracting a great deal of attention on both sides of the Atlantic," Edward revealed.

"A British colony?" John echoed in disbelief. "As I recall, our last attempt at creating a colony in America ended in disaster about a century ago."

"This colony is quite different," Edward explained. "It's been created for the express purpose of giving well-educated men like yourself the freedom of pursuing their own destinies without restrictions from society. The colony contains an atmosphere of culture and refinement, an environment for stimulating intellectual and cultural pursuits. At the same time, colonists have the chance to explore the opportunities that America offers to everyone."

John took a hefty gulp of brandy. From all indications, his father held a keen interest in this absurd scheme. And he suspected the duke intended to spark his interest in the concept, as well.

But John couldn't imagine himself living in a colony situated in a foreign land. After all, he was accustomed to the finest that life had to offer. He couldn't fathom life without servants catering to his whims, fine wines at every meal, or an ample selection of beautiful women at his disposal.

"Surely you don't think I belong in this new colony," John finally contended.

Edward puffed on his cigar for a long moment. "As a matter of fact, I think you would be an excellent candidate for this new British venture in America."

A sickening feeling rolled through John. He'd heard that some gentlemen were encouraging their younger sons to establish new lives for themselves in America. But he never suspected his own father, the Duke of Havenshire, would consider the idea of banishing his younger son from the motherland.

"You're sending me into exile, then." John couldn't suppress the anger in his voice. "You're casting me aside like some—"

"I'm not doing anything of the sort." A shadow of sadness flickered across Edward's face. "I have no desire to banish you from my life, John. You're my son, and I want nothing but the best for your future."

"Then why do you want me to go to America?"

"To take charge of your own destiny." Edward heaved a weary sigh. "You must think of your future, John."

"I can take charge of my destiny without leaving England," John argued. "I have no desire to live in some fledgling colony halfway across the world."

"But you haven't heard about the opportunities that are awaiting you there." The duke leaned forward in his chair. "The colony board has secured thousands of acres in Tennessee for the settlement, and colonists can purchase tracts of land from the board for establishing their homes and livelihoods. I'm convinced that the colonists who purchase prime parcels will make handsome profits for themselves as the colony grows and prospers. In fact, I'm one of the major investors in the venture. And if you agree to manage my investments in the colony, I will provide you with a generous monthly stipend for your trouble."

John regarded his father with interest. He hadn't realized the duke had provided capital for launching the venture. Perhaps there was more credence to the project than he'd realized. "You want me to oversee your investments in the colony?"

The duke nodded. "And I want you to create a fulfilling life for yourself, too. With your monthly remittance, you should have more than enough money to purchase some of the most desirable parcels in the settlement. What you do with the land, of course, is your decision. You could let the acreage to other colonists—further increasing your income—or you could hold on to your investment until the time is ripe for reselling. But you could also establish a business or build your own home on the property."

John lapsed into silence, absorbing his father's words. He'd heard of the vast fortunes being made in America. Men like John Rockefeller and Cornelius Vanderbilt were building vast empires in the New World. Untold riches were waiting for the man with an eye for wise investments and the determination to take advantage of the rich resources in his surroundings.

"I assume the colony is fully operational, then," John surmised.

"The formal opening will take place in the fall, but a number of Englishmen have already become residents of the new colony," the duke explained. "A grand hotel and a fine restaurant in the colony are providing temporary accommodations for new residents until they can get settled into new homes. And 'Rugby' has been chosen as the name for the settlement in honor of the school here in England, the alma mater of one of the colony's founders."

"A touch of merry old England in America," John quipped.

"With a name like 'Rugby,' it's unlikely the colonists will forget their British heritage," the duke remarked. "It's my understanding that Rugby resembles an English village of sorts. Since it's located a short distance from Cincinnati, Ohio, I suspect residents can travel into the city to attend a symphony or opera or the like, much in the same way that we journey from Havenshire to London."

Over the course of the next hour, Edward continued to elaborate on the British settlement. John learned that an abundance of minerals, timber, and wildlife in the region provided colonists with the means of becoming a self-sufficient community. He heard about the detailed designs of English gardens and parks in the colony. He discovered that the climate was superb, the scenery breathtaking, the cuisine divine.

"And it's not as if you'll be living among strangers," the duke pointed out. "More than likely, you'll know many of the colonists. Already several of my acquaintances have arranged for their younger sons to become residents of Rugby."

John shifted uneasily in his chair. For some unexplainable reason, the insane notion of carving out a successful life for himself in America appealed to him in a way that nothing else ever had.

He suspected that building an empire of prosperity would not demand a large investment of his time. With his knowledge and skills, it was feasible he could accumulate a small fortune within the span of several months. At the very most, he could afford to devote one year of his life to creating a secure future for himself. And along the way, he could prove to everyone—even his own father—that he possessed far more ingenuity and determination than they suspected.

If he agreed to become part of this new venture, he could view the entire undertaking as a game. Winning, of course, would be his highest priority. And victory would be measured by the size of the fortune he was able to create.

"So are you in agreement to my proposal?" the duke probed.

John drew in a deep breath, reminding himself that the odds of winning were stacked in his favor. "I'll agree to this arrangement on one condition, Father. As soon as I make my fortune in America, I shall be free to return to England and resume my life here as Lord John Winslow."

"An excellent plan, my son. I'm certain you will have no regrets." The duke smiled triumphantly. "In all honesty, I'm delighted you've agreed to become part of this venture. It will give me a wonderful excuse for taking a look at Rugby for myself."

John's brows rose in surprise. "You're planning to visit the colony?"

The duke nodded. "Your mother and I have already agreed to visit you when the colony officially opens its doors this fall. Sabrina, no doubt, will accompany us."

"You must have been quite certain I would agree to your proposal." John grinned. "You're already planning to travel to Rugby, and I haven't even left England yet!"

"You'll be leaving soon enough. In fact, you need to tie up all your affairs within the next few days. Bid good-bye to your friends and acquaintances, as well. You'll be setting sail for America next week." The duke rose from the chair. "I have every confidence that you shall succeed in your endeavors, son."

"And I have every intention of doing so, Your Grace." John sprang to his feet and held up his snifter of brandy. "To the future."

Edward lifted his glass and offered a final toast. "And to your new life . . . in America."

Chapter 1

May 1880
Morgan County, Tennessee

Surely there had been some mistake.

Lord John Winslow tightened his grip on the reins as he guided his horse over the steep mountain trail. After two hours of trekking through the dense forests of the Cumberland Plateau, he was convinced the Duke of Havenshire had been woefully misinformed about Rugby's close proximity to Cincinnati. If his father's assumptions had been correct, he should have reached the British colony long before now.

He stared straight ahead, casting a suspicious glare at Clell Thornton, the bearded mountain guide who proclaimed to know "every whoop and holler 'round these parts like the back of my hand." At the moment, Clell was cautiously maneuvering his mule and wagon over the rugged terrain, seemingly unaware that the mule's lumbering gait was becoming a major source of irritation for John.

Perhaps Clell had taken a wrong turn somewhere along the trail, inadvertently lengthening the journey to Rugby, John speculated. But the notion vanished from his mind when he noticed the sagging framework of Clell's wagon. Laden with an assortment of trunks, crates, and mail pouches, the wagon creaked and groaned beneath the weight of its heavy load. No doubt, the cargo had considerably slowed their pace through the mountain gaps and passes.

Still, John had never dreamed the last leg of his journey would span the course of an entire afternoon. And he'd never fathomed he would be traveling through an untamed wilderness.

All traces of civilization had disappeared as soon as he'd departed Sedgemoor Station, the closest train depot to the British colony. For a time, John held hope of finding a quaint little British village just around the next bend as he'd ventured through the remote region. But now he wondered if he would ever set foot in civilization again.

John stole a glance at his companions, wondering if they were as frustrated as he. "I do hope this chap knows where he's going," he grumbled.

Lord Adam Barrington emitted an unlordly-sounding grunt of displeasure. "I just hope he knows where we are."

"I had no idea we were venturing into uncharted territory," Lord Grant Montgomery admitted with an uneasy laugh.

"Maybe this charming fellow decided to take us on the scenic route," John muttered.

Until that afternoon, Lord Winslow's journey had been rather enjoyable. The seas had been calm, the weather pleasant, during the twelve-day voyage across the Atlantic on the American Line steamer *Illinois*. And along the way, John discovered that two of his fellow passengers—Grant and Adam—were also bound for the British colony of Rugby.

Like John, both men were the second sons of well-respected lords, raised in the exclusive world of privilege and wealth reserved for members of the British aristocracy. They shared John's concerns and questions about establishing new lives for themselves in Rugby, and they agreed with his contention that their most pressing priority as new colonists was the procurement of able-bodied servants—particularly valets, cooks, housekeepers, and laundresses—to tend to their personal needs.

After the *Illinois* docked in Philadelphia, John ventured on to Cincinnati by rail with his new traveling companions, seizing the opportunity to learn more about each of the two lords.

From the start, John had taken an immediate liking to Lord Grant Montgomery. Though Grant's muscular, stocky build resembled the physique of a bull, his mild temperament and pleasant demeanor bore not a hint of bullish traits.

Forthright and honest, the sandy-haired lord readily admitted that he hoped to find a new direction for his life in Rugby. A theological scholar during his days at Oxford, Grant had intended to devote his life to the work of the church. But a growing disillusionment with the effects of his ministry had prompted him to relinquish his clerical robes and set sail for the British colony.

Despite Grant's placid composure, John wondered if the former minister had truly resolved the issues that had provoked his resignation from the church. Each time Grant spoke of his ministry, his eyes and voice were tainted with traces of regret.

Grant's thoughtful, considerate ways contrasted sharply with the guarded deportment of Lord Adam Barrington. At times, the rigid stance of Adam's tall, lean frame bore the uncanny likeness of a mountain cat poised to attack an approaching predator at any moment.

John scarcely noticed Adam's constant habit of wearing gloves until he caught a rare glimpse of the scarred flesh that marred the palm and back side of his left hand. Though Adam revealed that his hand had been burned severely during a disastrous fire that had claimed the life of his wife, he offered no further details about the tragedy. Still, John sensed the tragic event was the reason behind Adam's cynical—and sometimes bitter—attitude toward life.

In spite of Adam's shortcomings, however, his dry sense of humor and cryptic remarks provided a steady supply of laughter and good-natured camaraderie during the journey to Cincinnati. By the time the threesome arrived in the Ohio city, strong bonds of friendship had been forged among them.

During their brief stay in Cincinnati, the men purchased horses for their personal use in Rugby, then arranged to transport the animals by boxcar on the same train that would take them to the Cumberland Mountains.

It was mid-afternoon by the time the train chugged to a stop at Sedgemoor Station. A scrawny mountain man with a mail pouch strapped over his shoulder stood on the wooden platform, awaiting the arrival of the day's incoming mail.

As the British lords asked the conductor for directions to Rugby, the mountain man announced they were welcome to accompany him as he ventured back to Rugby with the daily mail. Eager to reach their final destination, John and his comrades hastily accepted Clell's offer. A few moments later, they were plundering through the mountain wilderness, following Clell's lead over the winding trail.

Now, weary of roaming through the endless maze of trees and mountains, John clenched his jaw in frustration. "How much longer before we reach Rugby, Clell?" he called out, his voice ringing with impatience.

"Now, don't you young fellas be gettin' yourselves in a tizzy," Clell cautioned, his words coated with a thick, twangy accent sounding like none other that John had ever heard. "We'll be gettin' there in a spell or two."

John grimaced. He had no idea how lengthy a "spell" was, but he had the feeling it was much too long to pacify him.

The murmur of male voices and the clop of horses' hooves drifted across the mountain slope, shattering the sylvan silence of the May afternoon. Coralee Hayes dropped a handful of wild berries into her willow basket, startled by the sounds wafting through the air.

Crouched beside a large blackberry bush, Coralee peeled back the branches and peered through the opening. Just as her gaze dropped to the narrow pass at the base of the mountain slope, a mule-drawn wagon rattled around the bend.

Coralee wasn't surprised to see that Clell Thornton was returning from his daily mail run to Sedgemoor Station. But she was astonished by the amount of cargo crammed into the bed of his wagon. Numerous trunks and crates were rattling against the wagon's sideboards as Clell prodded his mule over the winding trail.

She was still staring in disbelief at the load of baggage when three men on horseback came into view. The strangers surveyed their surroundings with interest as they trailed behind the wagon, talking among themselves in hushed tones.

Coralee edged forward, her curiosity mounting. The strangers were wearing the finest clothes she'd ever seen, garments bearing little resemblance to the simple homespun clothing worn by mountain residents. Their dark jackets and trousers were tailored to perfection, and black ties were draped around the stiff, winged collars of their snowy-white shirts. Fancy bowler hats were perched atop their heads, and gleaming leather boots were tucked into their stirrups.

She narrowed her eyes. Who were these strangers?

And then it hit her. *The Englishmen.*

For months, Coralee had been hearing about the foreigners who planned to create a colony and make homes for themselves in Morgan County, Tennessee. In fact, her family and neighbors had talked of little else in recent weeks.

More than twenty mountain natives, including Coralee's three brothers, had been hired by the British group to help with the construction of new buildings in the colony. Even Coralee's uncle, Paul Proffitt, a master carpenter from Boston who had been born and raised in Morgan County, had moved back to the Cumberland Plateau with his wife and daughter to supervise the construction projects in Rugby.

In recent days, Coralee had learned that a dozen or so of the Englishmen had already arrived to prepare for the official opening of the new settlement. But this was her first glimpse of the strangers who were invading her native land. And she was astounded by what she saw. Never in her twenty-four years had Coralee seen any man dressed in such finery.

"Get a look-see at this, ladies." Coralee glanced over her shoulder, catching the attention of her two cousins as they gleaned the last of the berries from an unusually large blackberry bush. "You've never seen the like in all your born days!"

Maggie McCarter, an auburn-haired beauty of seventeen, glanced up in surprise. Setting aside her basket of freshly picked berries, she hiked up her skirts and scampered over to Coralee. "What's goin' on?"

Rachel Proffitt followed closely on Maggie's heels, her diminutive form moving through the maze of blackberry bushes with an easy grace. Settling down beside her cousins, she stole a glance at the approaching strangers. "Some more Englishmen are arriving, it appears."

"But just look at them!" Coralee struggled to keep her voice to a whisper. "They're all dressed up in their fancy go-to-meetin' clothes."

Rachel laughed. "All English gentlemen dress that way, Coralee. Appearances are very important to them."

Waves of golden hair tumbled over Coralee's shoulders as she shook her head in disbelief. "But you'd think they were gettin' ready to pay a call on the Queen of England!"

"They probably know the queen," Rachel mused. "Pa says their families are very, very rich, and they can afford lots of fine clothes for themselves."

Coralee leaned back on her heels, appreciative of Rachel's knowledge about the Englishmen and their ways. A resident of Boston for nearly a decade, Rachel knew more about worldly matters than anyone Coralee had ever known. And in the year since she'd returned to Morgan County with her parents, she'd acquired a considerable amount of information about the developing British colony through her father's daily contacts in the settlement.

But there was more to Rachel than her worldly manner, Coralee readily conceded. Small and petite with dark hair and dark eyes, Rachel had blossomed into a polished, well-mannered young woman of twenty who possessed a cheerful nature and an optimistic attitude toward life.

Maggie cut through the silence with a troubled sigh, breaking Coralee's train of thought. "I heard tell these Englishmen's daddies are sendin' them here, but for the life of me, I can't figure out why. They must have done somethin' terrible wrong for their families to ship them all the way across the ocean from England."

"Not necessarily." Rachel tucked an errant strand of dark hair behind her ear. "From what I've heard, the Englishmen are eager to establish new homes here in Rugby. They're hoping to create a better future for themselves."

"Well, I guess that makes sense," Maggie mused. "But why do they need to build a whole town?"

"Because they're expecting hundreds of settlers to live in the colony," Rachel replied.

"Hundreds?" Astonished, Coralee slowly turned to face her cousin. "Are you certain about that?"

Rachel nodded. "The Englishmen believe this will be a real town someday, if everything works out like they want it to."

Maggie wrinkled her nose. "What do you think about all this, Coralee?"

"I don't rightly know what to think, Maggie," Coralee admitted frankly. "We've had these mountains all to ourselves for a long time, and we haven't seen many strangers passin' through. It might take us a spell to get used to havin' these Englishmen as neighbors. They look like they're mighty different from us."

Maggie stole another glance at the strangers. "They look pretty fine to me," she observed with a giggle. "Who knows? If our homeboys figure these foreigners are movin' into their territory, maybe they'll quit dillydallyin' around and take a notion to do some serious courtin'."

"Or maybe the Englishmen will take a fancy to do some courtin' of their own," Coralee said, giving Maggie a playful nudge. "You'd like that, wouldn't you, Maggie?"

"I can't think of nothin' I'd like any better." Maggie's eyes took on a wistful glow as she twirled an unruly strand of auburn hair around her finger. "I'd love for some fancy Englishman to come callin' on me. Maybe he'd take me away from this place and show me all the things in the world I'd like to see."

Coralee's teasing grin faded away. Headstrong and restless, Maggie was determined to escape from the drudgeries of working on the family farm. And her budding curiosity about the ways of a man and a woman had only intensified her restless yearnings in recent months.

Maggie heaved another sigh. "If these Englishmen take a fancy to anyone around here, I suspect it will be you, Coralee. When you walked into the meetin'house last Sunday, I heard some of the fellas say you were the prettiest creature they'd ever laid eyes on."

Coralee felt a heated blush rise to her cheeks. Over the years, she'd paid little mind to the butter-mouthed suitors who'd attempted to win her affections. In fact, it was difficult to keep from laughing aloud at their silver-tongued flattery. More than once, she'd heard that her eyes were as green as the lush mountain forests, her hair more golden than the setting sun. She'd even been told her lips were the exact shade of the wild scarlet azaleas that blossomed along the mountainsides in the spring-time.

Though she gave little credence to all the cajol-ery, Coralee found no reason to complain about what the good Lord had given her. God had blessed her with an ample bosom, a tiny waist, and a pair of long legs that had become shapely and strong from endless hours of hiking over the moun-tain trails. But none of that meant her appearance might be appealing to an Englishman.

Still, Maggie continued to press the issue. "Be-sides, the fellas 'round here have been fallin' all over themselves to get a chance to court you ever since Reuben passed on," she insisted.

"But I'm not hankerin' to find me a new man, Maggie," Coralee returned. "It's time for you and Rachel to have a turn at gettin' hitched. I already know what it's like to be a married woman."

But I don't know what it's like to be married to a good, decent man.

Unbidden images of Reuben flashed through her

mind, but Coralee refused to dwell on the unpleasant memories. She was far wiser than the naive girl who had married Reuben Hayes some six years before, and she had no intention of repeating her mistakes.

Her gaze drifted back to the three riders who were trailing behind Clell's wagon. The strangers were closer now, so close that Coralee could see their faces. But the instant she glanced at the first stranger, everything else in her range of vision faded away.

The man was alarmingly handsome. Dark hair peeked out from beneath his hat, and his eyes were a piercing shade of blue. Every feature of his clean-shaven face—the broad width of his jaw, the deep cleft in his chin, the straight line of his nose—formed an intriguing combination that totally mesmerized Coralee.

But there was more—much more—about him that fascinated her. There was something akin to a regal bearing in the set of his broad shoulders, a touch of haughtiness in the tilt of his head. Coralee even detected an air of determination in the thrust of his chin.

Captivated, she sprang to her feet to get a better view of the passing stranger. But just as she peered over the top of the blackberry bush, the man turned his head and glanced up at her.

Their gazes met and locked. Tension crackled through the air. Coralee froze, stunned by the power of the man's riveting gaze and the overwhelming sensations swirling through her.

With forced effort, she jerked her gaze away from the stranger and tried to calm her racing heart. Forcing a strained smile onto her lips, she reached for her basket of berries.

"I reckon we should be gettin' on home," she advised her cousins. "It's gettin' close to sundown, and there won't be a speck of daylight left before long."

As Maggie and Rachel scrambled to their feet, Coralee turned to leave, never once looking back at the passing stranger.

For one spellbinding moment, John wondered if he were hallucinating.

The last thing he'd expected to see on the side of the trail was a woman. Especially a woman with a glorious mane of golden hair tumbling over her shoulders, a woman whose beauty was so overwhelming that he could scarcely catch his breath.

Enthralled, John watched in stunned silence as the woman whirled and scampered up the mountain slope with two companions at her side. In the next instant, she had disappeared from sight, vanishing into a thicket of trees at the top of the slope.

"Did you see that?" John peered over at Adam and Grant, disheartened to discover that the men had been immersed in conversation, too preoccupied by their discussion to catch even a fleeting glimpse of the woman and her companions.

Adam frowned in confusion. "See what?"

John gave a careless shrug. "It was nothing, I suppose." He shifted his weight in the saddle, determined to banish the unsettling vision from his mind.

As they continued their trek through the narrow gaps and passes, John noticed a misty haze settling over the mountains. Aware that daylight was rapidly fading, he hoped they would arrive at their destination before nightfall.

A few moments later, Clell's wagon veered from the trail and rattled over a cleared patch of land. John followed closely behind the wagon, somewhat startled when two frame buildings came into view. Both structures were trimmed with wide porches and stone chimneys, but the larger of the two buildings contained a pair of dormers.

Clell halted in front of the smaller structure. "Reckon you folks could use some vittles about now," he mumbled, hopping down from the wagon.

John grimaced. He didn't want vittles. He wanted *food*. God only knew what vittles were. He wanted shepherd's pie, plum pudding, or a hearty serving of biscuits and jam. Vittles did not sound the least bit appetizing to him.

"Thank God we stumbled onto this place." Adam quickly dismounted. "I'm starving."

"How much longer before we get to Rugby, Clell?" Grant asked.

The mountain man's laughter echoed through the surrounding forest. "Why, you're smack-dab in the middle of it!"

Grant's jaw dropped. "This is . . . Rugby?"

"But this couldn't possibly be Rugby." Adam's eyes narrowed with suspicion. "There should be more to the colony than two buildings. Where's the rest of the settlement?"

"It's all around you, young fella." Clell spread out his arms. "Forty thousand acres of the prettiest country you'll ever see. And all of it's just waitin' for you."

Aghast, John stared at his surroundings in stunned disbelief. Where was the quaint British village that his father had so eloquently described?

A knot coiled in his gut. Beyond the two buildings, he saw nothing but masses of trees and mountains amid the misty haze and approaching twilight.

"Now, this here's the dinin' hall," Clell continued on. "My little woman does all the cookin' here, and I'd be willin' to bet my last dollar that you won't find no better vittles anywhere this side of the Mississippi."

One glimpse at his companions told John that Grant and Adam were as stunned as he. Still reeling in shock, John slowly dismounted.

Clell bounded onto the porch and hurled open the door. "Hitch up your horses, fellas, and come get your vittles for the evenin'."

Too numb to protest, John tied his horse to a nearby tree. But as soon as he entered the building, he stopped cold. Not even the servants at Havenshire Manor were obliged to dine in such ghastly conditions.

Rugby's sole dining establishment—the glorified "restaurant" of John's expectations—bore no resemblance to the lavish banquet facilities frequented by the British gentry in England. Formally dressed waiters and elegant place settings were notably absent here.

Nothing but long, barren tables of splintered wood, flanked by primitive benches of equal length, lined the one-room structure. Instead of being seated and served, patrons were expected to fetch their own meals. Diners were lined up along one wall, tin plates and mugs in hand, waiting to file past a hunchbacked mountain woman who was ladling the evening fare from a huge black kettle.

John edged his way into the hall, Grant and Adam close behind him. Every man in the room, he noticed, wore garments that resembled the clothes of the British working class—dark blue jerseys or plain shirts, breeches, and long boots. Yet, snippets of British accents told John that the crowd was comprised of Englishmen.

A sickening feeling rolled through him as he edged his way to the front of the serving line. In lieu of an enticing selection of foods, the menu for the evening consisted of one dish—some sort of cabbage concoction flavored with a mysterious, unidentifiable meat.

He had just settled down at one of the tables, Adam and Grant seated across from him, when a stout man came up beside them. "Welcome to Rugby," the man said in a distinctively British voice. "I'm Daniel Yarby, manager of the colony."

After the trio of British lords had introduced themselves, Daniel nodded with approval. "We've been expecting you. The colony board in London sent word that you would be arriving this month, and we've already prepared your living quarters."

John breathed a sigh of relief. After experiencing the horrors of the dining hall, he welcomed the opportunity to enjoy the comforts of a newly constructed inn. But his visions of a luxurious poster bed with plump pillows vanished as Daniel led the way from the dining hall and came to a halt in front of the framed building with dormers.

"Our new inn is still under construction," Daniel revealed. "At the moment, the cottage is our only source of lodging. The rooms on the first floor are already occupied, but we've reserved a large space for the three of you on the second floor."

John trudged up the narrow stairs, fully expecting that the basic necessities for sleeping—a mattress, some feather pillows, and a coverlet or two—would be waiting for him.

But when he entered the room, he stopped cold, mortified by what he saw. Suspended from the rafters were tangles of ropes knotted together to form something akin to huge swinging cradles.

Hammocks.

Adam groaned. "Good Lord."

Grant shook his head in disbelief. "What have we gotten ourselves into?"

John set his lips into a firm, hard line. "Hell, I believe."

Chapter 2

~~~~~

"Can you imagine what our friends and family in England would say if they could see this place?" Seated on the bank of a mountain stream, John idly tossed a pebble into the water.

A few feet away, Adam stared into the depths of the creek bed. "They wouldn't believe their eyes," he muttered.

Grant dragged a hand through his sandy hair. "Not a single soul from England would be willing to live here if they knew about Rugby's deplorable living conditions."

John nodded absently, lost in his thoughts. Seven days of living in Rugby had failed to erase his initial disillusionments with the colony. If anything, his disappointments with the place had escalated over the course of the last week.

The food in the dining hall still held no appeal to his British taste buds, particularly the mealy concoction known as "grits." And sleeping in a hammock was just as dreadful as John had suspected it

would be. On several occasions, he'd flipped out of
the blasted contraption and crashed to the floor in
the middle of the night.

Each morning, John arose with the hope that the
new day would provide him with a fresh perspective of his surroundings, a new outlook on the
prospects of establishing a temporary home for
himself in the British colony. But day after day, he
could find nothing appealing about the place.

Even his hopes of investing in a parcel or two of
land had been dashed. When he'd surveyed the colony's holdings with Daniel, John had been
astounded by the number of tracts being offered for
sale to the colonists. Encompassing a total of forty
thousand acres, the grounds were situated on a
high plain that stretched between the deep gorges
of two mountain streams, the Clear Fork River and
the White Oak Creek.

More than enough land was available for pro-
spective colonists, John assessed. But that was the
problem. It was senseless for him to pursue the notion of purchasing land as an investment. Why
would anyone let land from a fellow colonist if he
could buy a plot of his own? Worse yet, who would
want to buy anything here at all?

Out of the dozen Englishmen who had taken up
residence in the colony, most looked no older than
schoolboys. The remaining few were disagreeable
gents in their twenties and thirties who obviously
believed their mission in life was to make everyone
else as miserable as possible.

Disgusted with the living conditions, the investment possibilities, and most of his fellow colonists in Rugby, John had turned to his love of sporting activities for a snippet or two of pleasure during his first few days in the colony. He'd hunted game in the forests. He'd fished in the streams. He'd swum in the creek. And he'd even whacked a few featheries with his golf sticks on the one rare occasion when he'd been lucky enough to find a cleared stretch of land.

But in the absence of horse races and taverns and gaming halls, what more could a gentleman do?

There were no balls to attend in Rugby, no spirits to drink, no games to wager . . . and no women to pursue.

As far as John could tell, females were as scarce as British taverns in the mountains of Tennessee. He'd seen nothing more of the elusive, golden-haired beauty since his startling encounter with her on the trail. Other than the little hunchbacked cook in the dining hall, he'd not laid eyes upon a woman since he'd set foot in the settlement.

Now, bored and miserable, John was sorely tempted to head back to Sedgemoor Station and jump aboard the first train that came passing by. At the moment, he wanted nothing more than to escape from the clutches of this living nightmare.

As if reading his thoughts, Grant reached over and clapped him on the shoulder. "Look on the bright side, John," he urged. "The situation couldn't possibly get any worse than it already is."

"Reserve your judgment until we've eaten dinner, Montgomery," Adam cautioned. "We haven't sampled the evening fare yet."

Grant's mouth twitched with amusement. "Maybe thinking about something in England would help us forget about our problems here. Perhaps we should imagine we're off on a fox hunt or visiting one of our fathers' hunting clubs in the English countryside."

"Thinking about those things only makes me more miserable," Adam contended. "The servants' quarters at those hunting lodges look like palaces compared to our pitiful living arrangements."

"And the cuisine at my father's hunting club is superb." John's mouth watered at the memories of the savory dishes prepared by the club's chef. "Right now, I'd give my right arm for one bite of some decent food from home."

Home. Images of England clicked through his mind, accompanied by sounds and smells so vivid and startling that John felt as if he had been magically transported back to his native land. He could almost hear the rustles of silk and satin sweeping across a ballroom floor. Almost taste the succulent flavor of a fine burgundy wine on the tip of his tongue. Almost feel the excitement of winning a heated match of lawn tennis . . .

Lawn tennis. The mere thought of the game rejuvenated John's spirits. After an entire week of wallowing in his misery, he'd almost forgotten the sheer joy of playing the game.

Worse yet, he'd been far too appalled by his new surroundings to remember the competitive, winning attitude that he'd vowed to employ while he was here.

It's just a game, Winslow, an inner voice reminded him. *Don't concede defeat so easily.*

The thought of returning to England, defeated and beaten, sent a shudder of revulsion down his spine. Hadn't he vowed to make a success of his life here? And what good could result from leaving now?

John pulled back his shoulders with renewed resolve. He suspected he could tolerate life in Rugby far more easily if the place offered something familiar to him, something that reminded him of life in England. . . .

Seized by a sudden bolt of inspiration, John lunged to his feet. "A touch of civilization is what we need around here, my friends," he announced.

"You don't say." A glib smile accompanied Adam's cynical remark. "I would have never suspected such a thing."

"But if we're going to enjoy ourselves in a civilized manner, we'll have to be the ones to create our own entertainment," John continued on.

"What do you have in mind?" Grant asked.

"Perhaps we could construct our own lawn tennis court." Ideas for the project tumbled through John's mind so rapidly that he could scarcely latch onto all of them. "I saw the perfect site for a playing court when Daniel and I surveyed the colony's land holdings. It's a small plot of land, designated as one of the common areas for the use of everyone in the colony. The ground is fairly level, so we wouldn't have to worry about grading the surface for a playing area. And I suspect we could mark off the boundaries with rows of small stones or—"

"Slow down a minute, John. You're moving too fast for me." Grant leveled a curious glance at John. "You're deadly serious about this, aren't you?"

"What do we have to lose?" John challenged. "We have nothing better to do with our time and energy. Why not build something we can enjoy?"

"It would be nice to have a lawn tennis court around here," Grant conceded. "Something like a touch of home in the wilderness."

"Not a bad idea, John." Adam flashed a rare smile. "Actually, Jack sounds like a much more appropriate name for you. If you're willing to construct a tennis court, I'd say you're well on your way to becoming a jack of all trades here in Rugby."

John grinned. *Jack.* For some reason, he liked the sound of it. "Then Jack it is."

He chuckled. Life in Rugby was sorely lacking in some respects. No poster beds, no gourmet meals, no women or wine or song.

But, by George, they were going to have a lawn tennis court, the finest court in all of Tennessee.

Coralee ambled along the familiar footpath that led to her grandmother's cabin, the hem of her homespun skirt brushing against the wildflowers that lined the narrow trail.

She inhaled a deep breath, relishing the fragrant

scent of pine that assaulted her senses and the beauty of the May afternoon. She had just paused to admire the snowy-white blooms of a wild rhododendron when some unfamiliar sounds sliced through the air.

Whack. Thump. Whack. Thump.

Coralee stilled. What in heaven's name . . . ?

Rumbles of male laughter drifted through the forest. "Good play, Winslow!" a man bellowed in a deep voice that bore not a trace of mountain twang.

Those Englishmen again.

Curious, Coralee hiked up her skirts and abandoned the footpath, following the direction of the sounds through the forest. When she reached the edge of a small clearing, she stumbled to a halt, astounded by her discovery.

Three Englishmen were chasing after a ball, running across a rectangular plot of land that had been cleared and leveled into a smooth surface. Two of the men were positioned on one side of a waist-high net that divided the playing area into two equal parts, while the third man stood alone on the opposite side.

Each of the men clutched an odd-looking paddle in his hand. Taut rows of string were woven into a hollowed, oval-shaped core at one end of the paddle. As the players hit the ball back and forth to each other across the net, a resounding *whack* split through the air each time the ball collided against the forceful stroke of a paddle.

Coralee edged closer, intrigued by the sight of

the men and their sport. As she focused her gaze on the tallest of the three men, she admired the short pants and dark stockings that clung to the muscled length of his long legs. Though she'd heard about those newfangled pants for men during her last visit to Cincinnati, she'd never seen anyone wearing knickerbockers until now.

Her gaze roamed higher, wandering over the broad expanse of the man's shoulders, then drifting upward to his face. But as her eyes focused on the man's handsome features, her breath snared in her throat.

The Englishman. The man with startling blue eyes and an intriguing cleft in his chin. The same man who had haunted her dreams for the past two weeks.

Studying him now, Coralee became vividly aware of his athletic prowess. As the ball sailed over the net in his direction, he sprang into action. Never once removing his eyes from the flying object, he lunged across the playing area and swiftly took position to meet the ball as it hit the ground and bounced toward him. Then he hurled back his arm, let out a grunt, and slammed the paddle into the ball.

Waiting for his opponents' next move, he gripped the handle of his paddle and moved into a crouched position. Knees bent, arms tensed, eyes focused on the ball, he assumed the stance of a man who was ready to charge into battle at any second.

His movements and actions told Coralee far more than words could say. There was a fierce competitiveness about the man, she surmised, a determined spirit that said he would settle for nothing less than victory. Between his intense concentration and calculated movements, it almost seemed as if he were obsessed with winning the game.

Just looking at him, Coralee felt her pulse racing, her knees trembling, and a heated flush of excitement soaring through her. Though the man's demeanor was far too aggressive and threatening to be appealing to her, she couldn't seem to tear her gaze away from him.

At that instant, the ball skimmed over the net and whizzed toward him. With a swift, agile stroke of his paddle, the man hit the ball dead-center.

To Coralee's surprise, the ball soared straight up into the sky. She tilted back her head and followed the direction of the ball as it glided through the air. Peering over her shoulder, she watched in silence as the round object disappeared into a cluster of trees behind her.

She was still gazing toward the forested area when she heard the sound of approaching footsteps. "I wasn't aware we had a spectator," a man grumbled in a voice that was distinctly annoyed and very British.

"Oh, you don't need pay me no mind," Coralee said, whipping around. "I was just takin' a look-see at what you fellas were . . ."

As Coralee lifted her eyes to the man's face, her heart skipped a beat. Close up, the Englishman was far more handsome than she could have ever imagined.

Accustomed to strong, husky mountain men and their rugged, rough looks, Coralee immediately sensed that this man was different from any other male she'd ever known. There was a cultured air about him, a polished, refined demeanor that was both unsettling and intriguing to her.

She struggled to find her voice. "If you're lookin' to find that little ball of yours, I think you'd best take a look-see back there." She pointed over her shoulder. "I'm not an eagle-eye, mind you, but I'd swear on a stack of Bibles that it went flyin' over yonder."

The man's brows narrowed in confusion. Coralee wondered why he seemed so perplexed by her explanation. It almost seemed as if he couldn't understand what she was saying.

She planted a bright smile on her lips and broke the awkward silence. "I don't rightly know what you fellas are doin', but it looks like a mighty interestin' game to me. And I bet you're winnin' by leaps and bounds."

He stared at her in disbelief. "Why do you think I'm winning?"

"Why, you hit your little ball clear out of sight! I didn't see nobody else hittin' a ball that far."

Annoyance flickered across his intriguing features. "Victory is not measured by distance in lawn tennis," he said in a crisp tone. "A player is supposed to keep the ball within the boundaries of the tennis court."

"Where are the boundaries?" she asked, genuinely curious.

"We've marked them with rows of small stones," he explained, turning to head back to the court.

Coralee hiked up her skirts and trailed behind him. When she came to the stone markers, she shook her head in disbelief. "Well, I'm plumb perplexified about this little game of yours," she admitted.

A few feet away, a sandy-haired Englishman chuckled. "Actually, lawn tennis is rather simple," he assured her.

"If you'd care to learn how to play, we'd be glad to teach you," the other Englishman offered. "In fact, we could use another player for doubles matches."

"It looks like a heap of fun," Coralee returned, "but I really don't have much time for playin' games. And besides, I don't have a paddle for playin'."

"A paddle?" Confusion rippled across the face of the man with sandy hair. But as Coralee motioned toward the object in his hand, the man's face brightened with sudden understanding. "Back in England, these paddles are known as tennis rackets," he explained.

"Then things must be mighty different where you come from." Coralee glanced around the tennis court. "I never dreamed y'all were buildin' a place to play games. I figured y'all would be buildin' some cabins for yourselves if you're intendin' to stay here for a spell."

The tallest man stiffened noticeably. "Our future plans have not yet been finalized. Until then, the colony is providing our living accommodations."

"I see," she mumbled, though she didn't see at all. Coralee didn't understand why anyone would waste their time playing games when they could be building their own homes. Odder still, she had no idea why the dark-haired Englishman seemed so perturbed by her questions.

"I suppose I should start looking for the tennis ball," the tall Englishman muttered. "We only have a few of them, and I'd hate to lose one."

"I don't mind a-helpin' you look for it," Coralee offered. "I've lived here my whole entire life, and I know my way 'round these parts. In fact, I think I know perzactly the spot where it landed."

He motioned toward the trees. "Then you lead the way, ma'am."

As Coralee picked up her skirts, the Englishman fell into step beside her. "Seein' as how we're neighbors and all, you don't have to call me ma'am. I'm Coralee Hayes, but you can call me Coralee like everyone else does. 'Course, I still don't know what to be callin' you."

"It's Winslow. Lord John Winslow." He nodded in the direction of his companions. "And that's Lord Barrington and Lord Montgomery."

"Lord?" She stumbled to a halt. "Like in . . . Lord God Almighty?"

"I've never considered the comparison." A trace of subdued amusement glinted from the depths of his sky-blue eyes, and he looked as if he was trying very hard not to laugh. "But the term is the same."

"Well, I never heard the like." Coralee resumed

walking toward the cluster of trees. "If you're ask-in' me, I think it's mighty peculiar that all three of you fellas have got the same first name. You must be joshin' me."

The amusement in his eyes vanished. " 'Lord' is the proper term for addressing second-born sons of British nobility," he informed her in a curt tone.

Coralee wandered into the thicket of trees to look for some sign of the small ball amid the under-brush. "Still, it's gonna be awfully confusin', callin' all of you fellas Mr. Lord." She laughed aloud at the thought. "Y'all won't never know who I'm talkin' to!"

The line of his jaw hardened. "The appropriate greeting isn't Mr. Lord," he said. "It's Lord Bar-rington, Lord Montgomery . . . and Lord Winslow."

"We sorta do the same thing around here, I reckon," she said, spying the ball at the base of a hickory tree. She scooped the ball into her hand, then tossed it to the Englishman. "We're always puttin' a word in front of somebody's name, like Preacher Joe Bob and Uncle Harlan and Granny Clabo."

"How charming." He shoved the ball into his pocket and wheeled, heading back to the tennis court.

" 'Course, nobody 'round here uses the Lord God Almighty's name, except when they're cussin' up a storm," Coralee continued, close at his heels. "It's gonna seem mighty strange to be callin' you Lord."

He came to a dead stop. "Then just call me Jack," he snapped irritably.

"Well, now, that's a whole lot easier to be a-sayin'." She lifted a hand and wiggled her fingers at him. "Bye-bye now, Jack."

She picked up her skirts and walked away. Jack couldn't help but notice the sway of her hips and the glorious mane of thick, golden hair tumbling down her back.

"Bloody hell," he grumbled.

He couldn't deny there was a wholesome charm about her. Never had he seen anyone who was so unpretentious. Those forest-green eyes of hers held a permanent sparkle, it seemed, and her lips shimmered with a natural, rosy hue. Even the saucy tilt of her head was intriguing.

But she wasn't the kind of woman who could ignite a flame of desire in him. There was no polished air of refinement about her, no sophistication in her quaint manner of speech. Every time she opened her mouth, he'd struggled to interpret the meaning of her words. It almost seemed as if she were speaking a foreign language.

By the time he returned to the tennis court, he was wondering why Adam and Grant had been so receptive to the woman. Storming up to his friends, he scowled in dismay. "I can't believe you asked that woman to play tennis with us," he muttered. "Can't you see she's nothing but a commoner?"

Adam shrugged. "Quite frankly, I don't see any harm in inviting her to join us on the court. After all, we need a fourth player for playing doubles."

"But it doesn't have to be her," Jack snapped.

"What other choice do we have?" Grant gestured

toward the empty court. "How many other ladies do you see around here?"

Adam chuckled. "Besides the cook at the dining hall, she's the first female we've seen in weeks."

"Then the two of you can play all the tennis with her that you like." Jack scooped the tennis ball from his pocket and tossed it to Adam. "As for me, I want nothing more to do with the woman. We don't even speak the same language."

Chapter 3

Turning away from the Englishman, Coralee headed back to the footpath that led to Granny's cabin. She didn't know what to think about the man named Jack. And she didn't know what to do about the crazy emotions ripping through her.

At the moment, she was feeling as befuddled as when she'd plunged headfirst into the icy waters of the Clear Fork, bumped her head on a rock, and knocked herself senseless.

"You silly goose," she chided herself, stepping back onto the narrow trail. "What's gotten into you?"

Over the years, Coralee had learned to trust her instincts, gauging her emotions with little difficulty. From her point of view, life's choices were simple ones. Right was right, wrong was wrong, and there was no middle ground.

And she also possessed the assurance of knowing she belonged in her beloved mountains, the place where she had been born and raised. The serenity and beauty of the Appalachians, Coralee believed, were the reasons for her clear mind and logical thinking.

But all of her sound reasoning seemed elusive as she worked her way up the mountain slope. She'd never experienced all these troubling, confused feelings until these strangers had invaded her mountains, these men who called themselves "Lord" and had the funniest way of talking that she'd ever heard.

And never had she encountered any man who possessed the power to ignite a slow, simmering heat within her, a heat that was still smoldering long after they'd parted ways.

She felt a warm flush rise to her cheeks. She couldn't explain why little tingles had shot up and down her spine every time he'd looked at her. And she couldn't understand why he'd seemed so aggravated with her every time she asked a question.

"Maybe all Englishmen act that way," she mused aloud.

Within a few moments, she approached a log cabin hidden amid a cluster of trees. A spry little woman was seated in a rocker on the front porch, diligently maneuvering a needle through a large piece of colorful fabric on her lap.

Coralee paused, admiring the woman for a moment. Though her shoulders were stooped and her face was lined with wrinkles, Lelah Clabo's mind and hands were never idle. In fact, Granny Clabo possessed more energy than anyone Coralee had ever known.

Coralee's maternal grandmother had become her most trusted confidante since the deaths of her own beloved mother and father. Over the years, she never ceased to be amazed at the extent of Granny's wisdom. Granny's wise counsel ventured far beyond the realm of human understanding, garnering respect throughout Morgan County. The woman could predict the upcoming weather or the trustworthiness of a person's character with astonishing accuracy. And one word of warning from her lips bore more weight than the clenched fist of a three-hundred-pound man.

But hocus-pocus magic and satanic spells held no place in Granny's life. Like a prophetess of old, she depended on signs of nature and trusted her uncanny sixth sense for guidance through the journeys of life.

Now, as Coralee edged toward the cabin, Granny glanced up and smiled. "I knew you was comin' to see me, Coralee. My nose has been twitchin' all afternoon, and that always means somebody is comin' to pay me a visit. But I was expectin' you a tad earlier than this."

"I got waylaid for a spell," Coralee explained. "I saw some of those Englishmen playin' a game with a ball and a paddlelike thing that they call a racket, and I stopped to watch them for a while."

Granny's white brows rose in surprise. "You talked to these strangers?"

Coralee nodded. "We introduced ourselves to each other, and I helped one of them find a lost ball in the woods." She paused, not wanting to discuss the unsettling subject until she had the chance to sort out her chaotic thoughts about the Englishmen. "I was hopin' I could work on my quilt for a spell while I'm here."

Granny scooped her needlework into her arms and sprang up from the rocker. "Then let's mosey on inside," she insisted.

Coralee followed the woman into the cabin. Granny struck a match against the fire board and ignited the wick of an oil lantern. A soft beam of light flickered through the room, casting a warm glow over the simple furnishings and faded homespun rugs.

As Granny sank into a rocker beside the fireplace, Coralee glided across the room and removed an unfinished quilt from a wooden rack. She brushed her fingers across the intricate stitches, admiring her own handiwork.

She'd finished a good portion of the piecework during the winter. Cooped up in her cabin on snowy days, Coralee had passed the time by cutting swatches of fabric and sewing the pieces together by hand to create an appealing pattern of colorful designs.

By the time spring arrived, Coralee decided to finish the quilt at Granny's cabin. While Granny tended to her own needlework and weaving projects, Coralee stitched on her quilt, grateful for her grandmother's company.

Much of her future depended upon completing the quilt before her family's annual trip to Cincinnati in the fall. The sale of her quilt could provide enough money to purchase most of the basic necessities—sugar, salt, coffee, and the like—that she would need throughout the winter.

Now, Coralee held out the quilt, trying to figure out how much more time would be required to finish the rows of stitches.

"The womenfolk in Cincinnati like the wedding ring pattern the best of all," Granny noted. "I'd say you'll fetch a pretty price for your quilt."

"I hope so. Come fall, I'll be needin' a good price for it. Along with buyin' my staples for the winter, I'll be needin' a new pair of shoes." She peered down at the scuffed toes of her leather shoes and frowned. "This pair won't be lastin' much longer."

Her frown deepened as she sank into a wooden chair by the fireplace. "I wish I could think of a way to make a little pocket money before fall. I know I've got to buy me a good pair of sturdy shoes for clompin' through the woods every day, but I wish . . ."

As her voiced trailed off, Granny's head snapped up. "Go on, child. There ain't nothing wrong with wishin' and dreamin'."

"I don't mean to sound like I'm frettin', Granny," Coralee said, stitching on her quilt. "But I wish I had just a little extra money to buy me somethin' I don't really need. Somethin' fine 'n' pretty, like a pair of fancy slippers for wearin' to the hoedowns on Saturday nights. And maybe a store-bought dress for wearin' to the church meetin'house on Sundays."

"Wantin' somethin' pretty for yourself ain't a sin,

child. A woman needs somethin' pretty in her life
every now and then to make herself feel special-
like." Granny's voice was soft with understanding.
"Before your granddaddy passed on, he used to
bring me home a little treat every time he went to
Cincinnati. Sometimes it was a lacy hanky; sometimes it weren't nothin' more than a few sticks of
licorice. But those little treats of his made me happier 'n a lark."

"But havin' someone buyin' gifts for you is different from buyin' somethin' for yourself," Coralee
pointed out.

"Not if you don't have a man of your own.
Women who are fendin' for themselves—like you
and me—gotta look after their own selves." Granny
leaned forward, and her voice dropped to a whisper. "Let me tell you a secret, child, somethin' nobody knows but me. When I went to Cincinnati this
spring, I bought myself something I ain't never had
before. I bought it just for me, and I ain't had one
minute of regret for buyin' it."

Surprised, Coralee cocked her head to one side.
"What did you buy, Granny?"

"I'll show you." With a sly grin, Granny reached
down and peeled back the hem of her long skirt.
Peeking out from beneath the homespun fabric was
a white petticoat trimmed with a band of dainty
lace. "Now, ain't that the finest petticoat you ever
done laid your eyes upon?"

"It's beautiful, Granny." Coralee admired the
band of lace for a moment, then sighed with frustration. "But buyin' salt and sugar and new shoes

for everyday wearin' will take every penny I've got, even if I do get me a good price for my quilt. It don't do me a lick of good to be pinin' for somethin' I don't need. Wishin' and dreamin' may not be a bad thing, but makin' sure I got enough vittles to eat next winter is more important than spendin' time on foolish dreams."

Granny's smile faded away, and her eyes took on a sorrowful look. "If that no-account husband of yours had had a lick of sense about him, he'd have bought his wife a fancy trinket or two instead of squanderin' what little he had on all that corn likker."

Coralee winced, wishing for the millionth time that she'd heeded Granny's warnings about marrying Reuben Hayes. Everything Granny had predicted about Reuben had come true. She shifted uneasily in her chair. "All that's behind me now, Granny."

"Well, don't fret about it none," Granny cautioned. "And don't dash your dreams, neither, child. Somethin' tells me changes are a-comin' your way."

"Changes?" Coralee straightened her shoulders. Over the years, she'd learned that Granny's instincts were rarely wrong. And she'd discovered, firsthand, the wisdom of giving credence to her grandmother's predictions. "What kind of changes?"

"Good ones, I do believe."

"Then I'd like to think the pain will be goin'

away when I'm havin' my monthlies. That's the nicest change I could hope for."

"Believe me, child, everyone wants those awful pains of yours to go away." Granny chuckled. "I declare, when you're a-havin' those monthlies of yours, you can down a jug of corn likker faster 'n a bolt of lightnin'. Don't know many men who can top you when it comes to chuggin' down that likker."

"I don't make a habit of drinkin' that awful stuff all the time, Granny." Coralee felt a heated flush rise to her cheeks. "But it's the only thing that will make the pain go away durin' my monthlies."

"I ain't a-criticizin' you, child. Before your mother was born, I gulped down my share of corn likker when I was havin' my time every month, too."

Coralee frowned in confusion. "And what happened after Ma was born?"

Granny shrugged her narrow shoulders. "All that pain went away. Givin' birth to your ma jiggled my insides around, I reckon. All those cramps and aches and pains disappeared after I birthed her."

"Then maybe I should be thinkin' about birthin' a baby of my own," Coralee mused. "If it'll take away the pain—"

"First things first, child," Granny warned. "Don't you be gettin' the cart before the horse. You gotta have a husband 'fore you can make a baby."

Coralee sighed. The prospects of a man in her future—to say nothing of a newborn babe—were dismal, at best. Though more than a year had elapsed since she'd buried Reuben in the little graveyard behind the church meetinghouse, she held little hope of marrying again. By mountain standards, she was past the prime age for marriage. Most Tennessee girls married long before the age of twenty.

"Without a man—or a baby—in sight, I reckon I won't be givin' up my monthly dose of corn likker any time soon." Coralee grinned. "But since you're predictin' some changes are a-comin' my way, I 'spect I could still be hopin' for some relief from those awful stabbin' pains every month."

"Nothing but a babe will make a difference in your monthlies, child." Granny set aside her needlework, and the rhythmic creak of her rocker came to a standstill. "Last night I dreamed about you, Coralee. You were hitchin' up a mule to a cart. And that means changes are a-comin' your way."

"But I'm hitching up my mule to my wagon all the time, Granny. It's never made any difference up till now."

"This don't have nothin' to do with what you've been doin' lately." Granny edged forward in the rocker, her eyes bright, her expression full of excitement. "This was a dream, child. And dreams always mean somethin'."

"Do you reckon this means I'm gonna find a way to make me a little spendin' money?"

"Could be. But, then, I never knowed anything to change a woman's life like a handsome feller. Maybe there will be a new man in your life, a man who'll be bringin' good luck with him."

Visions of a handsome Englishman flashed through Coralee's mind, but she hastily banished them. Though Granny Clabo's predictions were rarely wrong, Coralee couldn't imagine how an outsider could play a role in her future.

"Good things are in store for you, Coralee," Granny predicted once again. "I feel it in my bones, child. You just wait and see."

"I wish Granny would have a dream like that about me." Maggie gave a wistful sigh as she placed a load of wet garments into a large basket at the banks of the creek. "I'm the one who needs some changes in her life," she murmured.

Seated on the creek banks beside her cousins, Coralee dipped a garment into the water. "Sometimes changes aren't easy, Maggie."

"Moving back here from Boston was a big change for me." Rachel twisted a wet garment between her hands, wringing out the excess water. "I love being here again with my family, but I still miss Boston at times."

"At least you've lived somewhere else besides Morgan County." Maggie rose and picked up her basket of laundry from the ground. "I reckon I'd best be hightailin' on back to the cabin. By the time I hang out these clothes to dry, Ma will be wantin' me to help with the lunch fixin's."

"I should be leaving, too, I suppose." Rachel placed the last of her laundry into her own basket.

"I'm planning on taking Pa's lunch into Rugby for him today."

As the two women turned to leave, Maggie peered over her shoulder and grinned. "Let us know when all those changes start comin' your way, Coralee."

"You'll be the first to hear any news," Coralee promised with a laugh.

But as her cousins departed, the smile on Coralee's lips faded away. She only hoped she would have some news to report to her cousins in the upcoming days. Although Granny's dream had occurred nearly a week before, nothing in her life had changed.

Every morning, she'd awakened with a wondrous sense of anticipation, certain a profound occurrence would take place at any moment. But her daily morning routine—feeding the chickens, milking the cow, and tending to her horse and mule—had maintained a sense of normalcy throughout the week. And nothing unusual had transpired when she'd visited with her brothers and their families, nor when she'd attended the Saturday night singings and Sunday morning preachings at the meetinghouse.

Not even the arrival of the Englishmen had made a notable difference in her life. She'd seen not a trace of the three lords since the afternoon of their tennis game.

But, then, she hadn't ventured near the lawn tennis court in recent days. She wasn't entirely certain she was ready for another encounter with the Englishman. The man provoked feelings in her that her own husband had not been able to arouse.

Reuben. Coralee leaned back on her elbows and sighed.

As a young girl, she'd always assumed she would have the same kind of marriage and family that her parents had shared. Surrounded by the love and laughter and warmth of her parents and three older brothers, Coralee had presumed all marriages were strong, all families full of love.

But after her marriage to Reuben, she'd rapidly discovered that all men were not as kind and loving as her father and brothers, and not all marriages were loving and strong.

Oddly enough, she'd been certain Reuben was the right man for her. She couldn't even remember a time in her life when she hadn't known him. Mountain born and bred, Reuben had been one of her favorite playmates as a child. By the time their childhood days had vanished, Coralee had fallen in love with Reuben's carefree ways and deep-throated laughter.

But her spirited, fun-loving groom became a bitter, rebellious man after their marriage. Within a few years, Reuben cared little for anything other than his supply of corn liquor, and secretive trips to Cincinnati often kept him from home for weeks at a time.

Since Reuben's death, Coralee had resigned herself to a future without a husband or children. Most of her efforts were focused on surviving from day to day in the isolated mountains. She scarcely wasted a moment, and she rarely indulged in day-dreaming and wishing for the impossible to happen.

Still, she couldn't deny that she cherished the notion of living the rest of her life in her beloved mountains with a handsome man by her side and a merry clan of children at her skirts. Only on rare occasions did Coralee dare to dream of having the life that she'd always assumed she would have.

But deep down inside, she knew her hopes for marriage and children were nothing more than foolish dreams. None of the mountain men held any interest for her. Outside of her kinfolks, the majority of men in the mountains were already married. The rest were either too old or too young for Coralee.

And she couldn't imagine being married to anyone who hadn't been raised in the mountains. Most outsiders deemed mountaineers as peculiar folks who were set in their ways. None of them seemed to understand why anyone would prefer to live in the isolation of the Appalachians instead of in a populated area like Cincinnati.

The rustle of leaves in the distance jolted her back into her reality. Appalled by the direction of her wayward thoughts, she gave her head a shake.

"Moanin' and groanin' about your lot in life won't do a lick of good, Coralee Hayes," she scolded herself, reaching for another garment in her laundry basket. "And you've got too much work waitin' for you to be thinkin' about foolish dreams."

Chapter 4

"**R**eady for another game?" Jack challenged.

Adam shook his head as he retreated from the tennis court. "You've already won three straight sets, Jack. Isn't that enough for one morning?"

Grinning, Jack tossed his racket into the air. "I never quit when I'm on a winning streak," he insisted, snatching the handle of the racket before it could hit the ground.

"Personally, I think we need something other than lawn tennis to occupy our time." Grant leaned back against the trunk of a sprawling chestnut tree. "We haven't done anything but play tennis since we finished building the court. And playing the same game over and over again for more than a week has gotten rather tiresome, as far as I'm concerned."

"Then perhaps we should think of another diversion for ourselves," Jack mused. "Would you gentlemen care to join me for a morning ride?

Maybe something will strike our fancy if we take a little excursion."

"You go on ahead," Grant insisted. "I've got some letters to write, and I'd like to get them posted today."

"I've had all the fresh mountain air I can stand for one morning," Adam quipped. "I'm going back to the barracks for a nice, long nap."

A few moments later, Jack was roaming through the Cumberland Plateau alone on horseback, scrutinizing the terrain with interest. He'd awakened that morning with an idea brewing in his mind, and he was anxious to see if the notion was a feasible one.

A matted growth of laurel and rhododendron prohibited riders on horseback from traveling alongside the banks of the Clear Fork. Yet, Jack suspected the meandering banks were the perfect site for creating a bridle path.

In recent days, he'd discovered that dreaming about ways to enhance his life in the colony somehow made the daily grind more tolerable. Instead of dwelling on his woeful living conditions, he was learning to focus his thoughts on ways to improve the place.

For the most part, his tactics were proving to be successful, keeping his mind occupied with uplifting concepts, preventing him from thinking too much about . . . *her*.

Memories of a golden-haired beauty tumbled through his mind, annoying him beyond all reason.

"Bloody hell," he grumbled, resolving to banish the enticing vision from his brain.

Approaching the mountain stream, he paused, considering the possibilities of building a bridle path. Would the colonists be willing to clear and grade the banks of the stream? Surely they would see the benefits of devoting a few days of time to the project.

He was still musing over the idea when a woman's voice drifted through the air. "Well, fancy meetin' you here."

Startled, Jack snapped around, surprised to see that Coralee was sitting by the creek, dipping a garment into the water. Beside her was a large basket filled with clothing. The morning sunlight cast a golden glow around her, highlighting her fair hair and delicate features.

In spite of his determination to steer clear of the woman, Jack managed a bleak smile. "Good morning," he muttered.

"Mighty fine lookin' creature you got there." Wringing the water from her clothing, she swept her gaze over his horse. "You musta looked high and wide before you found a horse with four white feet."

"I purchased him in Cincinnati," Jack said, wondering why she seemed so fascinated with the animal.

"I 'spected as much. Folks 'round here don't like to part with a horse like that, not at any price." She placed the wet garment over a smooth stone, then rubbed the flat edge of a worn stick across the fabric with quick, agile strokes. "Accordin' to my granny, a horse with four white feet brings good luck to its owner. And if my granny says so, it has to be true."

"Well, I hope your granny is right." He ran a finger along his neck, tugging at his collar. "I could use a bit of luck. I've been running a bit short of it lately."

She glanced up at him, concern glimmering from her eyes. "Got a spell of troubles?"

"Good fortune has been rather elusive since my arrival in the States," he revealed just as she placed another garment into the water. Watching in silence for a moment, Jack became acutely aware that none of his clothing had been laundered since he'd disembarked from the ship in Philadelphia. "At the moment, I don't even own a set of clean clothes," he mumbled.

"Well, then, you need to get busy a-warshin' those fancy garments of yours." She held out her stick to him. "You can use my battlin' stick, if you'd like."

"That won't be necessary," he snapped, appalled by the suggestion. In England, no one would dare propose that the son of a duke should wash his own clothes. Even if he weren't a titled lord, he would be highly offended by the implication. After all, laundering clothes was women's work, a task far too degrading for any man—especially a member of the British gentry—who professed to be of sound mind and reason.

"Suit yourself, then." She shrugged with indifference. "I reckon I don't have any objections if you want to be wearin' dirty clothes for the rest of your life."

"I have no intention of wearing soiled garments," he ground out, gritting his teeth. But even as he said the words, an uneasy feeling rolled through him. Until this moment, he'd never given any consideration to the laborious tasks of tending to his wardrobe. Up until now, George had always taken care of cleaning and pressing his clothes for him. "But I'd give a sizable fortune to someone who'd be willing to launder my clothes."

He didn't realize that he'd spoken the words aloud until her eyes widened with astonishment. "You'd be willin' to *pay* someone for a-warshin' your clothes?"

He nodded, somewhat pleased he'd stumbled upon the idea. "I'd pay a handsome sum as long as my garments are appropriately cleaned and pressed. And my shirts, of course, must be properly starched."

She wrinkled her nose. "I'd be scratchin' myself raw if I was wearin' starchy shirts 'round here. Those stiff collars of yours would make me itch worse than a bunch of chigger bites."

Though the term "chiggers" was not part of his vocabulary, Coralee's message was perfectly clear. Jack bristled with annoyance. Who did this woman think she was? In his native land, she'd be nothing more than a commoner. How dare she tell him how to dress?

Besides, no one criticized the clothing of Lord

John Winslow. The fine quality of his garments was a major source of pride for him. He employed the finest tailors in all of England, tailors who used nothing but the best materials for his clothing.

"My garments are quite appropriate for a gentleman of my standing," he informed her in a crisp tone. "If you've ventured outside of these mountains, I'm certain you must realize my wardrobe is very befitting for a man like myself."

"I know what the menfolk are wearin' in Cincinnati," she countered. "I go there once or twice a year."

"But your travels don't make you an expert on men's clothing," he shot back.

She lifted her chin, boldly meeting his gaze. "Common sense is what makes me an expert, Mr. Lord Jack Almighty. If you had a lick of sense, you'd see those white, frilly shirts of yours aren't practical in these mountains. It looks to me like you'd want to be wearin' some old clothes that you don't care to get ruint when you're roamin' through all these hills and valleys."

A slash of anger sliced through him. A mountain woman—obviously uneducated and unaccustomed to the ways of the world—had no business telling him what to wear.

He glared at her for a brief moment, intending to give her a piece of his mind. But as he looked down at her, something held him at bay.

She had no way of knowing that everything he owned was new, he realized with a jolt. Nothing in his possession was unfashionable or stained or faded from excessive wear. After one season, he passed along his garments to the servants, discarding them without a second thought.

"I'm quite satisfied with my wardrobe," he finally managed to say.

"It's nice to want to look dandy, all spruced in your fancy clothes. I like to get fancied up myself, at times. But 'round here, it ain't practical for me to be squished up and pooched out just for the sake of it. I can't move around good if I'm wearin' a ton of petticoats and all those other contraptions that city ladies hide beneath those fancy dresses of theirs."

As if to prove her point, she sprang to her feet with a graceful ease. Her simple blouse and skirt billowed around her, caught on the wings of a warm summer breeze.

Jack clenched his jaw. More than likely, he was more familiar with the contraptions concealed beneath a woman's gown—corsets, chemises, petticoats, drawings, stockings, stays—than she. During his frequent visits to the bedchambers of London's most desirable women, he'd mastered the art of removing all those unmentionables.

By his estimation, every woman in England wore undergarments to achieve an hourglass figure that nature had failed to provide for them. But the woman standing in front of him wasn't wearing any waist cinchers or bust enhancers or bustles, he sensed. She had no reason to wear them.

Peering down at her, John felt a stirring of desire rippling through him. The thin fabric of her garments revealed curves and swells that were unrestricted by cumbersome stays or corsets.

As his gaze roamed over the length of her, his mouth went dry with longing. Her full, round breasts were generous enough to turn any man's head. Coupled with the indentation of her tiny waist and the gentle swell of her hips, she had no need for the constricting undergarments that most women wore.

But the sight of her faded homespun skirt jostled him back into reality, reminding him that Coralee Hayes wasn't his kind of woman. She was far too plain, too unsophisticated, too common, to capture the interest of a titled lord. She possessed none of the cultured, polished sophistication of a British lady in the true sense of the word.

"Now, lookee here at my clothes," she was saying, retrieving a garment from her basket. "This here is my oldest dress. It's faded and patched in a place or two, so I wear it when I'm doin' my chores. When I'm pickin' blackberries, I don't throw a conniption fit if I get a little stain on the skirt or if I snag my sleeve on those thorny ole' sticker bushes 'round here."

She held up the garment, pressing it to her chest. Watching her, John felt a knot coiling in his gut. The servants at Havenshire Manor donned better garments than this woman owned. In fact, he suspected that the rags used for dusting the manor were more serviceable than Coralee's pitiful little dress.

Yet, this mountain beauty bore not a trace of

shame on her face. As she regarded her faded gown, he saw nothing but acceptance and practicality written into her expression.

She returned the dress to her basket, exchanging it for another garment. "Now this is my second-best dress," she continued on, holding up a gown with a lace collar that had seen better days. "I wear it to Saturday night singin's and to—"

"Saturday night singings?" he echoed, puzzled by the term.

She glanced up at him, her eyes filled with amusement. "You don't know what fun you've been missin' until you go to one. Everybody for miles around comes to the church meetin'house on Saturdays for a whole night of singin' their hearts out." She paused, snatching the last garment from the laundry basket. "And this here is my Sunday dress. I only wear it to Sunday preachin'. It's the best dress I got, and I take extra-special care of it. I wouldn't want nothing to happen to it before I can get to Cincinnati and sell my quilt."

"Your quilt? What does a quilt have to do with your dresses?"

"Why, everything." She placed the Sunday gown into the creek, gently swishing it through the crystal-clear water. "With the money I get from sellin' my quilt, I'm hoping to get me a new store-bought dress. And maybe some fancy new slippers, too, if I have enough money left after gettin' my supplies for next winter."

Listening to her simple list of hopes for the future, John couldn't explain why he felt an uneasy sensation rolling through him. Most of his female acquaintances—and even his sister—possessed dozens upon dozens of gowns and matching slippers for every dress.

Yet, he sensed he'd just seen every dress that this woman owned. And, remarkably, one new gown and a pair of fancy slippers were all she wanted.

He shifted uneasily in the saddle, vividly aware of the vast differences between them, more mindful of the stark contrasts between their two worlds than ever before.

Forcing aside his wayward thoughts, he gave his head a shake. "Aside from the fact that you don't approve of my clothing, would you be willing to launder my clothes?"

"That all depends on you." She peered up at him. "What price are you payin'?"

"One shilling per garment seems fair to me."

"Oh." Disappointment clouded her delicate features. "Well, I reckon we can't strike up a deal between us. I don't rightly know what I'd do with a shilling, even if I had one. I don't even know what a shilling is."

He laughed, genuinely amused by her forthright manner. "Then let's use an American term. How about two bits?"

"You're willin' to pay me two bits every time I warsh one of those fancy shirts of yours?"

"As long as you starch and press each one of them," he confirmed.

Coralee inhaled a deep breath, trying to steady her racing heart. Two bits for laundering one shirt seemed like a small fortune. For someone accustomed to bartering chickens for sugar and eggs for flour, laundering clothes in exchange for money sounded too good to be true.

But it wasn't a dream, Coralee silently assured herself. This was the change in her life that Granny had predicted, she was certain of it. Only a foolish woman would refuse the chance to make a little pocket money for herself. And in a few months, she'd have the means to buy those fancy slippers and that beautiful dress she'd admired in the store window during her last trip to Cincinnati.

"Then I reckon you got yourself a laundress, Mr. Jack." She flashed a smile in his direction.

"So when can you start?"

"Today, I reckon." She quickly surveyed her own meager load of laundry. "Pert near as I can tell, I'm might-nigh finished warshin' my own things. I could get started on the first batch of your laundry this afternoon if you're willin' to hike back to Rugby and fetch your clothes for me."

"That won't be necessary." He hurled one long leg over the saddle and swiftly dismounted. "You can get started right now."

He reached for the top button on his shirt. Coralee froze, watching in stunned silence. He said something more, but Coralee had no idea what that something was. As he shrugged out of his shirt, she was far too mesmerized by the sight of his bare chest to comprehend anything that he was saying.

Land sakes, the man was a sight to behold. Dark tangles of curls covered an intriguing chest that rippled with muscles more sleek and sculpted and beautifully formed than any other muscles she'd ever seen. And the rest of him was just as intriguing. His shoulders were broad, his neck thick, his arms firm and sinewy.

Her heart lurched crazily. What with having three brothers and a husband, Coralee thought she knew everything there was to know about the male physique. But she'd never seen a man who was put together like this one. He was breathtakingly gorgeous.

She knew she was gawking, but she couldn't seem to help herself. She was still standing there, staring at him, when the sound of his voice penetrated her thoughts.

"Is something wrong, Coralee?"

She tore her gaze away from him, shaking her head. "My mind was just wanderin', I suppose."

"I thought perhaps you'd never seen a man's chest before. Or perhaps you liked what you were seeing."

The arrogant tone of his voice and the amused quirk of his lips irritated Coralee beyond all reason. Tossing back her head, she crossed her arms over her chest and glared at him. "You should be ashamed of yourself, Lord Jack Almighty. Where you come from, ladies may not pay no mind to your insults. But barin' yourself ain't proper-like here in Tennessee. All the menfolk in these hills know they shouldn't be strippin' off their clothes in the presence of a lady."

"Pardon me, then." He bit back a smile. "I didn't

realize my behavior was so appalling . . . to a lady."

She heaved a weary sigh. "I'll give you the benefit of the doubt this time. But you'd better be behavin' yourself from now on. I wouldn't want you to be exposin' yourself to my two cousins. They haven't been hitched to a man like I have, and they're not used to lookin' at a strange man who's practically buck naked."

Lines of confusion crinkled his brow. "Are you saying you're . . . married?"

"Not anymore." She pursed her lips together. "I've been a widow-woman ever since my husband got himself killed last year." Not wanting to dwell on thoughts of Reuben, she lowered her eyes. "I'll be bringin' your shirt to the colony first thing in the mornin'. Just make sure you're wearin' another one when I get there."

Offering nothing more, she picked up the battling stick and focused her attention on scrubbing the rest of her clothes.

Jack turned to leave, more puzzled by Coralee Hayes than he cared to admit. He'd never known anyone quite like her, and he wasn't certain how to contend with the troubling thoughts whirling through his mind.

By British standards, she was nothing more than a commoner. Anyone who laundered clothes could never be considered a lady in the true sense of the word. Laundresses belonged in the ranks of the working class.

And a titled lord had no business associating with someone of such lowly status, he reminded himself sternly. At Havenshire Manor, he'd kept his distance from the household servants. Though some had lived at the Winslow estate for as long as he could remember, Jack couldn't recall a time when he'd exchanged more than a few words with any of them. Their conversations were limited to discussions about household chores, and he held not a snippet of interest in their personal lives.

After a lifetime of contending with servants, Jack knew he should regard Coralee Hayes as just another commoner who was providing personal services for him.

He mounted his horse to return to the settlement, trying to dismiss all thoughts of the intriguing woman from his mind. Not daring to steal another glimpse of her, he clamped his mouth into a firm, hard line.

But no matter how hard he tried, he couldn't ignore the heated rush of desire that was still throbbing through his veins. Couldn't forget the strained expression that had marred her delicate features when she'd revealed she had once been married.

"Bloody hell," he grumbled, settling into the saddle.

He grasped the reins, silently vowing to forget the unsettling encounter. The woman was a laundress, he told himself sternly, not the lady she insisted she was. Their definitions of a "lady" were as far apart as the Tennessee River from the Thames, and the sharp contrast between their differences held no common ground.

*   *   *

"You did a mighty fine job on that Englishman's shirt, Coralee." Sitting in a rocking chair on the porch of her cabin, Granny Clabo nodded with approval as she scrutinized the freshly laundered garment the next morning. "It's whiter 'n snow, and stiffer 'n lumber."

"That's what he was wantin', I reckon." Laughing, Coralee admired the starched shirtfront. "I'm hopin' he'll be givin' me some more clothes to warsh when he sees how good his shirt turned out."

"He'd be a foolish man if he didn't." The older woman smiled. "I got me a feelin' that you'll be pert near swamped with dirty clothes by this afternoon."

"I hope so." Coralee reached over and affectionately squeezed her grandmother's hand. "It looks like I'm gonna be gettin' that pretty new storebought dress and those fancy slippers after all, Granny. That good change you predicted in my life has finally come around, just like you said it would. And it's bringin' me the pocket money I've been wishin' for."

Lelah's fingers tightened around Coralee's hand. "Somethin' tells me you'll be seein' more changes, child. I ain't had no more dreams, mind you, but every bone in my ole' body is tellin' me that the changes in your life are just beginnin'."

"Then I reckon I don't have any cause to be worried as long as I've got you forewarnin' me about the future." Coralee's smile faded away, replaced with a troubled frown. "But there's still lots of things that perplexify me. For the life of me, I can't figure out these Englishmen. They're mighty particular about their clothes, but they don't seem too keen on learnin' how to keep 'em warshed and starched and pressed for themselves."

Granny shrugged. "Men are men, no matter what part of the world they come from, I reckon. Your Granddaddy Clabo never had a hankerin' for cookin' or warshin', either. In fact, I never knowed a man who did."

"But Rachel said these Englishmen have a heap of servants back in England, folks who cook and clean and tend to their clothes like we womenfolk do for our men around here," Coralee explained. "And if they got servants tendin' to all their chores, I'm wonderin' what their wives are doin' with their time all the day long."

Granny nibbled on her lower lip for a moment, appearing deep in thought. "I reckon they tend to their younguns," she finally said. "I don't rightly know what else they would be doin'."

"I don't either." Coralee rose and planted a kiss on her grandmother's wrinkled brow. "Well, I reckon I need to be gettin' into Rugby, Granny. I promised the Englishman I'd have his shirt to him first thing this mornin'."

"Then you'd best be hoofin' along, child," Granny advised, giving her a warm hug. "But I'm mighty glad you came droppin' by to show me that furriner's fancy shirt, though. It's might-nigh the purtiest thing I've seen in a heap o' Sundays."

Coralee laughed as she picked up her skirts and turned to leave. Handling the Englishman's shirt as carefully as if it were a fragile piece of china, she headed toward the colony.

Coralee had ventured into the small settlement on several occasions, becoming familiar with the layout of the site. Though she hadn't taken the time to survey the progress of the new development in recent weeks, she'd heard about the steady advancements in construction from her family. During the weekly Sunday gatherings of the Clabo clan, her brothers frequently mentioned their work on the new buildings, often launching into lengthy conversations about the projects with Rachel's father, Paul Proffitt.

Still, when Coralee entered the colony, she was surprised to find that the framework for the inn— the largest of the public buildings in Rugby—was nearly completed. She paused in front of the construction site, watching the workmen as they crawled over the wooden frame and pounded nails into slats of lumber.

"Hey there, pretty lady!" a man shouted.

Recognizing the voice of her oldest brother, Coralee swung her gaze to the top of the building just as a husky, bearded man hurled an arm into the air and waved at her. "You look like you're busier 'n a woodpecker this mornin', Harlan," she called out.

His laughter rumbled like peals of thunder through the morning air. "Can't argue 'bout that," Harlan replied, hammering another nail into the beam of the roof.

A second man, also bearded and stocky, scrambled across the rooftop, hammer in hand. "Besides, we ain't got time to argue," Wiley Bohanan insisted.

As her youngest brother flashed a grin in her direction, Coralee looked for some sign of her third sibling. "You got Crockett helpin' you up there, too?"

Wiley shook his head. "He's down at the sawmill, fetchin' some more lumber for us."

"Well, at least you're keepin' him out o' trouble this mornin'," Coralee said with a laugh. Pleased that her brothers seemed to be enjoying their work, she turned to leave.

She decided to begin her search for Jack in the dining hall. But as she headed toward the frame building, Jack opened the door and stepped onto the wide porch.

Coralee tried to ignore the frantic beating of her heart, tried to pretend the fluttery, breathless feeling in her stomach wasn't there. But she couldn't deny that the sight of him was wreaking havoc on what little common sense she had left. Undoubtedly, he was the most intriguing man she'd ever seen.

The rest of the men who were streaming out of the dining hall paled in comparison to Lord John Winslow. Most had relinquished their frock coats, pressed trousers, and starchy shirts in exchange for clothing more suitable for the rigors of mountain life—comfortable blue jerseys, sturdy jeans, and knee-high boots. But Jack was still wearing the standard attire of a British gentleman, and his dark, formal apparel set him apart from everyone else.

Though Coralee sensed that clothing wasn't the

only difference between Jack and his counterparts, she couldn't pinpoint the other factors that elevated him above the rest. At the moment, she was having too much difficulty catching her breath to think about anything in a rational, sane manner.

Breathing became even more difficult when Jack's eyes drifted in her direction, then roamed and lingered over the length of her in a slow, exacting way. Forcing herself to inhale a deep, steadying breath, Coralee planted a bright smile on her lips, placed one foot in front of the other, and marched toward him.

"I pressed and starched your shirt, just like you were wantin' me to," she announced, handing over the garment to him.

"Very nice." He fished into his pocket and retrieved a bright, shiny coin.

Observing his movements, Coralee couldn't help but admire his hands. Dark hairs were sprinkled across the tops of his long, agile fingers, and his nails were clean and neatly trimmed. Though no unsightly calluses or scars marred the surface of his skin, Coralee suspected those well-kept hands were capable of doing all sorts of masterful things, particularly where women were concerned.

The sound of his voice erased the wayward thoughts from her mind. "Are you ready to pick up the rest of my clothes now?" he was asking.

She struggled to regain her composure. "As a matter of fact—"

"Are you taking in laundry?" Adam stepped up to join them, curiously peering at the shirt in Jack's hand.

Another Britishman peered over Jack's shoulder, nodding with approval as he studied the garment. "If you're looking for some new customers, you've come to the right place, ma'am." After introducing himself as Daniel Yarby, the colony manager, the man added, "We've got enough dirty clothes to keep you busy until next spring."

"How much are you charging, ma'am?" a young Englishman asked.

"Two bits per garment," she replied.

"Sounds reasonable to me," one man assessed.

"Any price sounds reasonable for clean clothes," Adam remarked.

"Step in line, gentlemen," Jack warned with a good-natured chuckle. "I found her first." He glanced over at Coralee. "Are you ready to take in some more work?"

"I can start this afternoon," she offered, mentally assessing the situation. It made little sense to haul tons of dirty clothes to her cabin for laundering. Setting up a laundry tub in Rugby would provide much more convenience for everyone, she decided. "If you fellas have as many dirty clothes as you say you do, I reckon I should be settin' up a laundry tub right here in the colony."

Daniel stretched out an arm, motioning toward the creek that flowed along the border of Rugby. "Be our guest, ma'am," he insisted.

"Then I reckon I'd better get hustlin'," Coralee said, beaming with delight. "I'm gonna be busier than a bumblebee in a bucket of tar."

Chapter 5

Jubilant over her good fortune, Coralee raced toward the construction site of the new inn. She couldn't possibly lug the laundry tub to the colony by herself, and she needed the help of her brothers.

A bearded, burly man was unloading the last plank of wood from a crude wagon just as Coralee scrambled up to the work area. "Just the man I was lookin' for," she teased.

Crockett Bohanan rolled his eyes heavenward. "I had the feelin' trouble was headin' my way," he grumbled in mock dismay. "What are you needin', Miss Trouble?"

Coralee grinned. "I need you to bring my laundry tub to Rugby for me."

"For land's sake, Coralee!" Crockett dropped the plank to the ground. "What in tarnation are you gonna do with your laundry tub here in the colony?"

"What do you think?" she taunted with a laugh. "I'm settin' myself up a laundry business. And I've already got all my customers lined up! All the colonists want me to launder their clothes for them."

Crockett crossed his arms over his broad chest and frowned. "I don't rightly know if I like this idea of yours, Coralee. I'd hate to see my baby sister warshin' dirty clothes for these Englishmen every day."

"And why not?" Coralee challenged. "It's a good way to make myself some pocket money."

"But if those Englishmen know you're willin' to warsh those fancy pants of theirs, they might think you're willin' to let them get their hands on some fancy pants of yours."

"Oh, Crockett!" Coralee playfully swatted his arm. "They won't have any reason to think that. They'll realize I'm just here for warshin' clothes, and nothing more."

"But a woman can't be too careful, especially a woman as pretty as you," Crockett cautioned. "If any of these men start hasslin' you, I'll set them straight."

"And if I promise to let you know if anyone starts botherin' me ... will you help me get my laundry tub from the cabin?"

"I reckon so." Crockett grinned. "Hop in the wagon and let's get a move on."

Pleased to have her brother's support, Coralee climbed into the wagon and took a seat beside Crockett. As soon as they arrived at the cabin, Coralee dashed into the log dwelling and gathered up everything she would need for laundering clothes—lye soap, scrub boards, clothespins, and several pieces of rope. By the time she stepped outside, Crockett had loaded the tub into the back of the wagon.

When they returned to Rugby, Coralee quickly decided to set up her business near the creek that flowed behind the dining hall and the men's barracks. Knowing she would need fresh water for laundering clothes each day, she liked the idea of locating the tub a short distance from the colony's main water supply. As an added bonus, the spot provided convenient access for the Englishmen who wished to use her laundry services.

As Crockett unloaded the tub from the wagon, Coralee hastily strung a length of rope between two trees for drying clothes. By the time her brother had positioned the tub in place, Coralee's first customers were arriving, hauling out bundles of clothes from the barracks and depositing them beside the tub.

Crockett hastily excused himself, returning to the construction area for the afternoon. Left alone, Coralee hauled several buckets of water from the creek to fill the laundry tub and located some kindling to start a fire for boiling the water.

She had just placed a scrub board into the tub when Jack emerged from the barracks with a bundle of clothes slung over his shoulder. Dropping the bag of garments at her feet, he flashed a disarming smile. "I'll need all of my things laundered and returned to me in the morning," he announced.

His tone was authoritative, his manner condescending. Coralee bristled with defiance. "And if I don't obey your orders?"

His smile died on his lips. "Why wouldn't you? I thought you wanted to work as a laundress."

"I'm glad I've got the chance to make me some pocket money, the chance to help out you menfolk here in Rugby," she acknowledged. "But I'm not beholden to you for anything, Jack. You can't order me around like I'm some sort of servant."

He feigned innocence. "I don't believe I was issuing an order to you," he insisted, one corner of his mouth twitching with amusement. "It was simply a request. Nothing more."

Sensing that he was mocking her, Coralee lashed out at him. "Don't you deny it, Lord Jack Almighty. You know you were bossin' me just as well as I do. Why, I heard tell men like you have got bunches of servants back in England, servants you can order around to do all your dirty work for you. But nobody has servants here in Rugby, and you'd better start harnessin' that tongue of yours when you're askin' a body to do somethin' for you."

He took a step forward. "Would you reconsider my request if I rephrased it?" A second step brought him closer to her. "Or perhaps if I sweetened up my language a bit?"

She tossed back her head. "You could drench that mouth of yours with all the honey in the world, but I don't think it would sweeten up your way of talkin'. Somethin' tells me you're used to demandin' things, not askin' for 'em."

He edged closer still. "Then perhaps this will convince you that I'm sweeter than you think," he insisted, his voice husky and low.

If Coralee hadn't been so furious with him, she might have been more aware of his intentions, more prepared for what he was about to do. But she didn't have the chance to protest when he cupped her face between his hands and brought his lips down to hers. And once she felt the searing pressure of those sensuous lips moving across hers, she didn't have the willpower to pull away.

His mouth glided over hers slowly, smoothly, seductively, making her tremble from her head to her toes, sending tingles of delight up and down her spine. Until this moment, Coralee had thought she knew all about kissing. After all, she'd been a married woman, a wife to a demanding man. But Reuben Hayes's kisses paled in comparison to the heated touch of Lord John Winslow's mouth.

She'd never been kissed in such a slow, exacting way, never knew one kiss could make her ache with such fervent longing. The provocative touch of Jack's lips aroused feelings that Coralee didn't even know she had, feelings she thought had been buried long ago.

His hands moved from her face to her hair, then slithered down her back and settled around her waist. A moan rumbled from the depths of his throat, and he pressed her more tightly against him. But his movements sounded a silent alarm within Coralee, shattering the magic of the moment.

Land o' Goshen, what was she doing? This man had insulted her, treated her like a lowly servant. Yet, she hadn't uttered one word of protest since he'd pulled her into the circle of his arms.

She abruptly pulled back her head, ending the kiss. "Tryin' to butter me up with a kiss won't work, Lord Jack. First, you're orderin' me around like a servant, and then you're stealin' kisses from me! That's no way to be treatin' a lady."

Struggling to pull away from him, she pressed her palms against his chest and pushed with all her might. Jack stumbled backward and grasped the rim of the laundry tub in a desperate attempt to steady himself.

But the tub tilted to one side beneath the pressure of Jack's grip. Water splashed over the ground. Slipping over the wet surface, Jack struggled to regain his balance by clinging to the edge of the tub. Unable to withstand the increased pressure of his weight, the tub toppled over, spilling its contents and drenching Jack from head to toe.

By the time Jack shook the water from his face, he was shaking with fury. "Why didn't you watch what you were doing?"

Coralee bit back a smile. "Maybe I was too busy watchin' you," she said, grasping a bucket in each hand as she headed in the direction of the creek.

Jack stalked into the cottage and trudged up the stairs to the attic, leaving a trail of muddy, wet boot prints in his wake. As soon as he stormed into his living quarters, he reached for a towel hanging from a wooden peg on the wall. "Bloody hell," he mumbled.

A few feet away, Adam was languishing in a hammock, absently thumbing through the pages of a book. But as Jack plowed into the room, the Englishman stiffened in shock. "What in the bloody hell happened to you?"

"Isn't it obvious?" Jack snapped, plunging the towel through the mass of wet curls clinging to his scalp.

Adam tossed his book aside and bolted to his feet. "But how—"

"Don't even ask." Jack hurled the towel over his shoulder. "Let's just say it was a bloody accident and leave it at that. Quite frankly, I have no desire to discuss the matter."

Without waiting for a response, Jack wheeled and traipsed down the stairs. In due time, he would make amends with Adam for his rude behavior. But at the moment, he didn't want to be bothered with answering questions or offering explanations about his drenched state and foul spirits. Drying off—and cooling down—was his most pressing priority.

He exited the cottage, heading for a secluded spot that he had seen during his explorations through the settlement. A few moments later, he came to an isolated cove nestled between two forested slopes. Beams of afternoon sunlight were shimmering like spun gold across the flat patch of land, casting a luminous glow over the colorful wildflowers that dotted the landscape.

John lowered his long frame to the ground and shrugged out of his boots. Streams of water gushed from the linings, spilling over the sides and dribbling across the luxuriant leather.

He muttered an oath and set the boots aside. No doubt, the warmth of the sun would eventually dry out the leather, but he suspected the drying process would take several days. He wished he'd had the forethought to grab another pair of boots from his trunk before storming out of the cottage. At least he would've had the luxury of wearing dry boots for the rest of the afternoon.

But grabbing a clean set of clothes would have been impossible, he realized with a jolt. Other than the wet garments clinging to his skin, his entire wardrobe was in the possession of the blasted woman who was responsible for this sordid state of affairs.

"Bloody hell." He leaned back on his elbows and stretched out his long legs in front of him. If he could have peered into a crystal ball and foreseen the events of the afternoon, he would have never taken the risk of kissing Coralee Hayes. But, then, he'd never intended to kiss her in the first place.

When she'd balked at his request to return his clothes in the morning, he'd been stunned by her defiance. No one in a position such as hers had ever dared to question his authority. Infuriated by her argumentative manner and scathing remarks, he'd felt compelled to teach her a lesson or two about the dangers of defying Lord John Winslow.

So he'd mocked her, taunted her, practically laughing in her face as she'd scolded him for treating her with a lack of proper respect. But once he saw the sparks of fire glinting in her eyes, everything changed.

As her passionate spirit soared to life, the delicate features of her face had glowed with an exuberance that he'd never seen before, a beauty that both mesmerized and intrigued him. Within the space of a heartbeat, his anger and resentment had disappeared, replaced with a desire so strong and powerful that he nearly trembled from the force of it.

Acting on reckless impulse, he'd pulled her into his arms, never expecting that the feel of those full, rosy lips would set his loins aflame. But once he'd sampled a taste of her, he couldn't seem to pull away.

But then she'd pushed. He'd stumbled. The tub had toppled. And bales of water had literally drowned the flames of desire searing through him.

Now, with the warmth of the sun beating down on him, drying his clothes and renewing his spirits, a smile slowly worked its way onto Jack's lips.

Coralee Hayes was much too forthright and saucy for the likes of him. Yet, he couldn't help but admire her in a begrudging sort of way. After all, she'd attempted to set him in his place for stealing a kiss from her. Most women didn't possess that kind of tenacity.

His smile widened. The next time he kissed her, everything would be different. He would abstain from barking out commands at her, refrain from mocking her every word.

And above all else, he would make certain that a laundry tub was nowhere in sight.

*   *   *

By the time Coralee returned from the creek with fresh water for the laundry tub, Jack had disappeared from sight. The tub had been straightened to an upright position, she noticed, and the bundles of clothing left by her customers were still waiting to be laundered and pressed. The only lingering evidence of her heated encounter with Jack was a trail of muddy boot prints and a few puddles of water on the ground.

Coralee inhaled a deep, steadying breath, wishing all the turbulent emotions careening through her would evaporate as easily as the water that had spilled from the tub. When she'd pushed Jack away from her, she'd never intended for him to stumble and fall. She'd merely shoved him away because she'd been terrified of her own reactions to that searing, smoldering kiss of his.

"It doesn't matter now," she told herself, kneeling to start a fire with the kindling that she'd gathered down by the creek. "It was just a little kiss, and it won't be happenin' again."

Determined to forget the incident, Coralee turned her attention to the mounds of soiled clothing waiting to be laundered. Judging by the large bundles of garments scattered about, she had enough work to keep her busy for days.

She plunged into the first batch of clothing and sorted out the dark and light garments. By the time the water was boiling in the tub, she was ready to wash the first load of clothes. She had just placed several pieces of apparel into the scalding water when the sound of Rachel's voice drifted through the air.

"I just heard the news, Coralee!" Breathless with excitement, Rachel bounded up beside her. "Crockett just told me about your new business."

"Word travels fast, I reckon." Coralee motioned toward the piles of dirty clothes that surrounded her. "Maybe too fast, considerin' all the business that's been comin' my way."

Rachel's eyes widened in astonishment. "You don't have to wash all these clothes this afternoon, do you?"

Coralee shook her head. "No, but it looks like I've got me more business than I can handle by myself, Rachel. Do you reckon you could help me out? 'Course, I'm not askin' you to work for free. I'd be willin' to pay you for your help."

"I've never been fond of laundry day," Rachel admitted, "but it would be nice to earn some pocket money. I could work a few days each week for you, if you'd like."

"Maybe Maggie could help out, too," Coralee mused. "Judgin' by the number of customers who've dropped by today, I'm suspectin' I might need another set of hands around here."

"But I doubt Maggie's folks could spare her for more than a day or two at a time," Rachel said. "They depend a lot on Maggie for helping them out around the farm."

"I suppose you're right about that. It wouldn't do any good to ask Emmaline or Velma Ruth or Lucy Anne, either," Coralee surmised, a smile touching her lips as she rattled off the names of her sisters-in-law. "They got enough laundry of their own between all my brothers and their younguns."

"Perhaps you won't need anyone other than me," Rachel ventured. "Between the two of us, I believe we can handle a lot of dirty clothes."

"Maybe you're right, Rachel." Coralee grinned. "We'll get started, together, first thing in the mornin'."

The sun had barely crested the mountain peaks when Coralee arrived in the settlement the next morning. Eager to plunge into her work for the day, she scurried past the construction area. But as she neared the site where she'd left her supplies and belongings, she paused, surprised by what she saw.

Another laundry tub was sitting next to her old one, a tub much larger and newer than hers. Her brothers were congregated around the tin basins, laughing and talking with Rachel and her father. A few feet away stood a crude shack that obviously had been erected overnight.

Coralee picked up her skirts and darted toward the small group. "Are y'all plannin' to steal away my business?"

Paul Proffitt, a congenial man with thinning hair and a slender build, chortled in amusement. "We know better than to compete with you, darlin'."

"Mama wanted you to have this laundry tub of hers," Rachel explained. "It's too big for her to handle, and she thought you might like to use it."

"It's just our little way of wishin' you good

luck." Coralee's uncle nodded toward the three Bohanan men. "And your brothers here got up before
the crack of dawn to build a laundry shack for
you."

Coralee's gaze wandered from Paul to Rachel,
then shifted toward her brothers. Overwhelmed by
their thoughtfulness, she felt her heart swell with
joy. "I reckon I've got the best family in the whole
world," she said, giving each of them a warm hug.

Harlan grinned. "We reckoned you'd stay twice
as busy with two tubs and a shack for launderin'
clothes."

"And we figured you'd stay out of trouble for
twice as long," Crockett added, playfully tugging
on her hair.

"And we're hopin' you'll remember your poor
ole' brothers when you get paid for warshin' all
these clothes," Wiley said with a wink.

"Then we'd best be lettin' these womenfolk get
to work," Paul noted with a chuckle. He nodded
toward the construction area. "And we'd best be
gettin' to work ourselves, boys."

As the men shuffled across the grounds, Coralee
turned to her cousin with a smile. "Let's get busy,
Rachel. We got a heap of warshin' to do this mornin'."

Jack stood on the porch of the men's barracks,
arms folded across his chest, legs braced in a wide
stance, watching in silence as the four men left the
women to their work.

Ten minutes before, he'd stepped from the cottage, intending to head straight to the dining hall for breakfast. But when he'd noticed the small cluster of people surrounding Coralee across the way, he'd paused, lingering beside the cottage door, observing the unfolding scene with interest.

From the snatches of conversation drifting through the air, he'd been surprised to learn that the Bohanan men were Coralee's brothers. Jack had crossed paths with them on frequent occasions, even exchanging a few snippets of conversation with them from time to time. Well respected for their diligence and skill, the trio had garnered praise for their work from both colonists and mountaineers.

But even if Jack hadn't heard the mention of brothers or family, he would have known this was a gathering of kinfolk. The affectionate gestures, the caring looks, the teasing laughter, told him far more than words could say. It seemed as if there were no restrictions on the love that flowed so freely among them, no limits on the unconditional acceptance of each for the others.

Observing it all, he became acutely aware that his own parents and siblings were far more reserved than these mountain folk, far more restrained in displaying their emotions. Though he'd never thought he needed a sense of family in his life, Jack felt something gnawing deep inside him, something akin to a yearning to be part of a common bond once more.

He was still loitering on the porch, lost in his musings, when a colonist stalked out of the dining hall and slammed the door behind him.

Jack groaned. The majority of British natives residing in the colony were amiable gentlemen, but this particular chap was an exception to the rule. In the short time since he'd arrived in Rugby, Jack had already caught fleeting glimpses of the man's sour disposition. Some colonists claimed no other Englishman alive could rattle off as many oaths in a single breath without repeating himself as Lord Sturgis.

Now, Sturgis stormed toward Coralee wearing a scowl on a rather ugly face that bore a ruddy complexion and a long, crooked nose. "The lack of your progress is appalling, miss," he sneered, surveying the parcels of soiled clothing scattered around her.

Coralee stiffened noticeably. "We're just gettin' started," she said in a curt tone, "but now that we're all set up here, we'll be a-warshin' as fast as we can."

He tilted back his head a notch, peering down at her in a haughty manner. "I had expected that my clothes would be finished this morning."

"We're warshin' clothes in the order that we got 'em. If you'll give me your name, I'll check to see when—"

"You don't remember my name?" The man's face reddened with fury. "This isn't any way to run a business!" he roared. "Why, you should be—"

"Curb your tongue, Sturgis." Jack stepped up behind the man, clapping him on the shoulder. "If you rile this woman's temper, she's apt to give you a dunking in that laundry tub of hers. Believe me. I know."

Detecting a trace of amusement in Jack's voice, Coralee lifted her gaze to his face. To her surprise and delight, a hint of a smile was curving on his mouth, and his eyes were teasing and warm.

Little ripples of pleasure danced through her. In spite of the splashing finale of their argument yesterday, his demeanor held not a snippet of the resentment or anger she'd expected to see. Pleased that he possessed a good sense of humor, she couldn't suppress a smile from blossoming on her lips.

Sturgis, however, was still wearing a formidable snarl. "I shall return for my garments at the end of the day," he announced gruffly. Wheeling, he stomped toward the men's barracks.

Rachel stepped up beside Coralee, shaking her head in dismay. "I hope the rest of your customers aren't like that man, Coralee. I've never seen anyone so rude and demanding."

"Most of the colonists are more cooperative than Sturgis, I can assure you," Jack interjected. Shifting his gaze to Rachel, he gave a polite nod. "By the way, I'm Lord . . ." He hedged for an instant, then corrected himself. "I'm Jack Winslow."

Rachel offered a pleasant smile. "And I'm Rachel Proffitt."

"Proffitt?" His eyes narrowed briefly, then widened with sudden understanding. "I've spoken with your father on several occasions. Judging from the progress of the new inn, I've been impressed with his work."

"He built a lot of houses when we lived in Boston," Rachel explained. "Living up north isn't the same as living here, though. All of us—Mama, Papa, and I—are glad to be back in Tennessee."

"But it sounds as though you've brought a bit of Boston back with you," Jack noted with a sly grin. "You pronounce certain words a bit differently than most of the residents here."

Arching one brow, Coralee gazed pointedly at Jack. "Seems to me Rachel ain't the only one around here with a funny way of talkin'," she teased.

Jack's grin broadened. "Sometimes it's rather difficult to believe all of us speak the same language."

"Rachel might could do some translatin' between your fancy English talk and our mountain ways of sayin' things, but she's gonna be so busy helpin' me with all this warshin' that she's not gonna have time for anything else." Coralee reached for a pair of tin buckets. "If you can be sortin' out clothes, Rachel, I can be fetchin' some water for us."

"I'll give you a hand," Jack insisted, falling into step beside her. As they headed for the creek, he added in a low tone, "I just hope you don't get any ideas about shoving me into the water again."

"Somethin' tells me you don't have anything to worry about today." She cast a sidelong glance at him, vividly aware that he was still wearing yesterday's clothes, the same clothes that had been drenched with laundry water. From his strained expression, she surmised he was conscious of that fact, too. "I reckon you know better than to be stealin' a kiss from me again," she added, pointedly raking her gaze over the length of his wrinkled trousers and the width of his creased shirt.

"Yesterday's experience taught me a lesson or two, I'll admit." As they came to a halt beside the creek, he reached for the buckets in her hand. "I learned never to kiss you again when I'm standing next to your laundry tub. But I also learned something else, something that was rather surprising, even to me."

"What do you mean?"

He dropped the tin containers to the ground, then lifted a hand to her face and tucked a stray strand of golden hair behind her ear. Desire flickered from the depths of his eyes as he gazed down at her, and his voice became husky and low. "I discovered I liked kissing you, Coralee Hayes. I liked the way those lips of yours felt against mine. And I liked the idea of kissing you again."

Coralee's heart thundered in her chest. Hearing the seductive tone of his voice, seeing the flames of passion smoldering in his eyes, she felt a slow, simmering heat building inside of her.

Part of her wanted to dash away as fast as she could and escape from the threat of this enchanting man. But another part of her wanted to stay and experience the taste and touch of his lips on hers.

He leaned forward, edging closer, dipping his head toward hers. Coralee lifted her lips, waiting in breathless anticipation.

But just as she closed her eyes, Rachel's voice sang through the air. "We've got some more customers, Coralee!"

Hearing the sound of her name, Coralee nearly jumped out of her skin. Her eyes shot open, and she backed away from Jack without daring to meet his gaze.

"I'd best be gettin' back to work," she mumbled, reaching for one of the buckets. She hastily dipped the container into the creek, then whirled and scurried away.

Chapter 6

Coralee darted away from the creek, determined to avoid any further contact with Jack.
She had no intention of giving him the pleasure of
knowing that he was the cause of her disconcerted
state. At the moment, her cheeks were burning with
shame, her heart was tripping like mad, and her
breathing was ragged and shallow.

But the burdensome weight of the bucket in her
hand and the tangle of skirts billowing about her
legs prevented her from scampering back to the
laundry site at a brisk pace. Within seconds, Jack's
boots shuffled up beside her. In his hand was the
bucket that she'd abandoned on the bank of the
creek in her hasty attempt to escape from him.

Too flustered to acknowledge his presence, Coralee marched straight ahead and attended to her
new customers. Though she managed to mumble
her thanks when Jack dumped the contents of both
buckets into the laundry tub, she refrained from
saying anything more to the Englishman, hoping

her silence would convince him to go away and leave her alone.

She picked up a scrub board and a cake of lye soap. "If you'll do the rinsin', Rachel, I'll do the scrubbin'. Then both of us can hang out everything to dry."

Rachel rolled up the sleeves of her gown to her elbows. "Sounds like a good setup to me."

Coralee placed the scrub board and soap into the laundry tub while mentally preparing herself to come face-to-face with Jack again. But when she glanced up, he had disappeared from sight.

She breathed a sigh of relief and plunged her hands into the tub of water, intending to concentrate on her work. But as she methodically scrubbed the dirt from a particularly grimy shirt, her mind wandered back to that heart-stopping moment by the creek.

She'd been astonished when Jack had insisted that he was longing to kiss her again, even more astounded by the realization that she wanted him to kiss her, too. But the sound of Rachel's voice had destroyed that breathless moment of anticipation, jolting Coralee back into reality. Terrified by what had almost transpired, she'd turned away from Jack and fled, escaping from the man's disturbing presence.

Coralee cringed at the recollection, appalled by what she'd done. Tightening her hold around the soapy shirt, she jerked the garment through the water with quick, angry strokes.

It wasn't her desperate longing for Jack's kisses that disturbed her so. It was the fact that she'd scampered away from him like a frightened jack-rabbit, too consumed by trepidation to challenge the source of her fears.

Coralee slapped the shirt across the scrub board, furious with her cowardly behavior. "You yellow-bellied sapsucker," she mumbled to herself.

She couldn't recall another time in her life when she'd been so ashamed of her actions. Coralee had always tried to face the challenges of life with a spirit of determination, confronting each obstacle that crossed her path without hesitation. After all, problems and fears never disappeared by ignoring or avoiding them.

"Or runnin' away from them," she added aloud.

Resolving to face up to her fears in the future, Coralee pursed her lips together with renewed determination, then returned her attention to the work at hand.

At noon, Coralee and Rachel broke away from their work for lunch. As they sat beside the creek, they munched on the apples and carrots that Rachel had brought from home with her that morning.

"I'll bring our lunch tomorrow," Coralee promised. "And in a few days, I'll treat us to lunch in the dining hall. Harlan says the food is really good."

No longer restricted by limited finances, Coralee looked forward to visiting the dining facility for the first time. Many of the mountaineers who worked in the colony, including the Bohanan brothers, opted for eating lunch or dinner in the dining hall with the colonists instead of returning to their cabins for meals every day. Though the cost of each meal was deducted from the worker's pay, visitors to the dining hall—like Coralee—were required to pay cash for their meals.

"That will be a nice treat for both of us," Rachel said. "No matter what Miss Pearl plans to serve that day, I'm sure we'll like what she has to offer. She's a wonderful cook."

Coralee nodded in agreement, recalling the tasty dishes that Clell's wife prepared for church socials every month. "Let's see if these clothes are a-gettin' dry," she suggested.

To Coralee's delight, the warmth of the sun and the breezes whipping through the air had completely dried the clothing. Ready to begin the process of starching, pressing, and folding the garments, she hastily removed the apparel from the ropes that dangled between two chestnut trees.

Later in the afternoon, Coralee was pressing a pair of trousers when a wagon rattled through the settlement and came to a stop in front of the dining hall.

Clell leaped down from the wagon. "Mail's here!" he shouted, hurling a thick mail pouch over his shoulder.

Within a few moments, a number of colonists had gathered around the wagon. Clell dipped into the pouch and handed the first piece of mail to the

colony manager, who promptly called out the re-
cipient's name.

Judging from the expressions on the colonists'
faces, Coralee sensed they were eager to receive
some word from their loved ones in England. Each
time Clell presented another letter to Daniel, the
assembly of men edged forward, pressing closer to
the wagon, anxiously waiting to hear the next
name.

Coralee's gaze skittered across the crowd, then
lingered on the tall figure of a man who was standing apart from the rest. Her eyes wandered over
the dark hair that tumbled across his brow, then
her gaze traveled across the broad width of his
shoulders and roamed over his flat belly and trim
waist before meandering over the muscular length
of his legs.

As she admired Jack, a rush of longing swept
through Coralee. In all the world, she suspected
there could never be another man who affected her
like this one, a man who could leave her weak and
giddy and gasping for breath just by looking at
him.

She was still reveling in the delight of Jack's arresting features when Daniel announced that all of
the mail had been disbursed for the day. Amid
groans of disappointment, the men turned away
from the wagon, going their separate ways. Some
shuffled back to the barracks empty-handed, while
others set off in different directions with their mail
from home in tow.

But Jack gave no indication that he intended to

leave. Remaining rooted to the spot where he had been standing throughout the mail call, he cast a puzzled glance at Clell and Daniel. "Are you certain you've distributed everything?"

Clell peered into the mail pouch. "Ain't got nothin' else in here to give out, young fella."

"Bloody hell," Jack muttered.

"I know it's difficult to be patient," Daniel said, "but the mail sometimes takes weeks to arrive."

"At the moment, I'd settle for getting my hands on any kind of news from London." Jack raked his fingers through his hair in frustration. "At the very least, it would be nice to receive a copy of *Punch* or the *Illustrated London News*. If I'd realized it would take months for a couple of bloody publications to get here, I would have never ordered the blasted things before I left England."

Pivoting on his heel, he jammed his hands into the pockets of his trousers and traipsed back to the barracks.

"Poor Jack," Rachel sympathized with a shake of her head. "It must be awful not to get any word from home."

Coralee quietly placed a pair of pressed trousers on top of a stack of neatly folded garments. "Maybe having some clean clothes will perk up his spirits a bit," she mused aloud.

"Why don't you take his laundry to him?" Rachel suggested. "I can take care of everything here while you're gone."

Coralee inhaled a deep, steadying breath, knowing what she had to do. Thus, she gathered up the freshly laundered garments that belonged to the Englishman. "I won't be gone for very long," she assured Rachel.

Cradling the clothes in her arms, Coralee set off for the barracks. As she stepped onto the porch of the cottage, she planted a bright smile on her lips and approached the open door. But her smile faded away when she heard the rumbling of male voices inside the house. She slowed her pace to a halt, listening to the conversation with interest.

"I can't recall the last time I read a newspaper," Jack was grumbling. "I haven't the vaguest notion of what's happening in London—or anywhere else on the Continent, for that matter."

"If our motherland vanished from the face of the earth, it would take years for the news to reach us here," Adam contended.

"It almost seems like we're living in a different world instead of a different country," Grant added.

Peeping around the door frame, Coralee stole a glance at the three men. Gathered around a small table, intent on their conversation, they seemed oblivious to her presence. She edged forward, continuing to eavesdrop on the discussion.

"Our choices are more limited here," Jack continued on. "A few months ago, deciding which ball to attend and which horse to wager on were my most pressing decisions of the day. Now I consider myself fortunate if I have the chance to choose between pinto beans or fried potatoes for dinner."

"All the plans we made during our voyage from England seem rather foolish now," Grant added, shaking his head in disdain. "If you recall, we vowed that hiring valets and housekeepers and cooks would be our first priority when we arrived in Rugby."

A cynical smile broke through the scowl on Adam's face. "What blimey fools we were," he mumbled. "If we had known about the lack of suitable servants in this place, we could have brought our own cooks and valets and housekeepers with us."

"That would have been much more feasible than trying to find some acceptable servants among the mountain natives," Jack agreed. "And at least we would have been able to communicate with each other without any difficulty. I don't understand half of what these mountaineers are saying. In fact, I've never heard anyone butcher the Queen's English the way they do."

"You mean you reckon you don't rightly know what they're a-tryin' to tell you?" Grant mimicked.

Adam chuckled. "That atrocious mountain twang doesn't bother me as much as the food around here. As far as I can tell, these mountaineers don't use any seasonings other than lard. Everything in the dining hall is dripping in grease. When I asked the cook if she had any Worchestershire sauce on hand, she looked at me as if I'd sprouted two heads. And if I have to eat another meal of cabbage and ham hocks, I think I shall . . ."

Adam rambled on, but Coralee didn't hear another word. Deeply offended by the men's degrading remarks, she bit her tongue to keep from lashing out at them.

But she couldn't ignore the defensive instincts surging through her. Mountain customs and ways were an integral part of her life, the very foundation of her roots and culture. Life might be simple and unassuming in Morgan County, but it was the only way of life that Coralee had ever known, and she couldn't bear the thought of anyone demeaning her native traditions. How could she stand by and allow Jack and his friends to belittle mountain life without rising to the defense of her heritage?

Determined to defend her culture and salvage her wounded pride, she burst into the cottage. "Well, Miss Pearl might try to whip up a batch of that Worchestershire sauce you're wantin' if she knew what it was," she said in a crisp tone.

The men snapped to attention, obviously startled by her sudden appearance. Ignoring the surprise flickering across their faces, Coralee stepped up to the table and dropped Jack's laundry in front of him. Then she pulled back her shoulders and lifted her chin.

"If you fellas would quit moanin' and groanin' about what you don't have, you might appreciate what you do have a whole lot more. No, this ain't London, my lords. You're not livin' in that big place called England anymore. This is the United States of America, and you're livin' in the hills of Tennessee. But you're so busy missin' all those fancy things you're used to havin' at home that you're not enjoyin' what you've got here."

Adam bristled with indignation. "But we don't—"

She cut him off with a wave of her hand. "Now, if I was livin' in England, I'd want to sample all the fancy foods you have over there. I might not like the way you cook some things, but I'm sure I could find somethin' that tasted good to me. And I might get a hankerin' for some of my granny's turnip greens and black-eyed peas, but I wouldn't be rude to the person who got up before the crack of dawn to fix breakfast for me."

A sheepish expression crossed Adam's face, and he shifted uncomfortably in his chair. "I never intended to insult—"

"Miss Pearl is doin' the best she can, cookin' up all that food every day in that dining hall for you Englishmen. But if you don't like her grits or hog jowls or black-eyed peas, you don't have to be insultin' about it. Why, I bet you'd like lots of Miss Pearl's dishes if you gave 'em a chance. She makes the best polk salad in these hills, and her cucumber pickles are the tastiest things you could ever hope to put into your mouth. And if you'd tell her about some favorite foods of yours from back home that you're cravin', she'd probably be happy to try and whip 'em up for you."

"But I'm not a cook, and I don't know how to tell her to prepare my favorite dishes," Adam grumbled. "Even if I did, I doubt she'd understand half of what I was saying unless I used terms like 'vittles' and 'pecks' and 'heaps.' "

"Most of us 'round these parts think your fancy

English way of talkin' is mighty peculiar, too, Adam." Coralee's voice remained steady and low. "But you don't hear us pokin' fun of the peculiar way you talk, do you?"

"No, but—"

"We might do things differently and we might say things differently, but that don't mean neither of us are wrong. Now, Lord Jack here likes to wear his shirts stiffer than a dried cow's hide. I think it's plumb crazy for him to be wearin' those fancy shirts of his when he's out traipsin' in the woods. But he didn't pay no mind to me when I told him he should be wearin' his old clothes. And that's fine by me if he wants to get his fancy clothes dirty. It don't make neither of us wrong or right. He's got the privilege to have his own opinion, and I got the right to have mine. But I'm not gonna hassle him just 'cuz he's doin' somethin' I don't agree with."

Every muscle in Jack's body went rigid. "I never asked for your opinion, as I recall."

"The way I see it, you're not used to askin' for anybody's opinion. You're used to doin' as you please and gettin' other people to do your dirty work for you. I think you fellas are havin' a hard time comin' to grips with the fact that you don't have no servants 'round here, waitin' on you hand and foot. And if I'm hearin' you right, I 'spect you're thinkin' the folks 'round these parts aren't even good enough to be your servants." She crossed her arms over her chest and frowned. "Didn't your daddies tell you that everybody is equal in America? That nobody is better 'n anybody else?"

"Equality in America is nothing more than a grand illusion," Jack retorted. "Life isn't equal for everyone here."

Coralee met Jack's gaze without flinching. "Some folks may have more money or school-housin' or fancy clothes than others," she contended in a low, steady voice, "but that doesn't mean anybody's life is less important than somebody else's."

She picked up her skirts and swept out of the cottage. Jack bolted from the chair and raced after her. Catching up with her on the porch, he grasped her arm and spun her around to face him. "What's gotten into you, Coralee? What prompted that tongue-lashing from you?"

Anger flared from her eyes and voice. "How would you feel if everybody in Morgan County came waltzin' into your fancy house in England and poked fun at everything they saw or heard or tasted?" she challenged. "How would that make you feel, Lord Jack?"

Peering down into her upturned face, Jack saw a myriad of emotions etched into her delicate features. Her eyes were wide and glimmering with outrage, her cheeks flushed with a rosy hue. The dismay crinkled across her brow said her pride had been deeply wounded, but the determined thrust of her jaw told him that she would not tolerate any further ridicule of her heritage.

Jack released his hold on her arm, determined to ignore the rush of desire pulsing through him.

There was so much about this woman that he didn't understand, so much about her that baffled him. She saw no need to apologize for her humble way of life, and she leaped to the defense of her roots with a sense of pride that he couldn't help but admire.

He'd never known a woman with more spirit, more pride in herself and her way of life. And he'd never known a woman who had the audacity to speak her mind so freely. Was it any wonder she was becoming more and more fascinating to him with each passing day?

"How would that make you feel, Jack?" she prodded once again.

"Bloody well angry," he admitted with reluctance.

She twisted her mouth into a frown. "For the life of me, I can't figure out why you're stayin' here. If you don't like anything about livin' in Rugby, why don't you just pack up your go-poke and leave? Why don't you just go back to England?"

"I have my reasons for remaining here." He pulled back his shoulders. "I plan to make a nice future for myself in Rugby."

The natural arch of her brows rose higher. "And just what are you intendin' to do?"

"I'm considering several options. But it has never been my intention to stay here permanently, Cora-lee. I've always planned on returning to England as soon as I acquire a substantial amount of wealth from my endeavors."

"Oh." Something akin to disappointment flickered across her face, then abruptly vanished beneath an overly bright smile. "Well, I reckon you'll have lots of stories to tell about livin' here when you get back home. When all those English buddies of yours hear 'bout the hillbillies you left behind in Tennessee, they'll be splittin' their ribs from laughin' so hard."

Irritated by the caustic assumption, he stiffened noticeably. "I suspect their amusement would pale in comparison to the enjoyment you hillbillies are already deriving from the presence of Englishmen in your midst," he shot back impulsively. "You say you haven't ridiculed our speech, but something tells me that you and your friends are rather amused by everything else about us. I imagine our lawn tennis court has caused quite a stir around here. Telling your friends and family about the court, you probably were laughing hysterically."

"I haven't been laughin' about that tennis lawn of yours with anyone!" Coralee denied hotly. "You didn't see me laughin' when I saw you playin' tennis with Adam and Grant, did you? Why, when Adam asked me if I had a hankerin' for learnin' how to play that little game of yours, I told him I wouldn't mind if I could spare the time and had one of those paddle-rackets."

"If you were truly interested in learning how to play tennis, I'm certain Adam or Grant would loan a racket to you," Jack pointed out. "But, then, I don't think you would care for the game."

Her brows rose a notch. "You don't want me playin' tennis with you?"

He shrugged with indifference. "To be honest, I—"

"I reckon you're thinkin' I'm not good enough to be playin' with you." A hint of defiance glimmered from her eyes, and her voice took on an impertinent tone. "Or maybe you're afraid I'll whup the tarnation out of you on the court."

Jack flinched. His instincts warned him that she was taunting him, deliberately trying to provoke him into saying or doing something he shouldn't. But the competitive streak that kindled his spirit and nurtured his soul refused to ignore the challenge that she presented to him.

He set his jaw into a firm, hard line. "Meet me at the tennis court in an hour, Coralee. I'll have a racket waiting for you."

Chapter 7

❧

Jack was waiting at the tennis court, just as he'd promised, when Coralee approached the site later in the afternoon. Breathless from the ten-minute walk from the heart of Rugby, she absently wondered why Jack and his friends had situated the court on the perimeter of the colony's land holdings. Her own cabin was located closer to the court than the men's barracks or the dining hall.

But those thoughts disappeared as Coralee neared Jack. A straw hat was perched atop his dark curls, and two tennis rackets dangled from his hands. Coralee couldn't help but notice that he was wearing a set of clothes she'd laundered for him—a pair of buff-colored knickerbockers with dark stockings, and a white shirt and tie.

Her heart gave a crazy lurch. Though Coralee didn't understand why he insisted on dressing in such fancy clothes for playing games, she had to admit the garments looked wonderful on him. The short pants hugged his sinewy thighs, and the dark stockings emphasized the bulging muscles that rippled along his shins.

Absorbed in perusing his appearance, Coralee scarcely noticed the tight set of his jaw until he leveled a stern look of disapproval in her direction.

"I was beginning to think you weren't interested in learning how to play tennis after all," he remarked in a terse voice as she stepped up beside him. "You're late, in case you didn't notice."

"I would've been here long before now, but everybody in Rugby showed up at the same time, wantin' to pick up their laundry before I left for the day." She winced. "And I wasn't perzactly countin' on Vernon Sturgis inspectin' every stitch of clothes he owns, makin' sure I'd pressed out every little wrinkle."

"From what I know of the man, he can be quite annoying at times." The scowl on Jack's face disappeared, and his lips twitched with amusement. "Contending with Sturgis is an acceptable excuse for being late to your first tennis lesson, I suppose."

More disconcerted by the intriguing tilt of his lips than she cared to admit, Coralee shifted her gaze to the tennis rackets in his hand. "To be honest, I never heard tell of lawn tennis before you Englishmen got here."

"An English chap by the name of Wingfield invented tennis-on-the-lawn a few years ago," Jack explained. "Though the game hasn't been around for very long, it's become quite the rage in England. People are even competing in tournaments, vying for championships in the sport. In fact, the best players have been competing for the world championship cup for the last three years at a place in England called Wimbledon."

"Have you played in lots of tournaments?" Coralee asked, genuinely curious.

"A few." He shrugged. "I'll have to keep in practice while I'm living here if I expect to continue playing in tournaments when I return to England."

"Maybe you can start some tournaments of your own here in Rugby," Coralee suggested just as a strong gust of wind whipped through the air, rustling the branches of the surrounding trees.

She tilted back her head, observing the swaying motions of the branches of a maple tree located a few feet away from the tennis court. "If you're intendin' to show me how to hit that little ball of yours this afternoon, we'd best get a move on," she advised. "We're fixin' to get a gully-washer in a spell or two."

Jack peered up into the cloudless blue sky. Confusion shimmered from his eyes as he glanced over at Coralee. "What makes you think it's going to rain?"

"That tree over yonder told me so." Just as she pointed out the tree to Jack, another whoosh of wind swept through the tree's sprawling branches. "See how the wind is whippin' up those leaves on that silver-leaf maple? When you can see the back sides of those leaves a-flutterin' in the wind, all shiny and silvery-like—just the way they're lookin' right now—that means a big rain is comin' our way."

The quirk on Jack's lips told Coralee that he held little faith in the prediction. "Then I suppose we should proceed with your lesson while the skies are still clear." Biting back a smile, he handed a racket to her. "Are you ready to begin?"

"I reckon I'm as ready as I'll ever be." Clutching the racket in her hand, Coralee fell into step beside him, making her way across the court.

"Then let's start with a few basic rules," he said, coming to a halt. "The game starts when one player serves the ball across the net to the other side." Demonstrating the point, he tossed the ball into the air, drew back his racket, and hit the ball across the net with relative ease. "Your objective is to hit the ball back over the net. If you miss, your opponent gets fifteen points."

"Fifteen points?" She wrinkled her nose. "That sounds like a heap of points just for makin' one little mistake."

He chuckled. "There are other ways for your opponent to score points, I'm afraid. If your ball hits the net instead of sailing over it—or if you hit the ball out of bounds—your opponent still gets the fifteen points. The second time you fail to return the ball, your opponent's score goes up to thirty. The third time, his score reaches forty. And the fourth time you miss, he wins the game."

"Oh, my." She shook her head in dismay. "It don't take long to give away all them points, does it?"

"Actually, it can take several hours for good players to complete a set of lawn tennis," he revealed. "The sport is played in sets, and six games make up a set. Of course, each game must be won by two points, and each set must be won by at least two games."

Coralee offered a weak smile. "All these numbers are clutterin' my brain, Jack. I don't mean any offense, but do you reckon we can just skip over the rest of the rules for now? I was hopin' you'd give me some pointers on how to get that little ball across the net without hittin' it out of bounds."

"I suppose it wouldn't do any harm to show you a few of the basic strokes," he conceded. "We can always play some practice games later to familiarize you with the rules."

"First, show me how I'm supposed to hold on to this paddle-racket," she insisted. "It's kinda hard to get a grasp on the dad-blame thing without lettin' it slip away from me."

He held out his racket, wrapping his long fingers loosely around the wooden handle. "You always want to grip the racket like you're shaking hands with it," he instructed.

"That looks easy enough," Coralee remarked, mimicking the gesture.

He nodded with approval. "Now let's work on your forehand stroke. Just pull back your arm and swing the racket forward," he explained, displaying the stroke as if he were hitting an oncoming ball.

"Like this?" Coralee attempted to imitate the movement, swinging the racket through the air.

He shook his head. "You've got to keep your

racket level and steady to follow through on your stroke. Let me show you."

He placed his racket on the ground, then stepped up behind her and rested his right arm over the length of hers. With the touch of his sleeve pressed against her blouse, a tingling sensation shot through her arm.

"You can control the direction of the ball with the movement of your arm and the tilt of the racket," he said. Clasping a hand over her wrist, he guided her through the motions of the forehand stroke.

"I see," Coralee mumbled. Though she was trying very hard to listen to his instructions, she was far too distracted by other, more pressing matters to comprehend much of anything he had to say. She was acutely aware that his chin was practically resting on her shoulder, and she could feel the heat of his breath skittering across her neck. To make matters worse, the crushing weight of his arm was burning into her skin with the heated effect of a branding iron.

"Let's try it again." His voice sounded hoarse, strained. "This time, let's take it ... very ... slowly ..."

As he pulled back her arm, the world seemed to grind to a halt for Coralee. Everything around her— every sound and color, every movement and smell—seemed brighter and louder, more pronounced and vivid. She heard the rustle of fabric as their arms moved in unison, felt the grinding strength of Jack's muscles pressing against her.

And she sensed flames of desire searing through her with such intensity that she trembled from the force of them.

She turned her head ever so slightly, wondering if Jack had noticed the sudden tremor that had ripped through her. To her dismay and delight, she found herself looking straight into a pair of the most startling blue eyes that she'd ever seen.

"I think you're a very good student, Coralee." His voice was just above a whisper. "But I believe it's time to try some different strokes now."

The rackets hit the ground with a clatter, and his hand flew to her face. With an outstretched finger, he tilted her chin up, forcing her to meet his gaze. "I can't stop myself, Coralee," he warned, his eyes dark with passion, his voice husky and low. "I can't stop myself from kissing you again. Can't stop myself at all...."

The rest of his thought vanished beneath the crush of his mouth against hers. Stunned by the electrifying contact, Coralee clutched his shoulders for support before her trembling legs could give way beneath her.

His fingers plunged into her hair, supporting the back of her head as he ground his lips into hers with increasing pressure. Mesmerized by the seductive power of his touch, Coralee instinctively parted her lips, granting his tongue entrance into her mouth. But as her tongue swirled around his, the intimate touch evoked a fiery response from Jack.

He devoured her with hot, openmouthed kisses

that bore the greed and hunger of a starving man, a man who had been denied the taste of a woman for far too long. Caught up in the riveting sensations swirling through her, Coralee sensed she would give this man anything he wanted, any part of her that he might demand. Every inch of her was on fire for him, burning with a heat more fiery and intense than any she'd ever known.

"I can't ... can't stop, Coralee," he murmured against her mouth, his breathing ragged and shallow.

"Who's sayin' ... you have ... to stop?" she murmured back, pressing herself more tightly against the length of his hard, masculine frame. Curling her arms around his neck, she removed the straw hat from his head. As the hat tumbled to the ground, she splayed her fingers through his dark hair, relishing the soft feel of the thick strands.

Her response provoked a deep rumble from the depths of his throat, an urgency in the pressure of his touch. His hands glided across her shoulders, then drifted down her back, coming to a halt beneath her outstretched arms.

Her breath snared in her throat as his fingers edged their way along her ribs, then halted at the outer curves of her breasts, touching, feeling, exploring. And when he boldly cupped each of the generous swells in his hands, Coralee thought she would die from the intense longing that was blossoming within her. His long fingers grasped and fondled and massaged each swollen mound as if he could never get enough of them.

Coralee moaned, only vaguely aware of the wind whipping around them, the rumble of thunder in the distance, the sudden drop of temperature in the air. Lost in the fiery flames of passion that were consuming her, she was oblivious to anything other than the feel of his tongue swirling around hers, the touch of his hands caressing her breasts, the warmth of his loins pressing against her.

As he grasped the hardened tips of her nipples, squeezing them between his fingers, Coralee moaned again. "Don't . . . stop," she urged breathlessly. "Please . . . don't stop."

At that instant, a strong current of wind lashed through the air, unleashing a torrent of rain. The droplets poured down from the skies like tiny bullets, stinging their skin and soaking their clothes within a matter of seconds.

As a clap of thunder split the air, Coralee jerked away from Jack's embrace. "Let's get back to my cabin," she insisted.

She scooped up Jack's straw hat from the ground as he hastily retrieved the rackets. Then she grasped his hand and broke into a run, heading for the shelter of home.

Jack offered no protest when Coralee took the lead, guiding them over a maze of trails that meandered through the forested hills. Sheets of rain plummeted over the mountainous terrain, sweeping across the valleys and gaps without any signs of ceasing.

Just as a bolt of lightning flashed through the

sky, a quaint log cabin came into view. Through
the driving rain, Jack could see the silhouette of the
building's sharply pitched roof. The roofline sloped
over a porch that skirted the full width of the front
side. To the right outer wall of the cabin was a
chimney made of mountain stone.

Coralee raced ahead of him, sprinting onto the
porch and shaking the water from her hair. As
Jack's boots trudged across the planked flooring,
she pushed back the matted strands from her face
and laughed. "You're a sight for sore eyes, I'm
afraid."

Jack grinned, mindful that beads of water were
trickling from his hair and dribbling down his face.
Setting aside the tennis rackets, he leaned back
against one of the four thin, smooth-shaven logs
that served as posts to support the porch roof. "I
thought you would have been accustomed to seeing me like this by now." He rested his hand over
the wooden railing that stretched between the supporting posts. "Every time I kiss you, it seems, I
end up drenched to the bone."

Her laughter was bright and warm. "But this
time, you had advance warning," she reminded
him. "You'd been warned that rain was a-comin'
your way."

His smile vanished. Though he'd given little credence to the sighting of upturned leaves blowing
in the wind, he couldn't deny that he was baffled
by the accuracy of her prediction. "Just where did
you learn how to predict the weather?"

"My Granny Clabo learned me about watchin'

the leaves on silver-leaf maples," she explained. "Granny knows all about the signs of Mother Nature."

"Then your granny must be a very insightful woman," he remarked absently, not fully convinced that anyone could foresee the future with total accuracy.

"Rain isn't the only thing she can foretell," Coralee insisted. "She's always taking note of signs of nature. Come August, she'll be countin' up the number of fogs settlin' along these ridges. For every heavy fog that comes along durin' August, we'll have the same number of heavy snows come wintertime. And the number of light fogs on the plateau in August tells Granny how many blue darters we'll be gettin' during the winter."

"Blue darters?" he echoed, unfamiliar with the term.

"That's when it's colder than the devil's heart with just a light dustin' of snow," she explained. "Everybody 'round these parts depends on Granny to predict what kind of winter we'll be havin' so we'll know how much food we should be a-stockin' up to last till spring. Durin' the summertime we know we're in for a bad winter if Granny sees that hornets are a-nestin' close to the ground, or if woolly worms are black on each end and brown in the middle."

Jack chuckled. "Sounds as if she has her predictions down to a fine art."

"There ain't nobody in this world like my Granny Clabo." Coralee sank into a rocker on the porch and removed one of her shoes. "I reckon we'd best be takin' off our shoes so we can let 'em dry out by the fire."

Jack plopped down on the planked flooring. Shrugging out of his boots, he shook his head in disdain. "My boots just started feeling comfortable again from their last drenching," he muttered.

"Quit grumblin', Jack," Coralee urged, springing to her feet. "We're gonna catch our death of cold stayin' out here. Let's get inside and get ourselves dry."

She darted into the cabin. Jack followed closely at her heels, his wet stockings shuffling across a puncheon floor of huge poplar logs. The logs were at least two feet wide, worn smooth from years of use.

Coralee scrambled toward a fireplace built of smooth mountain stones and mortared with clay. Logs rested on two round stones in the cavernous opening, stones that Jack presumed were a primitive form of andirons. Next to the logs, an iron pot was suspended from a hook and rod that dangled from the interior of the chimney.

Coralee placed her shoes on the hearth, then ignited the logs in the fireplace. As the fire roared to life, crackling and popping, shedding a soft golden glow over the room, Jack studied the interior of the cabin with marked interest. Never before had he set foot in a dwelling constructed from logs that had been chinked together with clay.

A wooden shutter with leather hinges sealed the one small window in the dwelling, masking the outdoor light. Over the fireplace, a wooden fire board held a handsome clock that appeared old but functional. The pendulum swayed to and fro, rhythmically ticking away the seconds. Above the clock, a shotgun with powder horn and leather pouch for ammunition hung from wooden pegs.

He swept his gaze across the room. A walnut bed covered with a colorful quilt was pushed against the log wall to his left. A rocking chair sat by the fireplace, while two straight-backed chairs flanked a small oak table. The remaining household equipment and furnishings were scant. Except for a few pots and pans, it appeared everything else was homemade.

All in all, it bespoke a primitive existence. Jack swallowed hard, suddenly feeling out of place and very uncomfortable. The storage sheds and barns at Havenshire Manor, buildings that housed the Winslow livestock and grains, were loftier than this woeful little shack.

He'd suspected Coralee's living quarters were simple and quaint, but he'd never expected anything so primal and uncivilized. Never expected to find anything so bereft of material goods.

Back in England, he'd scarcely glanced at the paupers and beggars who'd crowded the streets of London, paying little mind to the outstretched hands and tin cups that had clamored around him when he'd exited one of the gaming halls. But now, he couldn't help but wonder if those wretched souls were living in conditions any better than this.

It wasn't that the cabin appeared dirty or unkempt. On the contrary, everything seemed clean and tidy. But the stark barrenness, the lack of material goods, in the simple dwelling stunned Jack beyond words. How could this woman survive in such primitive conditions?

He was still perusing the room when the sound of Coralee's voice broke into his thoughts. "You need to be a-gettin' out of those wet clothes of yours," she advised. "I'll be fetchin' you something to wear while those fancy pants of yours are gettin' dry."

Before he could protest, she was hoisting herself up a ladder that was nailed flat against the log wall and scrambling into a small loft above the main room. In the next instant, a pair of men's breeches was sailing down from the loft.

"I 'spect these clothes will be droopin' on you a tad, but they won't be swallowin' you up. And they'll keep you from catchin' your death of cold, too." She peered down at him and grinned, then tossed a homespun shirt and a pair of socks in his direction. "Give me a holler when you're finished dressin'."

She pulled back from the rim of the loft, disappearing from sight. He set his boots beside her shoes on the hearth, then gathered up the clothing strewn about the room. Just as he picked up the last garment, she poked her head over the loft edge once again. "I plumb forgot you'd be needin' to dry off," she said in an apologetic tone, sending a towel flying through the air.

"Thanks," Jack muttered ungraciously, too disconcerted by the pitiful condition of the ghastly clothes to offer a decent word of gratitude. The very thought of donning the homespun garments sent a shudder of repulsion down his spine.

But what other choice did he have? He was sopped to the bone, so soaked he was shivering, and his own clothes were dripping with water and forming puddles beneath his stockinged feet.

With a shrug of resignation, he stripped off his wet garments and toweled dry. To his surprise, his quaking ceased as soon as he donned the clothing that Coralee had provided for him. Though the breeches hung loosely around his trim waist and the sleeves of the shirt were patched at the elbows, the garments were soft and warm and astonishingly comfortable. For one of the few times in his life, Jack had to admit that he felt quite content without the constricting collars and cuffs and starched shirtfronts of his standard attire.

But he'd burn in hell before he'd admit as much to Coralee.

"I'm decent," he called out, plunging the towel through his wet hair.

The patter of bare feet rippled across the loft. Coralee descended the ladder with an agile grace, wearing a faded dress that he immediately recognized. Other than the wet white blouse and skirt slung over her shoulder, he'd never seen her wearing anything else than the faded calico.

She padded across the puncheon floor, clutching a hairbrush in one hand. "You're lookin' like you feel a whole lot more comfortable now that you've put on some dry clothes."

He shrugged. "I can't say I'm totally at ease wearing clothes that don't belong to me."

"Those clothes that you're wearin' belonged to my husband, Reuben." She draped their wet garments over the backs of two wooden chairs. "I don't have any use for 'em, now that he's dead and gone, but I couldn't see throwin' 'em away. I figured I could always cut 'em up and use the fabric when I'm puttin' a quilt together."

An uneasy feeling rolled through Jack. The notion of wearing homespun clothing held no appeal to him, but the morbid thought of donning a dead man's garments repulsed him beyond words. Knowing the homespun clothes had once belonged to Coralee's dead husband only made matters worse. He cringed, appalled that he'd agreed to wear the garments in the first place.

"Now, don't you be frettin' yourself none about wearin' Reuben's things. Nobody is gonna see you 'cept me," Coralee assured him. "A body would have to be dead from the neck up to come callin' in the middle of a chunk-washer like this one." A soft smile curled at the corners of her mouth. "But, then, not too many folks come callin' 'round here even when it's bright and sunny."

He could understand why. The cabin was tucked away in a remote part of the county. And Morgan County was located in the middle of nowhere. "Don't you ever get . . . lonely?"

Her brows rose in surprise. "Why would I get

lonely? I've got my Granny Clabo, three brothers, three sisters-in-law, pert near to a dozen nieces and nephews, a heap of cousins, and two sets of aunts and uncles livin' here. I don't have the chance to get lonely." She warmed up her hands beside the fire. "I reckon we need us some hot apple cider to take the chill off our bones."

Jack watched in silence as Coralee removed a crock from the shelf and poured its contents into the iron pot from the fireplace. Then she returned the pot to the fire, hanging the handle through the hook of the iron bar, and waited for the flames to heat the cider.

Jack inhaled a deep breath, enjoying the scent of cider filling the room. And when Coralee presented him with a mug of the steaming liquid a few moments later, he was delighted to discover that the cider tasted as good as it smelled. "Ah, this is wonderful," he praised.

Smiling, Coralee settled down in the rocking chair near the fire, hairbrush in one hand and mug of cider in the other. Jack hunkered down on the braided rug at her feet, resting one arm across an updrawn knee, suddenly feeling very content and not knowing why.

He closed his eyes, listening to the crackle of the fire, the tick of the clock on the fire board. Finding the patter of rain on the roof and the creak of Coralee's rocker somewhat soothing, Jack became vaguely aware that he was noticing the simple things of life in ways he'd never considered before now.

Still, his contentment with the moment failed to erase the questions that lingered in his mind. He opened his eyes and glanced over at Coralee. "I don't understand why you're living alone here, Coralee. Wouldn't you rather live with one of your relatives?"

She set her mug on the hearth. "I love my granny more than anything in this world, but we're too stubborn and ornery to live together. We'd be peckin' at each other like a pair of old hens if both of us were tryin' to rule the same roost."

"But what about one of your brothers?"

"My brothers have got their own families to be frettin' about." She ran the brush through her hair. "They've got enough mouths to feed without bein' bothered with the likes of me. And now that I'm a grown woman, I'm not their responsibility."

A proud spirit of independence filled her voice and her eyes as she continued. "Besides, my roots go down deep here in this place. My daddy built this cabin with his own two hands, and my brothers and I grew up here. When Daddy and Mama passed on, my brothers decided to build their own homesteads. Since all of Daddy's land was divided up betwixt the three of them, they wanted me to have the old home place for my own, along with the land that stretches between here and Granny Clabo's cabin."

"That would have never happened in England," Jack remarked. "The law would have required that your father's estate be passed down to your oldest brother. The rest of you would have been entitled to little or nothing."

She wrinkled her nose. "Well, it's a mighty good thing we don't have a law like that here in Tennessee. If we did, I wouldn't have a roof over my head to call my own." Sighing, she idly brushed the golden strands that tumbled over her shoulders. "I reckon it all worked out for the best. My brothers have got so many younguns that none of 'em could have squeezed their families into this little cabin. They've got much bigger places for themselves now."

"So I guess this cabin must hold lots of happy memories for you," Jack speculated.

"My childhood memories of living here are very happy ones," she said very slowly, "but as for the time when I was a married woman..." She gave her head a shake. "Those memories aren't happy at all."

Jack cringed. He didn't particularly care for listening to women talk about their husbands, dead or alive. He'd heard enough tales of woe from the married women he'd secretly courted in England. "I didn't mean to pry," he said uncomfortably.

"I wouldn't be tellin' you anything I didn't care for you knowin'." She leaned back in the rocker. "You know, when you were askin' if I get lonely livin' here by myself, I was thinkin' that I hadn't been lonely at all since Reuben got himself killed last year. 'Course, I got myself plenty to do. If I'm not chasin' down my chickens, I'm quiltin' or tendin' to my chores. And now I'm launderin' clothes for most of the colony, too."

A sense of amazement suffused Jack. How could Coralee smile about her plight in life? The woman was simply struggling to survive, he thought. She scrounged for the basic necessities of living, hoarding food for the cold months ahead and battling against the odds to earn enough money for one measly dress and one pair of shoes.

He was still contemplating the situation when the still, small sound of her voice shattered his thoughts. "But to be honest, I've never felt more lonesome in my life than when Reuben and I were livin' here as husband and wife."

"What do you mean?"

"Reuben wasn't much company. He was always wantin' somethin' he didn't have. I don't think there's nothing wrong with havin' hopes and dreams, mind you, but Reuben couldn't be content with anything. Once he got somethin' he'd been wantin', he didn't care for it anymore. He was too busy wantin' somethin' else to enjoy what he had." Her voice grew very soft and quiet. "I reckon that's why he didn't have much use for a wife after he got hitched up to me. He started dippin' into his corn likker more and more, disappearin' for days at a time. And then . . ."

She swallowed thickly. "One afternoon, he got himself so full of corn likker that he could barely put one foot in front of the other. But he got to mouthin' off and told half the men in the county that he had himself a woman in Cincinnati, and he was takin' off to stay with her for a spell. Folks say when he got on that horse of his, he was so drunk that his head was bobbin' every which way, lookin' like it was gonna fall plumb off his neck."

"So you didn't see him leave?"

She shook her head. "When he left the cabin that mornin', he told me he was gonna be helpin' out on the McCarter farm for the day. I didn't know he'd been takin' off for Cincinnati until Clell come knockin' at my door that afternoon. Clell is the one who told me Reuben's horse got spooked by somethin' and threw him against one of the big boulders juttin' out along the trail to Sedgemoor Station. Said Reuben smashed his head plumb open, gettin' himself killed dead on the spot." She paused. "And Clell told me why Reuben had been on his way to Cincinnati, too."

Jack clenched his fists into tight balls, furious with the scoundrel for betraying his wife and bringing such needless pain into her life. "It must have been terrible for you to lose your husband and discover that he'd betrayed you at the same time."

"Any love I ever had for Reuben died soon after we got hitched up." She shrugged. "It's over and done with now. I don't clutter my mind with thinkin' about it anymore. I'm tryin' to focus my thoughts on gettin' me that store-bought dress and shoes in Cincinnati come fall. And it looks like I just may get 'em, considerin' I'm gonna be makin' some pocket money from takin' in laundry."

Jack's throat tightened with emotion. At the moment, he wanted nothing more than to take her away from the backwoods of Tennessee and show her all the pleasures that life had to offer, all the pleasures that she'd been denied for so long. For some unexplainable reason, he found himself yearning to present her with the dress and shoes that she longed to have, wanting to fulfill every desire of her heart.

And he wanted . . . *her*.

Lord, she was beautiful. The soft glow of the fire was highlighting the golden hue of her hair, emphasizing the beauty of her delicate features. He drank in the sight of her, sitting there, studying the sweep of her jaw, the deep green of her eyes, the sensuous curves of her lips.

His gaze lingered on her mouth for a moment, then dropped to the swell of her breasts. Desire, hot and searing, ripped through him.

He dragged his eyes away from her, reminding himself that the driving force behind the heated stirring of his loins was nothing more than an overwhelming urge to have his physical needs fulfilled. After all, an eternity or two had elapsed since he'd ventured between a woman's soft thighs, plunged his hard, swollen shaft into a sweet inner core that was wet and hot and throbbing with need.

Convinced that deprivation alone had provoked his ravenous state of longing, he glanced back at Coralee. Any woman—not just the golden-haired beauty seated in front of him—could have evoked the ache in his groin, the tremble in his hands, the beads of perspiration forming along his brow.

He forced himself to resume the conversation,

hoping a discussion would ease the throbbing pain in his loins. "So why haven't you remarried?" he probed.

Apparently oblivious to Jack's frazzled condition, Coralee gazed into the fire. "None of the homeboys 'round these parts have struck my fancy, I reckon. Besides, I've already been hitched up once, and I'd rather be seein' my girl cousins gettin' themselves some men of their own."

"But I'm rather surprised you don't have scores of suitors calling on you," he admitted frankly. "Isn't there one special beau in your life?"

"Mercy, no. I haven't had any jularkers comin' 'round here since Heck was a pup." The slight smile on her lips suddenly vanished. She snapped around to face him, stiffening noticeably. "I wouldn't have been lettin' you take liberties with me this afternoon if I'd been promised to somebody else," she said, her voice bristling with defensiveness.

A sly smile crept onto his lips. "Some women—even married women—don't mind sharing their affections with more than one man."

"I don't rightly know how you could be thinkin' that way about me." Suspicion glinted from her eyes. "But maybe you are thinkin' that since I've had me a man before that it wouldn't be too hard to get me wantin' to have a man again."

Jack winced, unable to deny the accusation. Though he'd never consciously considered Coralee as a prime candidate in the game of seduction, he supposed the thought had drifted through the recesses of his mind in recent days. After all, experience had taught him that women who were familiar with the pleasures of a heated romp between the sheets were much more willing to convey their affections without emotional entanglements. He'd always steered clear of young, virginal ladies, knowing their expectations were much different. Their innocent, naive ways demanded that any physical display of affection must be accompanied by such atrocities as marriage and loyalty and love.

The prolonged silence and his grim expression apparently confirmed Coralee's suspicions. "I'm beginnin' to understand now, Lord Jack. You're just wantin' a woman, aren't you?"

"I won't deny that the pleasures of feminine company have been absent from my life for far too long," he admitted frankly. "To be honest, I—"

"I don't reckon you need to be sayin' anything more, Jack. I didn't fight you down at the tennis court when your hands was wanderin' all over my body 'cuz I thought you were wantin' *me*. I didn't realize you weren't bein' particular, that you'd settle for any warm body wearin' a skirt who might come passin' by your way. But if you're thinkin' I'm gonna spread my legs for you just 'cuz you got your pecker all swelled up, you can pick up your buttocks off my floor and get yourself back to Rugby right now."

Anger slashed through him. Quaking with fury, Jack reached out and snatched his boots from the hearth. "I have no intention of staying here another moment," he snapped, shoving his feet into the damp leather and tying a knot in the laces. "Why should I waste my time consorting with a backwoods woman who holds no appeal to me?"

Lunging to his feet, he yanked his clothes from the back of the chair and hurled them over his shoulder. Then he stormed across the puncheon floor and hurled open the door, never once looking back as he bounded from the porch, surged into the forested hills, and plunged into the driving rain.

Chapter 8

A gust of wind and rain blasted through the front entrance of the men's barracks as Jack hurled open the door and stormed inside the building. Jolted by the blast of damp air in the room, Adam and Grant looked up from their card game and froze in stunned disbelief.

The cards in Adam's gloved hand slipped from his grasp and dropped to the table. "What in the bloody hell . . . ?"

"What does it look like?" Jack slammed the door and plowed into the room.

"It looks like you got caught in the rainstorm"— a pained expression crossed Grant's face—"wearing someone else's clothes."

"How observant of you," Jack growled. He lunged toward the stairs, annoyed by the men's intense scrutiny of his appearance. Though he had no reason to be shameful of his drenched condition— anyone, after all, could get caught in a rainstorm without warning—the notion of being seen in a ragged set of homespun clothes was a different matter entirely.

He had just grasped the handrail on the staircase when Adam called out to him. "Hold on a minute, Jack. Don't you want to tell us what happened?"

Jack wheeled, his hair and clothes slinging beads of water around him. "There's nothing to explain. The storm came up before Coralee and I could—"

"Coralee?" One corner of Adam's mouth twitched. "You've surprised me, Jack. I wouldn't have guessed you were the type who would be attracted to a mountain wildcat."

"I never said I was attracted to her," Jack denied swiftly. He dragged a hand through his wet hair and wished he'd never mentioned the woman's name. "I simply gave her a few pointers on playing lawn tennis."

"I thought you would have been furious with her after the way she lashed out at us today." Grant scooped up the game cards from the table and piled them into a neat stack. "As for me, I'm still licking my wounds. Some of her points were rather sharp, to say the least."

"That's because mountain cats attack with sharp claws." Adam bit back a smile. "The woman certainly has a way with words, I'll admit. I don't know that I've ever heard another female speak her mind the way she did."

"A British lady would never dare to be so outspoken." Jack winced. "Of course, Coralee has already reminded us of the differences between our cultures."

Grant shuffled the deck of cards in his hands. "Actually, I think she offered some good suggestions today. It wouldn't hurt us to look for the good around here instead of grumbling about the bad all the time."

"That's easy for you to say." Jack tugged at the drenched sleeves of his homespun shirt. "You're not soaked to the bone and freezing to death."

"But you've apparently taken Coralee's advice about wearing old clothes for traipsing through the woods," Adam pointed out.

"These homespun rags are only temporary, I can assure you." Jack grasped the wet garments draped over his shoulder. "My own clothes got drenched when the storm came up. When Coralee and I arrived at her cabin, she insisted I wear this homespun garb until my own garments were dry. But then . . ." He grimaced. "But then we had words, and I left."

Grant grinned as he raked his gaze over Jack's rain-soaked clothes. "Maybe it would have been better if you'd stayed."

"No telling what might have happened if you hadn't gone back out into the storm." Adam's voice was taunting and low. "A rainy afternoon . . . a cozy mountain cabin . . ."

"Drop it, Adam. I've already said I was simply giving the woman a tennis lesson." Jack plopped down at the foot of the steps and yanked off his water-soaked boots. "God only knows I have nothing better to do with my time."

"I suppose all of us need something constructive to do." Grant absently shuffled the deck of cards again. "If we had some sort of project to keep us busy, we probably wouldn't sit around complaining so much."

"After we built the tennis court, I considered the possibilities of creating a bridle path along the banks of the Clear Fork." Jack shrugged. "In the end, I figured it would be too much work for the three of us. Clearing and grading the riverbanks would require a lot of physical labor."

"Maybe the rest of the colonists would be willing to help," Grant suggested. "Who knows? They may like the idea."

"I suppose it wouldn't hurt to discuss the possibilities with them," Jack mused.

"You can bring up the issue in the morning when all of us are together in the dining hall for breakfast." Adam tapped his gloved fingers on the table, motioning for Grant to deal the cards. "As for now, it's time for another game."

"A bridle path?" The cynicism in Vernon's voice reverberated through the dining hall. "Why in the bloody hell do we need a bridle path around here?"

Jack leveled a hard glare at the disgruntled colonist. "For our own enjoyment," he answered in a clipped tone.

During the last quarter hour, the colonists in the dining hall had listened attentively as Jack outlined his proposal for creating a bridle path along the banks of the Clear Fork. Though the majority had expressed their interest in the project with nods of approval, Vernon Sturgis had voiced numerous objections. Now, Jack was rapidly losing his patience with the man's constant stream of questions and interruptions.

"If all of us work together, the project shouldn't be too difficult," one of the younger colonists reasoned.

"I think it's a bloody good idea," another piped in.

Still, Vernon balked. "If you chaps want a bridle path so badly, why don't you take up a collection, pool your funds, and hire some mountaineers to do the work for you?"

"Most of the local residents are already employed by the colony, working at the sawmill and construction sites," Jack explained. "As colonists, we're the only available source of labor in Rugby. If we want a bridle path, we'll have to be the ones to create it."

Vernon shuddered. "If you blimey fools want to break your backs and blister your hands, go ahead and be my guests. As for me, I have no intention of digging ditches like some common laborer. I'll find a better way to spend my time."

As Vernon marched out of the dining hall, Jack glanced around at the remaining colonists. "Vernon has made a valid point, gentlemen. This project will require a great deal of physical labor—the type of work we're accustomed to delegating to members of the working class. But if you're not opposed to rolling up your sleeves and getting dirty for a week or two, I believe we can work together and construct a fine bridle path for our own pleasure."

"I'd be willing to help," one man offered.

"It would be nice to have something constructive to do for a change," another agreed.

"And we'd have something to show for our efforts," added a third man.

One by one, the remaining gentlemen offered their assistance. Within a few moments, every man in the dining hall had volunteered to work on the project. By Jack's estimation, nearly two dozen volunteers had offered to render their services, including four newcomers who had resided in Rugby for less than a week.

Pleased with the show of support, Jack grinned. "It's settled, then. We'll start clearing the banks of the Clear Fork right after breakfast in the morning."

As the discussion came to a close, the group quietly disbanded. Some picked up their forks and resumed their meals, while others lined up for their servings of grits and ham from the cook's kettle. Several men who had already eaten the morning fare quietly left the facility.

Seated alone at the table, Jack lingered over a mug of hot tea, grateful the men had accepted his proposal. Clearing the way for a bridle path would require a great deal of his time and labor, not to mention the efforts of planning and preparation for the project.

And God only knew he needed an engaging venture in his life. Jack desperately hoped his involvement in the ambitious plan would consume all of his energy and block everything else from his mind ... especially all thoughts of a fiery-tempered mountain beauty.

"Blasted woman," he grumbled, still infuriated by the events of the previous afternoon. His heated exchange with Coralee had haunted him throughout the night, and the dawn of a new day had not diminished his anger. Even now, as he recalled the parting words of their conversation, waves of fury swept through him.

He slammed down his mug and bolted to his feet. "It's just a damn game," he muttered as he stalked outside.

But that was the problem, he realized with a jolt. His boots clattered to a halt on the porch as the revelation gripped him, swift and hard.

Coralee Hayes had caught onto his game of seduction. She'd seen his motives as clearly as if she'd been peering through a glass windowpane. Worse yet, she wasn't willing to become a participant in his favorite sport, nor did she care for following his rules. All of which meant he was losing at his own game.

Jack was still fuming as he glanced across the grounds and noticed that two men were making their way toward the laundry shack. Though he'd seen the pair working at the construction site of the inn, he'd taken little notice of them amid the mass of mountain natives who arrived for work each morning in Rugby. But, now, he observed the two men with interest as they struck up a conversation with Coralee.

The tallest of the pair, a husky man with a thatch of bright red hair, flashed a good-natured grin at Coralee. "How much would you charge me for warshin' one of my shirts?"

"Two bits, Simon." Coralee grinned back at the man. "Just the same as I charge everyone else."

Simon's dark-haired companion clutched his throat in mock horror. "You wouldn't give us a special rate?"

"Why should I?" she shot back. "I don't give a special rate to anyone else, Zach."

"But I thought we were special, seein' as how we've known you since you was knee-high to a grasshopper," Zach returned.

"You are special to me," Coralee insisted, laughing. "I dance with the two of you more than anyone else at the hoedowns, don't I?"

Simon's grin widened. "Come to think of it, I reckon you do."

Jack clenched his fists into tight balls. Though Coralee had denied any interest in local men, her present actions were sending a far different message.

Coralee Hayes might not be schooled in the art of etiquette, but she instinctively knew how to warm up to the male gender, he observed. At the moment, she was flashing that honey-sweet smile and batting those lashes of hers with the skill of an accomplished flirt.

Unable to endure another moment of the troubling sight, Jack stormed across the porch and marched past the laundry shack without a glance in Coralee's direction. Without thinking, he headed in the direction of the weathered barn that housed the colony's horses.

A multitude of emotions ripped through him, emotions he'd never known existed until now. No longer could he deny that he wanted Coralee. At the moment, Jack wanted nothing more than to claim her as his own. He wanted to devour every enticing dip and swell, explore every hidden, secret part of her that he had not yet had the chance to taste and touch and explore.

But that was all he wanted. Jack didn't want to admire her courage and strength or care about her happiness. Didn't want to listen to her dreams or hear about her family. He didn't want to have any feelings for her at all, other than feelings of physical attraction.

Yet, he couldn't seem to control the avalanche of emotions crashing through him. In spite of Jack's determination to shield his heart, uninvited emotions were invading his thoughts and gnawing away at the very core of his soul.

He closed his eyes and groaned. What had happened to Lord John Winslow? Where was the titled aristocrat with the elusive heart and cavalier ways? Was he still the same man who had mastered the art of seduction, never allowing himself to fall prey to the allure of a woman's charms? Or was he actually starting to *care*?

"Bloody hell," Jack grumbled. He stalked into

the barn and hoped a morning ride would erase the chaotic emotions whipping through him.

As Simon and Zach turned and walked away, Coralee slapped the scrub board into the laundry tub with such force that water splashed into her face. "I should wring that man's neck," she muttered. "If anyone ever deserved to be strangled—"

"Good heavens, Coralee!" Rachel's eyes widened in shock. "Simon and Zach didn't say anything offensive. They were just—"

"I'm not accusin' Simon or Zach of anything. It's Lord Jack Almighty who's got me madder 'n a wet hen. Did you see the way he marched right past us with that nose of his stuck up in the air?"

"Actually, I didn't see—"

"Well, thank the good Lord that He spared you from the sight," Coralee snapped.

A mixture of concern and confusion glimmered from Rachel's dark eyes. "Why are you so angry with Jack?"

Coralee leaned against the laundry tub and heaved a weary sigh. "Let's just say I thought we were startin' to have feelin's for each other. But then I found out Lord Jack doesn't have any feelin's at all."

Rachel paled. "You and . . . Jack?"

Coralee nodded glumly. "I should have known better than to let an Englishman turn my head."

"I never realized . . ." Rachel gave her head a shake. "I suppose I should have suspected as much, considering the way he's always dropping by here and talking to you. But I didn't think you were interested in finding a man for yourself after the way"—she grimaced—"after the way Reuben treated you."

Coralee pulled her hands from the soapy water and sighed again. "When Reuben got killed, I figured I'd never get married again, never in a million years. I was hurtin' somethin' terrible when I learned about all the awful things he did behind my back. Still, I reckon that didn't stop me from wantin' to have a man in my life again someday, the kind of man who will treat me real special-like." She placed a soiled shirt into the tub just as a fresh surge of anger ripped through her. "But Lord Jack Winslow certainly isn't the man for me."

"Perhaps the situation isn't as dismal as you suspect, Coralee. I've noticed the English seem much more guarded and reserved about expressing their feelings than the rest of us. Maybe Jack is simply being cautious, or perhaps you've misunderstood—"

"I haven't misunderstood anything," Coralee insisted. "Jack made his intentions perfectly clear."

At that moment, one of the colonists approached the laundry shack with a bundle of soiled clothing in hand. As Rachel scurried to tend to the customer, Coralee attempted to focus her attention on her work. But her thoughts lingered on the events of the previous afternoon, no matter how hard she tried to push them away.

When Jack declared he wasn't interested in the likes of someone like her, she'd decided that nothing would give her more pleasure than yanking the roots of his hair from his head. His heartless remark had deeply wounded her, and she'd given serious consideration to seeking revenge against him.

But his callous disregard for her feelings had wounded her even more. How could he pull her into his arms with such soul-jarring passion, then declare that he cared nothing for her? As far as Coralee was concerned, the Englishman had taken liberties with her that no man—other than a husband, of course—should dare to take with a woman outside the bonds of marriage.

To make matters worse, she'd been plagued with shame for her own lack of judgment. Why hadn't she resisted the man's charms? She'd been a fool to allow a man like Jack Winslow to turn her head. Only a pea-brained idiot would have fallen into his arms without restraint and permitted him to have his way with her without once offering a word of protest. But what had she done? She'd actually encouraged him *not* to stop!

Coralee scrubbed a grimy shirt with all the force she could muster. All in all, she was terribly confused about her feelings for Jack Winslow, and she wasn't certain how to deal with the conflicting emotions swirling through her.

She was still thinking about the situation as Rachel placed the customer's bundle beside the laundry tub. "So much has been happening around here this morning that I haven't had the chance to tell you about some exciting news, Coralee. Last night, Pa told Mamma and me that he's going to build us a new house . . . right here in Rugby!"

Coralee glanced up, surprised by the announcement. "I thought the colony was just for Englishmen."

"Pa said the colony board has decided to open the settlement to anyone who wants to establish a home here. He thinks lots of families from up north will be interested in moving to Rugby. And maybe some families from England, too."

"I hope Uncle Paul can get your new house built before all those folks get here." Coralee grinned. "They'll be wantin' him to build new houses for them."

"He's got to finish the colony's public buildings first," Rachel explained. "But he promised he'd start working on our house just as soon as the new inn opens up. He and Mamma are already talking about what kind of house they want to build. I think they're leaning toward a design that would complement the English architecture of the rest of the buildings in Rugby."

"That must be awfully excitin' for them." Coralee picked up another bundle of clothes for scrubbing. "How do you feel about livin' in Rugby, Rachel?"

"It will be different from living in our cabin," Rachel admitted. "But I think it will be nice to have some neighbors close by—as long as they're nice."

Coralee offered a weak smile, suddenly grateful that she was not the one who was planning to move into the settlement. Judging from one particular Englishman's behavior, she suspected that nice neighbors in Rugby would be few and far between. And she could certainly live without neighbors like Jack Winslow.

Jack galloped over the narrow trail, determined to think of an endeavor that would yield a handsome profit for him during his stay in Rugby.

The brisk morning ride had cleared the maze of muddled thoughts from his head, just as he'd hoped. As he'd plundered through the forested hills and galloped through the quiet coves, he'd become mindful of the importance of occupying his mind with thoughts of something other than Coralee Hayes. If he intended to withdraw from his pursuit of the mountain woman, he needed to focus his efforts on another type of challenging game.

He headed back to the settlement, pleased with the magnificent performance of the horse he'd purchased in Cincinnati. Every man needed a horse as fine as this one, he thought.

The passing notion suddenly became a source of intrigue for Jack. Who wouldn't be willing to pay a hefty sum for a fine animal such as this? Horses were indispensable commodities, especially for the men who lived and worked in these isolated mountains. No one could survive in this remote region for very long without a horse at his side.

Why couldn't he breed horses? He could buy the livestock in Cincinnati, then bring the creatures to Rugby for breeding. No doubt, he could easily hire a few of the mountain lads to work for him as stable hands and groomsmen. And the rest would be simple. He merely needed a few stalls for the horses and a parcel of land for grazing and training the creatures.

As Jack surveyed his surroundings, he quickly dispensed with the idea of purchasing one of the large tracts of land along the perimeter of Rugby. If any portion of the colony held the potential of increasing in value, it was the heart of the town site. Already, the rough trails that had been cut through the settlement were taking the shape of village roads and streets.

Jack's vision for his future came into clearer focus when he returned to the settlement and perused the vacant lot adjacent to the construction site of the new inn. The plot appeared large enough for his purposes, it seemed. And the mere position of the land next to the inn meant that it held more promise of increasing in value than other tracts in Rugby.

He was still surveying the plot when he caught sight of Daniel near the construction site. He swiftly dismounted and approached the colony manager. "Tell me, Daniel. Is this parcel of land still available for purchase?"

Daniel nodded. "No one has indicated any interest in it."

Jack's pulse accelerated. Purchasing the lot was a gamble, he knew. But something deep inside of him sensed it was the right thing to do. And every instinct he possessed told him that the odds of making a success of his venture were highly favorable.

As Daniel rattled off the size of the lot and

named a price, any doubts that might have lingered in Jack's mind quickly faded away. One monthly remittance from his father would easily cover the cost of the land.

"Sold," Jack announced firmly.

Surprise flickered across Daniel's face. "There's no need to rush into a decision, Jack."

"But there's no need in delaying the matter, either," Jack insisted. "I would like to get my plans under way as soon as possible."

"We can draw up the paperwork, if you'd like." Daniel heaved a troubled sigh. "But you can't take possession of the property for several more weeks."

"What do you mean?"

"The colony board is the legal owner of the property," Daniel explained, "and all documents pertaining to the transfer of property within the colony must be approved at the board's office in London. Sending documents across the Atlantic—and back again—is a rather slow process, I'm afraid. More than likely, it will take several weeks—maybe even a month or two—before you'll have any legal rights to the property."

"And I can't occupy the site until I have a clear title to the land in my possession," Jack surmised.

"I'm afraid so," Daniel confirmed.

Jack closed his eyes and groaned. He had no intention of permanently living in this primitive wilderness. The longer it took for him to get started on building his fortune, the longer he would have to stay. He'd hoped to lay the groundwork within a few days, put his plans into motion within a few weeks. But without legal claim to a parcel of land, how could he get started on building a new life for himself?

"Bloody hell." The bitter sting of disappointment ripped through him. At the moment, Jack was sorely tempted to head down the mountain and jump on the first train he could find. He should have known nothing would work out the way he'd intended. Should have known there was no hope of a future in this wretched place, no matter what he tried to do.

He was still considering the possibilities of leaving Rugby when the sound of Daniel's voice intruded into his thoughts. "So what would you like to do, Jack? Do you still want to make an offer on this piece of land?"

The questions pierced through Jack, deep and hard. Was he prepared to meet the challenges of life in this rough, untamed land? Could he overcome the obstacles that would be certain to ensue?

Or was he ready to admit defeat now?

He straightened his shoulders, reminding himself that the game had just begun.

"Let's draw up the papers and get them off to London today, Daniel." Jack turned and headed toward the barracks, hoping they could complete the transaction before he had the chance to change his mind.

Chapter 9

───∞─────

In spite of Jack's determination to steer clear of Coralee, he couldn't resist the urge to steal a glimpse of her when he emerged from the men's barracks the next morning.

But as his gaze wandered in the direction of the laundry shack, he was surprised by what he found. Though Rachel was working diligently—alongside a young woman with auburn hair, a woman who was not familiar to Jack—Coralee was nowhere in sight.

He jerked his gaze away from the shack and stepped down from the porch. Perhaps Coralee was running an errand or delivering a batch of laundry to one of the colonists. But whatever she was doing, it was none of his concern, he reminded himself just as a crackling noise sliced through the air.

Jack peered in the direction of the construction site and noticed that several workers were removing nails from one side of an immense wooden shipping crate. Curious, he walked over to the area. When Jack reached the site, the workers removed the final board from the crate and began hoisting furniture from the wooden container. As the men hauled the items into the building, Paul Proffitt glanced over at Jack and grinned. "Looks like we're ready to put the final touches on this place," he remarked. "These crates of furniture just arrived from England last night."

"I hadn't realized the building was so close to completion." Jack watched with interest as the workers pulled a mahogany bed from the shipment. He'd almost forgotten that most people spent their evening hours in soft, comfortable beds. Eager to bid farewell to his hammock, he silently resolved to become the first occupant of the new inn—and the first to occupy the mahogany bed that the workers were hauling into the building.

"I've already assigned most of my workers to other projects," Paul explained. "This afternoon, we'll be startin' on a church building. And next week, we'll be layin' the foundations for a few cottages."

Jack smiled. "Sounds like we're finally getting a touch of civilization in Rugby."

An hour later, Jack discovered another reason to smile. When he arrived at the banks of the Clear Fork after breakfast, he was pleased to find that the colonists seemed eager to tackle their new project. And by the time he returned to Rugby for lunch, he was amazed by the amount of work that had been accomplished in so short a time. The men had cleared a large portion of the matted growth of rhododendrons and laurels from the creek banks as they'd worked side by side throughout the morning. And they'd promised to work at the project each morning until the bridle path was completed.

Jack was still musing over the day's accomplishments as he headed in the direction of the dining hall for the noon meal. But as he strode past the laundry shack, the sound of Rachel's voice broke into his thoughts.

"We haven't seen much of you around here in the last few days, Jack," she remarked in a pleasant tone.

Grinning, he stumbled to a halt. "I've been rather busy of late," he lied smoothly.

"We've been rather busy, too." Rachel nodded toward the woman standing beside her. "Maggie here is helping out for a few days."

"I don't have much of a likin' for warshin' clothes, but I reckoned I could help out for a spell, seein' as how Coralee and Rachel and me are cousins and all," Maggie explained. "But I'm just pitchin' in for Coralee until she gets to feelin' better."

A tiny beat of alarm pulsed through Jack's veins. "Coralee is . . . ill?"

"She's having a great deal of pain," Rachel revealed, "but I suspect she'll be back to her old self in a day or two."

"Until she gets back her strength, stayin' at home is the best thing she could do—for herself and for everybody else 'round here," Maggie insisted.

Jack's heart skipped a beat. "So her condition is . . . contagious?"

"Oh, no. You can't catch anything from Coralee." Rachel bit back a smile. "Unless, of course, her foul mood rubs off on you."

"Believe me, I love the woman like a sister, but I'm not gettin' anywhere near her today." Maggie picked up a basket of wet garments. "I reckon I'll hang these clothes on the line while you're rinsin' out the rest of this load, Rachel."

As the women returned to their tasks, Jack frowned in confusion. Both Maggie and Rachel had been vague about the nature of Coralee's ailment, and he couldn't understand why. What was wrong with the woman?

He was still pondering the question when Grant stepped up beside him. "How about a set of lawn tennis after lunch?" Grant asked.

"Sounds good to me," Jack agreed hastily, welcoming the chance to focus his thoughts on something other than Coralee.

On the tennis court, Jack put forth his best efforts, centering his concentration on the ball as it whizzed back and forth across the net. Between his agile movements and skillful strokes, Jack easily won the set, defeating Grant in four out of six games.

"Congratulations, Winslow." In a gesture of true sportsmanship, Grant extended his hand to Jack at the completion of the set. "You're a hard man to beat on the tennis court, you know."

"What can I say?" Jack grinned. "Winning is my sole objective."

"At the moment, my only objective is getting some rest before dinner." Grant sighed, wiping the perspiration from his brow. "Between working on the bridle path and playing tennis with you, I don't have an ounce of energy left for anything. I'm heading back to the barracks."

"I'll catch up with you later, then." Jack picked up the tennis ball from the ground. "I think I'll stay here for a while and practice my backhand."

Ten minutes later, however, Jack realized that practicing tennis wasn't what he truly wanted to do. Restless and discontent, he retreated from the tennis court. But as he walked away from the site, he couldn't ignore the reason for the uneasy feelings that were assaulting him. And he couldn't dismiss his mounting concern for Coralee's welfare.

"Bloody hell," he muttered. Unable to resist the temptation of checking on the woman's condition, Jack set off in the direction of her cabin.

When he reached the log dwelling, he paused in front of the structure and surveyed his surroundings for a moment. During his last visit to the cabin, the heavy downpour of rain had prevented him from getting a good look at the place.

A split rail fence stretched out from each side of the building, then rambled along the edge of a rocky field behind the back of the house to provide a barricade for the livestock. At the moment, a horse, a cow, and a mule were grazing in the stone-covered field. A small barn was located near one corner of the fence, and a few chickens were pecking along the ground.

Everything else about the place seemed familiar to him. But as Jack stepped onto the porch, he became vividly aware of the surrounding silence. Other than an occasional cluck from the chickens, not a sound could be heard. Compared to the stillness hovering about the cabin, the thump of his boots shuffling across the planked flooring sounded like claps of thunder.

Trying to quell the frantic beat of his heart, he inhaled a deep breath and knocked on the door. "It's Jack, Coralee," he called out.

"What in tarnation are you doin' here?" she snapped back.

Judging from the spiteful tone of Coralee's voice, Jack suspected his visit would not be a lengthy one. "Rachel and Maggie said you weren't feeling well, and I thought—"

"Then why are you hecklin' me? Can't you let a woman die in peace?"

Jack gritted his teeth. "Just open the bloody door, Coralee," he demanded impatiently.

"Open it yourself." She paused. "It's not bolted."

Jack hurled open the door and plunged into the cabin. But he'd taken no more than three steps across the room when he stumbled to a halt, disturbed by what he saw.

Coralee was curled up on the bed, the walnut bed that was pushed against one wall of the cabin. Her hair was wild and tangled, and she was hugging her knees to her chest. Bare toes peeked out from beneath the hem of her white nightgown, and dark circles appeared beneath her eyes.

"What are you doin' here?" she demanded.

He edged closer, appalled by the deep lines of

pain etched into her face. "I just came by to see if you needed anything . . . or if I can get something for you."

"You don't have what I need." She glared at him.

"What do you need?" he asked, genuinely curious. "Perhaps I could find it for you."

She lifted her head from the pillow, grimacing. Scooting across the bed, she propped her back against the headboard and stretched out her legs in front of her. "All I need is a heap of corn likker." She reached for a jug on the table beside the bed and drained the contents of the container into a tin mug. "It's the only thing that'll take away the pain."

Jack stared in stunned disbelief as Coralee tilted back her head and downed the entire mug without once pausing to catch her breath. "You must be hurting . . . very badly," he managed to say.

"I'm hurtin' worse than a jackrabbit snared in a trap." She winced and clutched her abdomen. "'Course, I don't know why you should care. From the way you were mouthin' off when you stormed out of here a few days ago, I got the feelin' you don't care if I'm dead or alive."

"That's not necessarily true, Coralee." Jack sighed. "In all honesty, I'm beginning to realize that my behavior has not always been befitting of a gentleman, especially where you're concerned."

"Well, you haven't been treatin' me like a lady should be treated, if that's what you're gettin' at." She pushed back a tangled mat of hair from her cheek with the palm of her hand. "I may not have had any fancy school-housin', mind you, but my mamma didn't raise a bunch of fools in this cabin. I know when a man is tryin' to take advantage of me."

"I haven't tried to take advantage of you, Cora-lee. I've simply tried to enjoy the pleasure of your company," Jack argued, keeping his voice low and steady. "And considering the way you were responding to me when the skies broke loose over the tennis court, I thought you were enjoying my company, as well."

"But that was before I found out I don't mean any more to you than a hill o' beans."

Jack kneaded the nape of his neck in frustration. "I don't think you know how I feel about you," he returned, not fully understanding it himself. "But I can assure you I'm dreadfully concerned about your ill health at the moment."

"I don't know how you're thinkin' you can prove that to me," she mumbled, slurring her words.

Jack edged closer to her. "I'm here, aren't I?"

Her head snapped up, and something akin to astonishment flickered across her face. "I reckon you are," she murmured, her voice soft and low. "I reckon you must care more than I—"

She halted, clutching her stomach. Then she squeezed her eyes shut and let out a moan that sliced straight through Jack's heart. Propelled by sheer terror, he raced across the room and dropped to his knees beside the bed. "You need a doctor, Coralee. Where can I find a doctor for you?"

"We don't have a doctor in Morgan County,

Jack." Eyes shut tight, she rocked to and fro, grimacing in anguish. "Besides, I don't need no doctor. What I need is some more . . . corn likker."

Jack leaned back on his heels, troubled and confused. He had no idea what to say or do, no comprehension of what the woman must be going through.

Slowly rising to his feet, he picked up the jug from the table. Though the container was empty, the lingering smell was potent and strong. Judging from the formidable scent, Jack suspected that a hefty man would be reeling for days after gulping down a dose or two of the mountain brew.

He returned the jug to the table, wondering why the trenchant liquor had not yet eased her pain. It appeared she'd guzzled down more of the caustic liquid than most men could consume in a week.

At that instant, she opened her eyes. "What are you starin' at?" she snapped irritably. "Haven't you ever seen a woman in pain before now?"

He shook his head. "Not pain like this."

"But don't women back in England have . . . monthlies?"

Monthlies. Jack wanted to crawl into a hole and stay there for an eternity or two. Why hadn't he suspected as much?

He should have realized. All the signs—the excessive crankiness, the abdominal pain, the stabbing cramps—had been obvious. Over the years, he'd encountered dozens of women who'd experienced the same symptoms, but in much milder doses.

But, then, he'd never known a woman like Coralee, he reminded himself. Never known any
woman who nursed her pain by chugging down
jugs of mountain brew, who expressed herself in
such plainspoken language. And he'd never known
any woman who used such flagrant displays of
emotion to communicate her feelings.

All in all, she was an intriguing creature, he
thought, a smile curling at the corners of his mouth.

"English women are just like women in every
other part of the world, Coralee," he finally answered. "And some of them experience ghastly
pains every month, just like you're having now."

"God bless their English souls," Coralee murmured just as a hiccup assaulted her. After lunging
for her pillow, she flopped onto her stomach. "Now
I got—*hic*—the dad-blame hiccups," she moaned.
"My back is hurtin' like the—*hic*—devil, and my
likker jug is—*hic*—bone-dry."

"I still don't know what to say or what to do for
you, Coralee," Jack admitted.

She lifted her eyes to his face. "Instead of just—
hic—standin' there gawkin' at me, you could be
puttin' yourself—*hic*—to good use. I wouldn't be
moanin' and groanin' so much—*hic*—if you were
rubbin' away the pain—*hic*—in my back."

Jack's gaze skittered along her backside, and
panic ripped through him. After he touched her,
what would happen then? He was well aware she
was hurting. But once he felt that soft flesh beneath
his fingers, would he have the strength to pull
away?

He was still floundering for an answer when his gaze drifted back to her face. Her eyes were pleading, imploring him to take away her pain. How could he refuse such a simple request?

"Well, what are you waitin' for?" she snapped. "Are you gonna rub my back or not?"

"I'm always anxious to accommodate a lovely woman who expresses herself with such eloquence and charm," he chided, kneeling beside the bed.

"If you're so anxious—*hic*—get yourself busy rubbin'," she urged.

Jack inhaled a deep, steadying breath, then placed his hands along the curve of her back. She was warm to the touch, soft and inviting. "Where does it hurt the most?"

"Down low." She burrowed her face in the pillow, muffling her words. "In the small of—*hic*—my back."

He pressed his fingers along the base of her spine. "Here?"

"Ah, yes . . ." she purred, closing her eyes.

Jack closed his eyes, too. He'd already noticed her gown was thin and worn, revealing more than he was prepared to handle at the moment. Settling for the feel of her skin through the cotton gown, he gently kneaded her taut muscles.

It was sweet agony, touching her, feeling the curves and hollows along her torso. But as he massaged her tender flesh, Jack knew he could never take advantage of the woman. When the timing was right, he would claim her as his own—but he wanted her to be an eager, willing participant in his game of seduction.

He continued to rub her back, applying gentle pressure to her skin with the tips of his fingers. Within a few moments, her hiccups faded away and most of the tension dissipated from her muscles.

Jack edged back and noticed that her breathing was steady and even. Rising, he expelled a sigh of relief. She was resting comfortably now, and there was nothing more he could do. Between his awkward attempt at massaging her back and her zealous consumption of the potent mountain brew, she was sleeping peacefully for the moment.

He quietly slipped out of the cabin and closed the door behind him. Just as he stepped onto the porch, he heard the sound of approaching footsteps. He glanced up, startled to see a short, grayhaired woman marching up to the cabin carrying a large jug in her hand.

"I'm Lelah Clabo," she announced, her eyes narrowing with suspicion. "And who might ye be?"

"Jack Winslow, ma'am," he replied, somewhat surprised by his own answer. The name had rolled off his tongue as easily as if he'd been repeating it for years.

"Well, you're a brave man, Jack Winslow." The spry little woman stepped onto the porch. "At this time o' the month, not too many folks have got the gumption to come callin' on my granddaughter."

"And now I know why," Jack replied, biting back a smile.

She raked her gaze over the length of him. "But you don't look like you've been in a cat fight. I don't see any scratches on your hands or face, and your clothes don't have any tears in 'em."

"Luck must have been with me today." Jack chuckled. "Actually, I never felt as if I were in danger of being physically attacked. But as for a verbal assault . . ."

The woman nodded with complete understanding. "There ain't nothin' Coralee won't say when she gets to feelin' poorly. She starts hissin' worse than a riled-up rattlesnake." Lelah set the jug on the floor, then took a seat in the porch rocker. "We've learned just to stay out o' sight and leave her be for a few days every month. When it's all over, it's like nothin' ever happened. One day, she's snappin' off your head. The next day, she's sweeter 'n a bucket of sugared yams."

Jack expelled a frustrated sigh as he leaned against one of the porch posts. "Don't you know of some sort of remedy for her, Mrs. Clabo?"

Lelah shook her head in dismay. "Monthlies are just one of them things that we womenfolk have to accept. Some women—like Coralee—get the curse worse than others, and they learn to deal with it the best they can. 'Course, the only way Coralee knows how to get through the pain is by drinkin' corn likker. I figured she was runnin' out by now, so I brought her another jug for tomorrow."

"But surely there must be a better solution for her than corn liquor."

Sadness shadowed the woman's lined face.

"There isn't another remedy for Coralee, I'm afraid, seein' as how her man is done dead and all."

"I'm not certain I understand, Mrs. Clabo," Jack admitted. "What's the connection between Coralee's late husband and all the agony she endures every month?"

"It means she can't get in the family way, son. Givin' birth is a surefire cure for gettin' rid of all them aches and cramps. When a baby is growin' inside the womb, it jiggles all the mama's inners 'round and 'round. After it's born, everything gets put back right inside the mama, and all her pain goes away."

"I wasn't aware . . ." Jack felt a flush of embarrassment creeping along his neck. "I didn't realize . . ."

"I didn't mean to get you all flustered, Jack." Lelah sighed. "To be honest, I'm not even sure havin' a baby is the remedy for every woman who hurts like the devil when she's havin' her monthlies. All I know for sure is that it worked for me, and I reckon it could work for Coralee, too. But since she don't have a man in her life, she sure can't have no baby."

"Perhaps she'll eventually remarry," Jack pointed out.

"I'm not real certain about that," Lelah admitted. "Somewhere in that head of hers, she's got the notion that she's done had her chance at love. She thinks she don't have no hope of her ever gettin' hitched again. Trouble is, she's wantin' a family in a bad way, and wantin' a special man of her own, too. But that pride of hers won't let her admit it to anyone." She peered curiously at Jack. "You got family?"

"My parents reside in England," he offered, "along with my sister and brother."

Something akin to sympathy flickered across her face. "It must be tough on you, livin' so far away from your family and all."

"It's been more difficult than I expected it would be," he admitted candidly.

"It's not good for a man to be away from family." Lelah pushed up from the rocker. "You just come on over to my cabin for Sunday dinner, Jack. I got a heap of kinfolks 'round these parts, and we all eat dinner together at my place every Sunday after preachin'. It'll do you good, bein' with a big family for a while."

"I appreciate the invitation." Jack offered a strained smile, finding little appeal in the thought of fraternizing with a mountain clan for an entire afternoon. "I'm afraid I must decline your offer, however. I wouldn't want to impose on your family's time together."

"Why, you won't be imposin' at all," she insisted. "You just come straight on over to my cabin from the church meetin'house after the preachin' is done on Sunday. I'm kin to pert near half the congregation, so you won't have no problem findin' my place if you just follow the crowd as they're leavin' the meetin'house."

Jack struggled to maintain the smile on his lips. "I don't believe I would feel comfortable attending worship services, Mrs. Clabo. Quite honestly, I've never cared a great deal for that sort of thing."

"Then that's all the more reason why you need to go." Displeasure glinted from her eyes. "Nobody comes to Sunday dinner at my house unless they go to preachin' first. That's the rule, and there's no arguments 'bout it. But as soon as you get yourself to preachin', you're welcome to Sunday dinner."

Listening to the formidable tone of her voice, observing the stern expression on her face, Jack knew Lelah Clabo was not a woman who could be easily swayed. He suspected the feisty little lady wielded more power over her family than any male could ever hope to possess. And only God could help the poor fool who dared to undermine her authority.

But Jack Winslow was not a foolish man. He gave a cordial nod, acknowledging the conditions she'd set forth without committing himself to anything. "Then I hope I shall have the pleasure of your company again in the future, Mrs. Clabo," he said as he left the cabin.

Chapter 10

When Coralee arrived at her grandmother's cabin the next afternoon, Granny Clabo was sitting beside the kitchen table and humming a cheery mountain tune under her breath. The skirt of her apron was laden with pole beans, and her nimble fingers were plucking strings and removing stems from the beans in a steady, rhythmic motion.

A large bowl on the table brimmed with freshly snapped beans, while a smaller container held the strings and stems that Granny had already gleaned from the vegetables. At her feet was a basket filled with more fresh beans waiting to be snapped.

As Coralee shuffled across the puncheon floor, Granny Clabo glanced up, her eyes widening in disbelief. "Land o' Goshen, child! I wasn't expectin' you to get back on your feet this soon."

"I wasn't expectin' to, neither." Coralee grinned sheepishly as she pulled out a chair and joined her grandmother at the table. "I reckon all that corn likker musta done the trick."

Granny chuckled. "You was sleepin' like a babe

when I came by to bring you a fresh jug of likker yesterday afternoon."

"I didn't even know you'd dropped by until I saw the jug on the table this mornin'." Coralee grabbed a handful of beans from the basket and dropped the green stems into her lap. "I reckon I overdrank myself on all that corn likker yesterday. It musta knocked me flat on my backside, considerin' I slept straight through till late this mornin'."

"And you weren't hurtin' any more when you woke up?"

"Not perzactly." Coralee heaved a weary sigh. "All them pains in my belly went straight to my head for a while. For the first few hours after I got myself out of bed, I couldn't hear anything but a bunch of drums gongin' between my ears."

Granny quickly swept her gaze over Coralee, assessing her appearance with a critical eye. "You look like you're farin' pretty good now. Why, you even got your hair tied back with a purty red ribbon!"

"I gave myself a good scrubbin' from head to toe after I got up." Coralee tossed some snapped beans into the bowl on the table, then picked up another cluster from her lap. "I thought I'd pull my hair back from my face today, just to be doin' somethin' different for a change."

Granny's lips twitched. "And here I thought you was gettin' yourself all fancied up just in case that English fella came droppin' by your cabin today."

Coralee's hands stilled. "The English fella . . . ?"

"That fella named Jack," the older woman explained. "He was fixin' to leave your place 'bout the time I got there yesterday. We met up on your porch and had us a nice little chat."

"I see," Coralee mumbled, shifting uneasily in her chair. She dropped her eyes to her lap, uncomfortable with the turbulent emotions careening through her.

All of her life, Coralee had shared everything with Granny Clabo, everything from her deepest secrets to her most daring dreams. But never once had she mentioned the name of Jack Winslow to her grandmother.

Knowing she hadn't intentionally avoided the subject somehow eased the twinges of guilt that were pricking away at Coralee's conscience. After all, what could she have said about the man? She hadn't been capable of setting aside her jumbled emotions long enough to gauge her true feelings about Jack Winslow. Since the moment she'd met him, doubts and fears had been assaulting her, clouding her thoughts and distorting her common sense.

Coralee tossed another handful of snapped beans into the bowl. "After contendin' with me yesterday, I reckon Jack was wishin' he'd never set foot on the place," she finally managed to say.

"He didn't act like he was in a hurry to leave," Granny mused. "In fact, he seemed right worried about you, child."

Little tingles of apprehension skittered along Coralee's spine. During Jack's unexpected visit, she, too, had sensed that he'd been truly concerned about her. Yet, she'd scoffed at her instincts, convincing herself that too much corn likker had addled her brain and thwarted her perceptions by the time he'd arrived at the cabin.

But now, Granny Clabo's observations validated Coralee's initial feelings about Jack's regard for her. And with the confirmation from her grandmother, Coralee realized why she'd become attuned to the depths of Jack's feelings.

Quite simply, he'd demonstrated just how much he cared about her. Obviously, her absence in Rugby had been troubling to him, or he wouldn't have bothered to hike up to the cabin and check on her. But during the time they'd spent together at the cabin, Coralee had noted his concern in dozens of other, subtle ways—like the apprehension glimmering from his eyes, the compassion in his touch, the worried tone of his voice.

And all of those unspoken messages told Coralee that Jack Winslow cared more for her than he was willing to admit.

Baffled and unsettled by the revelation, Coralee pursed her lips together in a tight line. She'd been convinced he was nothing more than a heartless scoundrel when he'd denied all interest in her and stormed out of the cabin on that dreadful rainy afternoon. But his actions the previous day had told her far more than words could ever say. Was he waging a battle against his emotions? Perhaps verbally denying his true feelings?

Coralee was still trying to find some answers to her questions when the sound of Granny's voice drifted into her thoughts. "I thought it was right nice of that Jack fella to come checkin' on you," Granny was saying. "In fact, I invited him to have Sunday dinner with us, as long as he was willin' to follow our family rule of goin' to preachin' first."

"Oh, Granny." Coralee groaned. "What makes you think Jack Winslow would be wantin' to have Sunday dinner with the Clabo clan?"

"Lord o' mercy, Coralee. If you have to be askin' a question like that, all them jugs of corn likker must be turnin' your brains to mush." Merriment danced in Lelah's eyes. "But if you'll take a peek into that lookin' glass over yonder on my dresser, I can guarantee you'll find the answer you're searchin' for."

Coralee couldn't suppress a smile. "But can that lookin' glass tell me anything else?"

"That all depends on what you're wantin' to know, child." The gaiety vanished from Granny's wrinkled face, and her voice took on a serious tone. "But I reckon it can tell you a heap of things if you're willin' to take a good, hard look at that purty face starin' back at you."

Coralee's smile faded away. Realistically, she knew Granny was right. Hidden truths were lurking within the depths of her soul, truths that could provide solutions to life's problems. And if she looked deep inside herself, she would be certain to find answers to her questions.

Trouble was, she might uncover some answers that she wasn't prepared to accept. And she might even discover that her feelings for the Englishman were growing into more—much more—than a passing interest.

Disconcerted by the possibility, Coralee cringed. She promptly rejected the notion of probing too deeply into the recesses of her heart, fearful of what she might find. Resolving to set aside the disturbing thoughts, she pulled back her shoulders and lifted her chin.

"A lookin' glass won't tell me nothin' I don't already know, Granny," she chided, hoping she sounded more confident than she felt.

Splat.

Jack awoke with a start, jolted from a deep sleep by an eerie sensation that he couldn't identify.

Splat, splat.

Two drops of moisture hit Jack's face. Stunned, he bolted upright and vaulted like a jackknife in the hammock.

Splat, splat.

The droplets skirted past Jack and plummeted to the floor just as a clap of thunder crackled through the air. In the next instant, a bolt of lightning streaked through the dark skies, shooting a bright flash of light through the dormer windows before disappearing from sight. Exposed wooden beams along the slope of the ceiling creaked and groaned beneath the force of the wind and rain hammering against the barracks, while wayward branches from surrounding trees scraped across the roof of the building and clattered against the shingles.

Splat, splat.

Jack steadied the hammock with his hands, then lunged to his feet. "Bloody hell," he grated.

He paced across the length of the room, his irritation mounting each step of the way. He was learning to accept grits and hog jowls. He was even adapting to the isolation of the mountains in a peculiar sort of way. But being awakened in the dead of night by a bloody leak—directly over his head, nonetheless—was more than any Englishman should have to tolerate.

Another clap of thunder rumbled in the distance, followed by a crack of lightning that illuminated the room for a split second. Stealing a quick glance at Adam and Grant, Jack discovered that both men were sleeping soundly, seemingly undisturbed by the raging storm.

He slowed his pace to a shuffle, dragging his bare feet across the pine floor. Jack supposed he shouldn't be surprised that the howling winds and driving rains had not awakened his companions. The men had collapsed into their hammocks shortly after sunset, exhausted and spent after a long, laborious day of clearing brush from the banks of the Clear Fork.

Working alongside the other Englishmen, Jack, too, had been weary by the time he'd returned to the barracks for the night. And if leaks from the roof had not landed in his face, he suspected he would still be sleeping as peacefully as his friends.

Scowling, Jack silently vowed to remedy the situation at the first light of dawn. Noticing that the wind and rain were diminishing, he stalked back to his hammock. He lowered his long frame into the net of rope, reversing his sleeping position to shield his face from the threat of additional splatters. Within a few moments, he drifted off into a restless slumber.

By the time Jack awakened the next morning, the sounds of rain and thunder had been replaced by a soothing silence. Noting the pair of empty hammocks at the opposite end of the room, Jack surmised that Adam and Grant had already departed for the dining hall.

He peered through the dormer window. Ribbons of sunlight were streaming through the glass panes, and puffy white clouds were billowing through the morning sky.

But the change in weather failed to cheer Jack's sullen spirits. Disgruntled from his restless night, he tore away from the window.

A few moments later, he was dressed for the day. He stomped down the stairs, reaching the last step just as Daniel Yarby emerged from one of the rooms on the main floor.

"Good morning, Winslow." A pleasant smile accompanied Daniel's greeting.

"Good morning?" Jack balked, glaring at the man. "Considering I spent the night in hell, I find it rather difficult to believe that this morning could be a good one."

Daniel's smile vanished, replaced with a frown of concern. "What do you mean?"

"I'll show you." Jack wheeled and stalked up the

stairs. Daniel trailed closely behind him, following in puzzled silence.

When they reached the top story of the building, Jack hurled open the door and motioned for Daniel to enter the room. "The roof leaked during last night's storm," he explained, pointing out the puddles of water on the floor. "And it leaked directly on me."

Daniel grimaced. "Egad, Winslow. No wonder you're in such a foul mood."

Jack crossed his arms over his chest and scowled. "You're the colony manager, Daniel. What do you intend to do about this?"

Daniel tilted back his head, peering up at the wet, dark rings that marred the wooden beams. "I'm not quite certain what to do," he admitted. "We never intended for this building to be a permanent structure in Rugby. It was constructed for the sole purpose of providing temporary housing for new colonists until they could make arrangements to build their own homes."

Jack clenched his jaw, trying to contain his anger. "But we have no other alternatives for living quarters until the inn opens for business," he reminded the Englishman, his voice strained and low. "And surely you can't expect anyone—especially those of us who are accustomed to much finer accommodations—to live in such deplorable conditions, even on a temporary basis."

Daniel kneaded the nape of his neck and sighed. "Perhaps the roof won't leak again," he said. "After all, last night's storm was rather unusual. Normally, the weather here in Rugby isn't so—"

"Quit making excuses, Yarby." The last vestiges
of Jack's patience slipped away from his grasp.
"This isn't a difficult problem to solve. Fixing a
bloody roof shouldn't require a lot of effort from
anyone."

"But the construction crews are already behind
schedule," Daniel pointed out. "They're trying to
complete several projects before the official opening
of the colony this fall. Quite frankly, I don't see
how they can take the time to—"

"They'll have to make the time," Jack interrupted
in a curt tone. "Unless, of course, you would like
to exchange sleeping accommodations with me. I
feel certain that the first floor of the barracks would
offer a much more comfortable environment than
the attic during the midst of a thunderstorm."

Daniel heaved a frustrated sigh. "All right, then.
I'll inform Paul Proffitt about the damage to the
roof. Perhaps he'll send over a crew this morning
to make the repairs."

Without another word, Daniel turned and retreated from the room.

After convincing the colony manager to take immediate action on repairing the roof, Jack supposed
he should be feeling rather smug or—at the very
least—triumphant. But for some unexplainable reason, he couldn't dredge up a snippet of delight
from the depths of his irritable soul.

He edged toward the window and aimlessly
peered through the glass panes. Several colonists
were making their way toward the dining hall for

their morning meal, leaving a trail of muddy boot prints in their wake.

Jack groaned. Obviously, the ground was too soft for playing a game of lawn tennis or working along the banks of the Clear Fork this morning. And until the sun dried out the ground, he had not a single project or endeavor to occupy his time.

"Bloody hell," he mumbled in disgust, wondering how much longer he would have to wait for the title to his land. If the blasted paperwork from London had arrived by now, his morning could have been a productive one. Instead of whiling away his time, he could have been clearing the vacant lot beside the new inn.

He felt a knot of frustration coiling in his gut just as the figure of a golden-haired beauty came into view. Tensing, Jack narrowed his eyes, startled by what he saw through the window.

The bedridden woman of two days before, the woman who had been writhing in agony, now appeared free of all pain. As if transformed into an enchanting waif, Coralee was bending and stretching with relative ease, draping wet laundry over a rope that swayed between a pair of chestnut trees. Her movements were fluid and agile, Jack noticed, and her limbs were relaxed and lithe. By all indications, she bore not a trace of the crippling, mind-numbing pain that had invaded her body less than forty-eight hours before.

Jack continued to scrutinize Coralee with interest. After securing the damp clothing to the line, she picked up a bucket and headed for the creek, ease and confidence in her stride. A few moments later, she was pouring the contents of the bucket into the laundry tub, greeting her first customer of the day. And all the while, she was laughing and smiling, acting as though she hadn't a care in the world.

Confounded by her demeanor, Jack ripped his gaze away from the window. Heading for the dining hall, he stalked through the barracks and lunged through the door. But his confusion intensified when he neared the site of Coralee's laundry business. The sound of laughter was bubbling up from her lips as she chatted with Rachel, and her face was awash with something akin to pure delight.

Bewildered, Jack halted in his tracks. Why in the bloody hell was she so cheerful? Coralee Hayes had nothing to be cheerful about. She lived in a primitive cabin, and her worldly possessions were few. The extent of her social life was limited to Saturday night singings and Sunday morning sermons. During the rest of the week, she scrubbed clothes for other people like a bloody slave, hoping to earn a pittance or two.

And once each month, it appeared, she suffered more pain than most humans were obliged to endure in the span of a lifetime. If he'd been forced to bear the piercing agony that she'd experienced within the last few days, Jack figured he wouldn't be faring nearly as well as she. More than likely, he would still be nursing his wounds, angry and resentful that he'd been inflicted with such unbearable torment in the first place.

Yet, as he strode toward her now, Jack became vividly aware of an uncanny sense of serenity that was enveloping the woman, wreathing her like the glow of an ethereal cloud. The smooth line of her brow held not a single furrow of worry, and the narrow set of her shoulders conveyed not a hint of tension or pain. Humming merrily under her breath, she seemed quite content—even peaceful—with herself and her surroundings.

Jack shook his head in disbelief. By his estimation, Coralee's lot in life was a dismal one, at best. Yet, she accepted the situation without reservation or complaint. It almost seemed as though she were totally oblivious to her plight.

As Jack stalked toward her, Coralee glanced up from her work. "You're lookin' mighty perplexified this mornin', Jack," she observed candidly. "Somethin' clutterin' up your mind?"

"You, for one," he grunted, "among a few dozen other things."

"Me?" Her eyes widened incredulously.

"Yes, you," he snapped. "Two days ago, I was convinced you were on the verge of inhaling your last breath." He raked his gaze over her in a slow, exacting way. "But, apparently, you've made a speedy—and complete—recovery."

Laughing, she placed a scrub board in the laundry tub. "I'm feelin' as fit as a fiddle today, thank goodness." Her laughter dissipated into the morning air as she stole another glance at him. "But that

sneer on your face tells me somethin' else is troublin' you this mornin'."

Annoyed by her perceptiveness, Jack frowned. "I
always sneer when I don't get enough sleep," he
growled. "That blasted storm kept me awake half
the night."

"Well, maybe you'll be farin' better after you eat
yourself some breakfast." She inhaled a deep
breath; a smile touched her lips. " 'Course, just
breathin' in all this beautific weather should make
you feel a heap better, too. I haven't seen a day as
pretty as this in a coon's age. All that rain last night
left everything smellin' fresher and lookin'
greener."

"I don't detect any difference in the way things
look or smell around here." Jack swept his gaze
across the grounds. "This place still looks like an
uncivilized wilderness to me."

Coralee pursed her lips together, quietly lather-
ing a grimy shirt with a cake of lye soap for a few
moments. When she finally lifted her eyes to his
face, Jack was stunned by the warmth and concern
shimmering from her gaze. "There's somethin' I
want to show you, Jack, somethin' I've been wantin' you to see," she revealed, her voice soft and
low. "Come supper time, do you reckon you could
meet me down by the Clear Fork?"

He shrugged with indifference. "I suppose I
could. But I doubt you could show me anything I
haven't already seen. I've explored most of the area
by foot and by horseback."

"But it's easy to miss seein' things if you don't

know what you're lookin' for," she pointed out.

"Then perhaps you should tell me exactly where I should be looking for you this evening," he suggested. "The Clear Fork covers a lot of territory in Morgan County, you know."

"You can meet me at the spot where I was warshin' clothes on the day when you came ridin' up on that good-luck horse of yours," she instructed. "And bring an empty belly with you, too. I'm gonna be cookin' us up two of the thickest, juiciest beefsteaks you done ever laid your eyes upon."

Both surprise and skepticism pulsed through Jack's veins. Surely an ulterior motive was lurking behind Coralee's generous invitation. He couldn't imagine what she wanted him to see, and he had no idea why she was insisting on cooking dinner for him.

At that moment, one of the colonists stepped up beside them. "Here's my laundry for the week, Miss Hayes," the man announced, dropping a bundle of garments beside the laundry tub. "When will my clothes be ready?"

"That all depends." Coralee scrambled to untie the parcel. "Will you be needin' me to starch and press a heap of fancy shirts for you?"

"You should find about three shirts in my laundry bag," the man answered. "Of course, I may have more . . ."

Leaving Coralee to her work, Jack turned and walked away, still puzzled about the prospects of the evening that lay ahead.

Chapter 11

Coralee added two tin plates and mugs to the basket of goods that she had packed for her evening picnic with Jack. "That should be everything we'll be needin', I reckon."

She swept her gaze through the cabin to check for other items that could be useful during the outdoor meal. "We could use somethin' to sit on while we're eatin'," she reminded herself when she noticed the quilt that was spread across the bed.

She quickly folded the quilt and placed it on top of the basket, suddenly mindful that her hands were trembling and her heart was thundering in her chest.

"You silly goose," she chided. "You don't have anything to be nervous about. You're just sharing a meal with Jack, and nothing more."

She picked up a brush from her dresser and hastily ran the bristles through her hair. But as she lifted her eyes to the looking glass hanging on the wall, her breath snared in her throat.

Her eyes were sparkling with excitement, and

her cheeks were splotched with a rosy hue. Her skin glowed with a healthy vigor, and her lips bore the hint of a satisfied smile.

All in all, she looked very much like a woman in love.

"Nonsense," she told her reflection. "I invited Jack to share dinner with me this evening because I want him to see this place through my point of view. I'm not tryin' to get him to fall in love with me. Why, I don't even know if I *want* to be fallin' in love with him!"

But even as she voiced the words, Coralee had no explanation for the giddy, wondrous feelings swarming through her.

Unwilling to explore the reasons for her elated state, she tore her gaze away from the mirror and returned her brush to the dresser. Then she picked up her basket of goods and headed for the banks of the Clear Fork.

Dappled rays of afternoon sunlight glistened through the trees that bordered the Clear Fork as Coralee spread the faded quilt over the grassy bank. "Now we got ourselves a nice place for sittin' down and eatin' our supper as soon as the beef-steaks get done," she mused aloud.

A few feet away, the flames of a low-burning fire crackled and popped. Whirling, Coralee scurried to inspect the pots that were dangling from an iron rack over the open flames.

A few feet away, Jack propped one shoulder against the trunk of a sturdy white oak tree and

watched in silence, somewhat taken aback by Coralee's energetic efforts to prepare their evening meal.

Coralee removed the lid from a black kettle, us-
ing a rag to shield her hand from the hot cookware.
As a gush of steam spouted up from the pot, she
dipped a ladle into the boiling water and spooned
generous helpings of boiled potatoes onto a pair of
tin plates.

Next, she turned her attention to two thick slabs
of beef that were sizzling over the red-hot surface
of a large stone next to the fire. After stabbing a
fork into the meat to see if it was cooked, she
placed the broiled steaks on the dinner plates. "I
reckon we're ready to eat now," she announced,
holding out a plate to Jack.

He edged forward with reluctance. "I didn't realize this would be so much trouble for you," he
said, accepting her offerings with an uneasy smile.

"Why, this isn't any trouble at all," Coralee insisted, removing a tin pot from the fire. The enticing aroma of freshly brewed coffee wafted through
the air as she poured the steaming liquid into a set
of mugs. "'Course, I don't reckon a supper like this
one could compare to the fancy meals you're used
to gettin' back in England," she said, placing a mug
in Jack's hand.

"Actually, potatoes and beefsteak are served
quite frequently in Britain." Carefully balancing his
drink and food, Jack lowered his long frame to the
ground.

Coralee settled down beside him, the hem of her

skirt billowing around her as she sank onto the faded quilt. "I always know I'm gettin' some good-tastin' beef when Maggie's folks—the McCarters—slaughter off a few head of cattle from their farm. Trouble is, that only happens three or four times a year, and I sure do get a hankerin' for a nice cut of beef betwixt slaughterin' times. There's nothin' in this world like the taste of a juicy beefsteak."

Jack stabbed a fork into a potato, wondering why she was sharing what little she had with him, bothered and angry that he even cared.

He lapsed into a brooding silence, unable to shake the gnawing apprehensions that had been building inside him throughout the day. He didn't understand why the prospect of spending the evening with Coralee had rattled him beyond all reason, couldn't comprehend the reasons for his current frazzled state of mind.

The stark simplicity of his present circumstances—picnicking by a stream, eating from a tin plate, practically living like a commoner—was a world apart from the pomp and circumstance of his old life in England. Yet, consorting with titled aristocrats at formal functions and wooing the hearts of bejeweled ladies had never once evoked the measure of anxieties that were tormenting him now.

He crammed a generous slice of beef into his mouth, somewhat startled to find that the taste was far more delicious than he had anticipated. Broiled to perfection, the steak was tender and juicy, palatable and savory.

Yet, he still had no idea why Coralee was sharing her dinner with him. He glanced over at her, wishing she would reveal the motives behind her invitation. But as his eyes drank in the sight of her loveliness, his breath caught in his throat.

He couldn't deny she was a beauty, a genuine beauty in the true sense of the word. Everything about her—the delicate curves of her lips, the forest green of her eyes, the enchanting gold of her hair—radiated with an inherent loveliness. She had no need for the powders and paints that many women plastered upon their faces, layer after layer, hoping to improve—or attempting to mask—their natural features.

But all the regal ladies and elegant marchionesses in the world had never disconcerted him the way this simple mountain beauty was unsettling him now. With one glimpse of the woman, his heart was thundering in his chest and his pulse was racing like mad.

Irritated with his lack of control over his own emotions, Jack ripped his gaze away from her and concentrated on eating the food on his plate. He had just placed the last bite of steak into his mouth when Coralee broke the silence that had hovered between them throughout the meal.

"I didn't see hide nor hair of you after our little chat this mornin', Jack," she remarked, her voice light and breezy. "You musta been mighty busy with yourself today."

"Busy?" he scoffed. "If sleeping counts as an industrious activity, I suppose you could say I was busy for most of the afternoon." He gulped down the coffee from his mug. "Quite frankly, I decided to take a nap because I had nothing better to do with my time. The ground was far too muddy for playing lawn tennis. Working on the new bridle path wasn't a possibility, either. Some of the twists and turns along the creek banks are rather steep, and I didn't want anyone—myself included—to take the chance of slipping down a muddy embankment."

"I heard some of the Englishmen talkin' today about that bridle path of yours. They were sayin' ya'll got a heap of clearin' done yesterday."

Jack nodded. "The project has been progressing quite nicely until today."

"I wouldn't mind takin' a look-see at what all you've been doin' lately," Coralee said. "Betwixt bein' down in the mouth and doin' heaps and heaps of laundry, I haven't had much of a chance to be traipsin' around the Clear Fork in the last few days."

"We've been working along a section of the creek that isn't very far from here," Jack revealed. "We could walk over to the site after we've finished with dinner, if you'd like."

"I'll have these feet of mine sot to run just as soon as I get the supper dishes warshed up." She peered down at the empty plate in Jack's lap. "Looks like we've eaten every bit and grain of the beefsteak, but a whole mess of taters is still boilin' over the fire. If your belly isn't full—"

"I've eaten more than enough, I'm afraid," he

insisted, suddenly aware that he should be expressing his gratitude for all that she'd done. "It was a wonderful dinner, Coralee. In fact, I can't remember the last time I enjoyed a meal that was any better."

Her cheeks blossomed with a rosy hue. "Thanks," she murmured, obviously pleased and slightly flustered by the unexpected praise.

Without another word, she sprang to her feet and collected the soiled dinnerware and utensils, then scampered to the edge of the creek. After dipping each item into the water and scouring each with sand to clean it, she dried the articles and packed them away into her large willow basket.

While Jack extinguished the remains of the fire, Coralee removed the quilt from the ground and shook out the bits of grass that were clinging to the fabric.

"There's no reason for haulin' all these supper fixin's with us while we're walkin' along the bridle path," she remarked, draping the folded quilt over the top of the basket. "These things aren't goin' anywhere till I get ready to head back to the cabin in a spell or two."

A few moments later, they were making their way along the banks of the Clear Fork. Mountain breezes, fragrant with the scent of fresh pine, whispered through the air as they headed toward the bridle path.

Ambling alongside Coralee, idly scanning his surroundings, Jack was astounded by the range of sounds swirling around him. The Clear Fork, it seemed, was practically singing a song of its own.

The crystal-clear water rendered a soothing melody of sorts, babbling and gurgling over a multitude of smooth stones that were embedded into the floor of the creek. But as the current followed the slope of the land, tumbling down sharp inclines and cascading over protruding stones in the creek bed, the lilting tune gave way to a symphony of harmonic crashes and roars.

The music of the Clear Fork was still ringing in Jack's ears when they reached a narrow strip of land that had been cleared of foliage and trees. Halting, Jack pointed out a steep embankment to Coralee. "Eventually, we'll be leveling out rough patches like this one, grading the surface of the ground to create a smooth course for the bridle path."

"This venture of yours is mighty fine, Jack. It'll be a right nice treat to ride along the creek banks on horseback for a change."

"I'm glad you like the idea," he said.

Coralee swept her gaze across the site, nodding with approval. "Come fall, I'd wager all those visitors to Rugby would be willin' to pay a nice sum for a guided tour of the mountains along this bridle path."

Jack shrugged. "Profiting from this project has never been my intention, Coralee. When I came up with the idea of clearing the banks of the Clear Fork to create a bridle path, I was merely looking for a constructive way to spend my time."

"You mean you were lookin' for somethin' to do

'cuz you were bored?" Coralee guessed.

"I suppose so." Jack kneaded the nape of his neck, expelling a frustrated sigh. "Back in England, boredom was never a problem for me. I always had somewhere to go, someone to see, something to do. But here . . ."

As his voice trailed away, Coralee frowned in confusion. "But here . . . ?" she probed.

Annoyance rippled through him. "I can't go to a concert or attend a horse race in Rugby. This place doesn't have golf links and gaming halls. Tennessee doesn't offer the diversions that were available to me in England. In fact, I'm beginning to suspect that this place has nothing to offer at all." He narrowed his eyes, sweeping his gaze across the horizon. "There's nothing but bloody mountains here, mountains that block the rest of the world from sight."

A stab of longing for England seared through him. At the moment, Jack suspected he would be willing to sever his right hand just for the chance to spend another afternoon in his native country.

Visions of crowded city streets lined with rows of brick buildings were parading through his thoughts when he felt the touch of Coralee's hand on his arm. The brief contact had the effect of a hot iron scorching his skin. Tensing, he snapped around.

"I got just the remedy to make you forget all those troubles and woes of yours," she offered, her upturned face aglow with a rosy hue.

He leveled a speculative glance at her. "What kind of remedy?"

"It's not a foul-tastin' medicine or magic brew, if that's what you're askin'," she explained. "All you got to do is get yourself workin' at somethin' every day. Hard work will make you forget your miseries like nothing else can."

Irritation sliced through him. "Why in the bloody hell do you think I've been building a bridle path with my bare hands?"

Blithely ignoring the offended tone of his voice, she sauntered away from the cleared tract of land. "But every Englishman around these parts is pitchin' in to help, and this project of yours isn't gonna last much longer," she pointed out.

"Still, it's serving a purpose at the moment," he countered, his words crisp and curt.

She drifted into a meadow that bordered one side of the bridle path. "But it's not the same as gettin' up every mornin', day after day, havin' a purpose to your life, knowin' you'll be workin' real hard at honin' your skills or gettin' yourself a trade."

"Yet, it's rather difficult to proceed with plans for your future when your present options have been curtailed." Jack stomped across the grass, catching up with Coralee. "I've decided to breed horses while I'm living in Rugby, and I've even offered to buy the vacant lot next to the new inn as the site for breeding and housing my stock. But until the legal title to my land arrives from London, my hands are tied. I can't start breeding horses on property that I don't officially own."

"But the longer you're sittin' 'round, grumblin' about what you're missin' back in England, the more miserable you're gonna be. If you'd quit your bellyachin' and start gettin' yourself to work every mornin', your arms and shoulders and back and legs will be achin' so bad by evenin' time that you won't even remember what you've been missin'."

Jack clenched his fists into tight balls in a vain effort to contain the fury ripping through him. "I've already told you why working isn't an option for me at the moment, Coralee."

"But somethin' tells me that you could find a way to get your business started if you really wanted to be workin'," she countered thoughtfully. "You had a heap of school-housin' back in England, didn't you?"

Jack nodded, somewhat puzzled by her sudden interest in his education. "I'm a graduate of Cambridge. It's one of the most prestigious universities in all of Britain," he informed her.

"And what did they learn you at that fancy school?" she asked.

"I completed all of the studies in British law, but my courses included instruction in other subjects like mathematics and philosophies through the ages."

"It's too bad you didn't get to study about takin' advantage of what you got in life," she teased, biting back a smile. "If you're askin' me, I reckon you musta missed the class that learns people how to get some common sense for themselves."

He glared at her. "I've never asked for your opinion, as I recall."

"Then I reckon you must be one of those folks who got too much pride to ask for anything." Her skirts billowed around her legs as she meandered across the meadow. "Have you ever thought about startin' a livery for the colony? I'd be willin' to bet you could hire out a heap of horses to all those folks who'll be payin' visits to Rugby come fall. And if your livery is located next door to the inn, nobody would be able to miss it when they come passin' through town. You could still be breedin' horses at the same time, too."

Jack stilled, amazed by the woman's insight. Though he'd never considered the prospects of owning a livery, the idea sounded quite feasible.

"And while you're waitin' for that important paper to get here from London," she continued on, "you could be checkin' with Daniel about gettin' started on clearin' out all the trees off that plat of land you're hopin' to buy."

His eyes narrowed in confusion. "What do you mean?"

Her shoes shuffled to a halt. "I heard tell that all the trees sittin' 'round Rugby belong to the colony. Do you know for sure if that's true?"

"It's my understanding that the board is maintaining timber rights to all of the colony property without regard to individual ownership," he confirmed.

"Then how come you can't go ahead and hack down all them trees next to the inn?" she inquired, genuine curiosity glinting from her expression. "Instead of wastin' your time moanin' and groanin', why don't you ask Daniel if you could be gettin' a rip-roarin' start on all those plans for your livery. Why, by the time that legal paper gets here, you could be ready to—"

"I don't need to hear any more, Coralee," Jack grated, appalled and infuriated that he hadn't thought of the idea himself. "I don't need anyone to tell me what I should or shouldn't be doing with my life . . . especially a woman who has no grasp of legal matters and no concept of how the world operates outside of these bloody mountains."

Incensed with his own lack of insight and furious with Coralee, Jack wheeled away. Plowing his way through the meadow, he stomped back to the bridle path, every muscle in his body rigid with tension.

He wanted to tell Coralee Hayes to mind her own business and to keep her nose out of his. He wanted to inform the woman that she didn't have a snippet of influence in his life. And he wanted to convince the sassy female that her suggestions and opinions were meaningless to him.

At that moment, the swish of a woman's skirt snared his attention. Jack whipped around, sweeping his gaze across the grassy meadow.

His eyes locked on the slight figure of a mountain beauty who was drifting through the meadow. Mesmerized, Jack froze in place, his cold, hard resolve disappearing into the air like a wisp of vapor.

Coralee was plucking wildflowers, dancing through the meadow with the grace of an accomplished ballerina, studying each bloom with the curiosity of an innocent child. Swathed in the glory of the setting sun, she looked like an ethereal angel winging her way through an earthly bed of colorful blossoms.

She glanced over at him, her face awash with delight. "Take a look-see at this, Jack," she urged.

Unable to resist her plea, Jack retraced his steps through the meadow. As he returned to her side, she was admiring the bouquet of flowers in her hand.

"Have you ever seen the like in all your born days?" she cooed. "This spray of flowers is gonna look mighty pretty sittin' in a milk pitcher on the center of my kitchen table. All these colors mixed together will be brightenin' up the cabin for days."

"Each different flower has a stunning hue of its own," Jack observed. "I don't believe I've ever seen anything quite like this red blossom. The shape of the bloom and the intensity of the color are rather unusual, I would suspect."

"These long red tubes are trumpet creepers," Coralee explained. "The lavender bloom is a purple raspberry, and this flamin' orange one is a butterfly weed."

"I didn't realize flowers held such a fascination for you," Jack remarked.

"I reckon there's a lot we don't know about each other," Coralee mused aloud, a shadow of darkness flickering across her face.

Turning, she rambled back toward the creek. Jack

had just fallen into step beside her when she stumbled to a halt, squealing with delight.

"This is a sight for sore eyes, that's for sure." Coralee nodded toward a stalk of flowers blooming in the distance. "Why, those mountain meadow lilies are growin' clear up to the sky!"

Jack followed the direction of her gaze. Though flowers had never captivated his interest, he couldn't deny that the blossoming stalk was resplendent with beauty. At least twenty lilies were blooming along the towering plant that stretched some eight feet above the ground.

They ventured back to the banks of the Clear Fork. Gardens of wild rhododendrons sprouted along the terrain, their snowy-white blossoms contrasting sharply against the dark, shiny green foliage of the plants.

After walking a short distance, Jack noticed that the terrain was becoming steep and rocky. "If I didn't know better, I'd swear we were climbing up the side of a mountain," he observed, trudging up the slope behind Coralee.

"This may not be a real mountain," she said, "but it's pert near close to one."

In spite of his vigorous strength, Jack was tired and winded by the time they crested the peak of the steep incline. As he stepped across the rocky ground, he frowned in dismay. "I don't see why anyone wants to bother with hiking up a cliff," he grumbled. "It's nothing but a bloody trouble, as far as I'm concerned."

"But that's why I wanted you to come here with

me this evenin'." Coralee's voice was soft and warm. "I've been wantin' you to see all this."

Jack's frown deepened. "You wanted to show me ... *this*?" he asked, glowering down at the jagged cliffs that plunged into the rippling waters of the Clear Fork.

"In a way," she answered. "I know I've been fussin' at you a lot about not appreciatin' what you got here. But in the last few days, I come to realize that you can't appreciate nothin' that you can't see."

"So you decided to bring me here and show me the beauty of Morgan County that I've already seen," he surmised.

"Not perzactly." She brushed back a stray strand of hair from her cheek. "We got different ways of lookin' at things, it appears. I was wantin' you to see Morgan County through my eyes, to look at things from my point of view."

"Then show me what you see," he challenged, finding her reasoning both absurd and irrational.

"That's what I'm wantin'," she insisted, "but I got some explainin' to do before you take your look-see." Coralee inhaled a deep, steadying breath. "I know the folks from 'round these parts—me included—aren't rich like you Englishmen. We don't have no servants or fancy clothes or fine houses. But we're rich in other ways, ways you're too blind to see until now."

"And now ... ?"

"Take a look-see over here, Jack," she invited with a sweep of her arm, motioning toward the scenic view that surrounded them. "How can anyone say we're poor mountaineers when we've got all this?"

Jack swept his gaze across the horizon, stunned by the breathtaking beauty of what he saw. The mountains were so numerous and tangled that it was hard to determine the spot where one mountain ended and another one began. Sharp, rocky ridges jutted along the slopes, covered with a dense growth of laurels, white oaks, and tall pines.

But it was the haze hovering over the mountains that fascinated him. For a fleeting moment, the misty vapor vanished, revealing a flash of silver from a mountain stream that was cascading down a hillside and disclosing coves and valleys.

In the next instant, the haze shrouded the stream and valleys from sight, enveloping, concealing, mystifying. All the while, the color of the mist was constantly changing, ranging from smoke gray to heaven's blue, casting light and shadows across the terrain.

"You know, I never seen all those fancy castles and churches where you come from." Coralee's voice was just above a whisper. "I reckon my eyes would be poppin' out of my head if I got the chance to see all them far-off places. But have you ever seen anything more beautiful in all the world than what you're seein' right now?"

Something tight and restricting gripped Jack's chest. "I can't say that I have," he admitted, his voice choked and strained. "I've traveled through all of Europe, a portion of Africa, and a great deal of the United States. But Morgan County must be one of the hidden wonders of the world."

"And it don't cost nothin' to look at," Coralee added. "I reckon God knew we mountaineers were too poor to pay for anything, so He just decided to give us all this for free."

Jack studied the view once again, overwhelmed by his change in perspective. Only a few moments before, rocky cliffs had been nothing more than dangerous obstacles and the mountain haze had been something akin to menacing fog.

He turned back to Coralee, silently acknowledging that the woman's wisdom about living surpassed all that he had ever learned from a book, garnering a new understanding of the woman and her world.

He drew in a deep, shuddering breath. "Only you could have made me see your world in a different light, Coralee."

Then he lifted her hand to his face and pressed his lips against the softness of her slender fingers, cherishing the moment in ways that he'd never dreamed possible before.

Chapter 12

Two weeks later, Daniel Yarby nodded with approval as he surveyed Jack's progress in clearing the trees from the property adjacent to the inn.

"You'll be finished clearing the lot by the time your paperwork arrives from London, Winslow," Daniel assessed. "And everyone has been extremely pleased to hear that you've decided to open a livery, too. All the guests at the inn will be certain to take advantage of letting horses during their stays here in Rugby."

"I just hope it doesn't take much longer for the papers to get here." Jack wiped the sweat from his brow with the sleeve of his shirt.

"They should be arriving any day now," Daniel predicted as he turned to leave.

Jack leaned against the handle of his ax, both weary and exhilarated. He'd enlisted the help of Adam and Grant to fell the trees from the land, but he'd garnered a deep sense of personal satisfaction from his own work. The fresh air was invigorating, and he was developing muscles that he'd never known he had. Better yet, he was mastering his own fate, forging his way to a better life.

Jack was still dreaming about the future when the shuffle of footsteps interrupted his thoughts. He whipped around, surprised to see Coralee scampering up to him.

"Taking a break from your work?" he asked.

She nodded. "I just wanted to take a look-see at your progress. And it looks like you've gotten a heap of work done today."

Pride surged through him. "It's coming along quite nicely, I have to admit." He motioned toward one corner of the lot. "Right here is the spot where I'm going to build the livery. It's going to be the finest livery that anyone has ever seen, a livery stocked to the brim with carriages and wagons and horses. I'll hire out the buggies and horses by the day or the week or the month to visitors staying at the inn or residents of Rugby who don't have their own means of transportation."

Excitement rushed through his veins as he swept his gaze across the tract of land. It almost seemed as though his plans and dreams were taking on new life as he voiced his thoughts about the future. Vivid images of the livery flashed through his mind, images with shape and form and substance that he'd never dared to imagine before.

"Behind the livery, I'll have a stretch of land for grazing and exercising my stock," he continued on. "And I'll have plenty of room for breeding horses, thoroughbreds like none other that anyone has ever seen. They'll be the finest horses this side of the Atlantic, and buyers will be clamoring to—"

He halted abruptly, catching himself, appalled by his lack of reservation. What had possessed him to ramble on like some mindless fool? He'd never intended to voice his aspirations so freely.

He cringed, convinced his musings must have evoked a smirk on Coralee's lips or a glint of amusement in her eyes. But as he turned his head ever so slowly and stole a glance at her, he was startled by what he saw.

She was standing very still, gazing across the plot of land that he'd chosen as the site for the livery. Her face was awash with a dreamy, wistful expression, and her eyes were shimmering with promises of hope for the future.

Jack felt something tight and restricting grip his chest. "For some reason, I thought you would be laughing by now," he admitted uneasily.

She looked up at him, surprised. "Why would I be laughin'? Granny Clabo says a body has got to do some dreamin' every now and then. Besides, your ideas about buildin' a livery and breedin' horses aren't anything to be laughin' about. When this fancy hotel opens up and all those folks from England start arrivin' to take a look-see at Rugby, they'll be needin' horses and buggies and the like."

"That's precisely what I suspect will happen, too. Of course, I always knew you believed we needed a livery in Rugby. You were the one who suggested the idea in the first place."

"But I was just talkin' about a livery," she

pointed out. "You're the one who is actually doin' somethin' about it."

"And I think the livery should produce a comfortable living for me." Jack set his jaw in a hard, firm line as his thoughts drifted back to his original idea for the use of the land. "But it's not the livery that will create the fortune I'm planning to make. It's breeding horses that will generate my wealth while I'm here."

"And then . . . you'll be leavin' Rugby after you get rich?" There was a slight tremor in her voice.

Jack peered down at her, an ache swelling in his chest. "It's never been my intention to stay here permanently, Coralee."

She forced a bright smile onto her lips. "Then I reckon you need to get busy makin' that fortune of yours. And I reckon I'd best be gettin' back to the laundry shack before—"

"Coralee!" a man's voice bellowed. "How 'bout payin' your brother a little mind before he's too old to hear anything you're sayin'?"

"I reckon I'll be seein' you later, Jack." Coralee laughed as she picked up her skirts to leave. "Right now, I've got to see what Crockett is hollerin' about."

She turned and headed for the construction site, grateful that Crockett had interrupted her conversation with Jack. Although she was disconcerted by the knowledge that Jack had no intention of remaining in Rugby permanently, she didn't care for him to see that the news was unsettling to her.

But as Coralee approached her husky, muscle-bound brother, she sensed that Crockett was troubled about something as well. His thick brows were narrowed with concern, and a frown of dismay appeared on his lips. "What's goin' on, Crockett?"

He settled down on the front steps of the inn and brushed away the sawdust from the space beside him. "Sit down here a minute with me, sister."

Coralee sank to the steps, alarmed by Crockett's serious tone. "Is somebody sick? Or hurt? Or . . . ?"

He shook his head. "It's you that's troublin' me, Coralee. I've been noticin' the way you've been eyeing that English fella, Winslow. And the look in your eye has got me worried. What's goin' on betwixt the two of you?"

"We're just . . . friends," she floundered. "He's been teachin' me how to play tennis, and I've been warshin' his clothes. But he's been mighty busy the last couple of weeks, clearin' off the lot here next to the—"

"I know what he's been doin' around here, Coralee. I've been seein' him every day while I'm working here at the inn. But I don't know what he's been doin' with my baby sister when I can't see him."

Coralee bristled with indignation. "I promised I'd let you know if any of these Englishmen were steppin' out of line, didn't I?"

"Yes, but—"

"Then you should know that I wouldn't break my promise to you, Crockett. Nobody—including Jack Winslow—has been hasslin' me about anything, or I would have been lettin' you know."

Crockett heaved a troubled sigh. "It's just that I don't want you to get hurt, I reckon. After all the things that no-account husband of yours did to you, I can't stomach the thought of any man—"

"You can't always protect me, Crockett." Coralee's voice was tender and low. "I love you for loving me, for wantin' to watch out for me. But you can't protect my heart from gettin' broken—especially if I'm the one who's giving it away."

Crockett expelled another long sigh and wrapped an arm around his sister's narrow shoulders. "If you want to be givin' your heart to someone, I reckon I don't have no say in the matter. But just don't let any of these Englishmen steal away that heart of yours . . . unless that's what you want, too."

Coralee leaned her head on Crockett's strong shoulder, her throat tightening with emotion. She could only pray that her heart would still be intact when Jack Winslow eventually returned to his home in England.

The sound of male laughter rippled through the air just as Coralee crested the hill near the lawn tennis court the next afternoon. She stumbled to a halt beneath the sprawling branches of a chestnut tree, listening with interest as she watched the scene on the court below.

"You're losing your touch, Winslow," Grant cajoled.

Adam nudged Grant with his elbow and grinned. "Or else we're getting better. I do believe

we've actually beat him in two matches this afternoon."

"Then we'd better quit while we're ahead,"
Grant said with a laugh.

Defiance glinted from Jack's eyes as Grant and
Adam turned and retreated from the court. "Afraid
of the challenge, are you?" Jack taunted in a crisp
tone. "You know I'm just having an off day."

"Something is causing your off day, Jack. I've
never seen you play so poorly." Grant tucked his
racket beneath his arm. "Do you think Coralee put
too much starch in your shirts?"

Jack glared at his companions. "Coralee has
nothing to do with my prowess on the tennis
court."

"But you've seemed a bit preoccupied today.
You haven't focused on your game like you normally do," Adam noted, his voice serious. "It's almost as though your thoughts are somewhere
else."

"Maybe you're more exhausted than you think,
Jack," Grant suggested. "After all, you put a lot of
hard work into the bridle path this morning."

Jack stiffened with resentment. "I am not tired,"
he snapped. "And I am not ready to quit playing
tennis until I've won a match."

Adam shrugged. "Then you'll have to play by
yourself, I suppose."

As Adam and Grant turned and walked away,
Jack slammed his racket to the ground and muttered an oath under his breath.

Coralee grimaced in dismay. It almost seemed as

though Jack were angry at more than himself and his friends. In fact, it appeared as if he were angry at the entire world and everything in it.

She lingered beside the chestnut tree for a few moments, hoping Jack's anger would dissipate swiftly. But as she made her way down the hill and crossed over the tennis court, the tight set of his jaw and the belligerent thrust of his chin told her that he was still seething with fury.

"You look hot enough to boil water in my laundry tub," she quipped with a teasing smile.

He snapped around to face her, every muscle in his body fraught with tension. "I gave away my game," he announced, his voice thick with rage. "Lord knows, I shouldn't have lost. I don't like to lose at anything—particularly lawn tennis."

"Don't be so hard on yourself, Jack. Everybody— even the best of players—loses a game every now and then. Nobody can win all the time."

"Well, *I* expect to win." He pulled back his shoulders with defiance. "I play to win, and I settle for nothing less. I don't tolerate losing in any form or fashion, at any time or any place."

Astounded by his adamant stance on the subject, she lifted her brows in surprise. "But it's just a game, Jack!"

"It's not just a game to me," he snapped. "I don't settle for second best. Nobody ever remembers who came in second. People only remember who comes in first place. The winner—not the loser—bears the name that no one forgets."

Though Coralee was perplexed by the man's ob-

session for winning, she struggled to understand
his reasoning. "If you were playin' in one of those
tournaments back in England that you were tellin'
me about, and you'd lost an important match, I
could see why you would be spittin' mad. But
you've just been playin' for fun with Adam and
Grant. Why, playin' with them here in Rugby
doesn't count for a hill of beans!"

"Everything counts." He retreated from the court
and sat down at the foot of a hickory tree. A pained
expression flickered across his handsome face, and
his voice grew distant and low. "When you're the
second son of a duke, you have to excel at everything you do."

Coralee sank down beside him. "What do you
mean?"

He gazed into the distance, his eyes taking on the
sorrowful glint of a man who had fought against a
host of demons for far too long. "I have an older
brother, Alexander. For as far back as I can remember, I've always known Alexander would inherit
my father's land holdings and wealth and title. Alexander—not me—is the one who will eventually
become the seventh Duke of Havenshire. But I've
always had to prove I'm just as good as—or better
than—the 'chosen' one in my family. All my life,
I've fought against the notion of being second best.
Just because I'm the second-born son doesn't mean
I always have to come in second place."

"But you didn't have anything to do with not
bein' the oldest son in your family," Coralee countered. "No one has any control over where or when

they're born. That's somethin' only the good Lord knows, and it's impossible for anyone to change. And if you can't do anything about changin' the circumstances of your birth . . ."

She left the rest of the thought unfinished as sudden understanding assaulted her. The order of Jack's birth wasn't the root of his misery. He was simply trying to hold on to his pride and self-respect, his esteem and his good name—all those things that matter most in a person's life.

Her throat tightened with emotion. She'd never seen this side of Jack before, and she was both intrigued and moved by his revelations. She'd never dreamed that Jack felt inferior to anyone. And she'd never realized he was constantly striving for victory in everything he set out to do.

"Eventually, I learned how to beat Alexander at everything," he continued on. "I excelled over him in tennis, golf, and every other sport in the world. But none of that helped me to overcome the stigma of being a second son when it came to snaring the affections of an acceptable lady."

Coralee's heart thundered in her chest. "You mean . . . a woman stole your heart?" she probed, not certain she wanted to hear the answer.

He nodded slowly, then dragged a hand through his dark hair. "I was engaged to be married to a lady by the name of Phoebe at one time. But that was before she discovered I didn't meet her standards of acceptability. And before she caught the eye of a firstborn son who expected to inherit a substantial amount of wealth and a distinguished title from his father."

An ache swelled in Coralee's chest. It was little wonder the man was so full of determination to claim victory in life. Obviously, he'd struggled to be in first place in other people's eyes. Acceptance was everything in his world, and a person's worth in life was determined by the order of his birth.

Coralee couldn't fully comprehend the extent of Jack's inner turmoil, nor the depths of the social structure or the proprieties in a foreign land. But she could fully understand why this man felt he had to prove his worth. And she ached for the anguish he must have experienced along the way.

"This woman must have hurt you very badly," she finally said.

"I think she wounded my pride more than anything else. She certainly didn't break my heart."

"You never loved her?"

He gave a careless shrug. "I don't believe so. I was fond of her, but I never truly gave the woman my heart, I suppose. Looking back on it now, I believe the wretched experience taught me a lesson about the value of viewing life as a game."

"You think all of life is a . . . game?" Coralee echoed in disbelief.

"Why not?" He pursed his lips. "Just consider Rugby for a moment. My father has invested a great deal of money in this colony, and he has entrusted me with the task of making a success of his investment. There will be winners and losers in this venture, just like there are winners and losers in any game. But this is one game I have no intention of losing. I'm determined to—" He halted abruptly and gave his head a shake. "Enough of this for now. I'm probably boring you to death with my philosophies on life."

"Maybe I should keep my mouth shut and listen to you more," Coralee said. "You haven't had the chance to talk very much lately. I keep spoutin' off at the mouth and don't give you a chance to say anything."

"I think I've just said more than enough for now," Jack insisted with a sheepish grin.

"I'm glad you told me about your reasons for wantin' to win at everything all the time." A sly smile curved on her lips. "But you should have asked me for some advice about winnin'. I know of somethin' that guarantees you'll win every game that you play. It's a mountain secret."

He held out his palms as an indication that she should back away from the suggestion. "If you're thinking about casting some sort of spell on me, don't bother, Coralee. It would be a waste of your time and effort. I don't believe in such nonsense."

"This isn't a spell," she insisted. "It's just one of Granny Clabo's remedies, but nobody knows about it except my older brother Harlan and me."

Skepticism glinted from his eyes. "If this is such a well-guarded family secret, why would you bother to tell me about it?"

"Granny said if anyone ever needed to know the secret, somethin' inside me would know. And that somethin' is telling me you should know about this secret, Jack." She reached for the red ribbon in her hair. "Now, hold out your left arm."

He followed her order, and she wrapped the silk ribbon around his biceps. The feel of the taut muscle beneath the sleeve of his shirt sent a tingling sensation through Coralee.

As soon as she'd tied the ribbon in place, Jack's eyes narrowed in confusion. "What's the meaning of this?"

"It's the secret, Jack! As long as you have a red ribbon tied around your arm, you'll win at every game you play."

"Is that so?" he taunted, obviously not believing her.

"It certainly is. I know it's a surefire way for winnin' because Granny Clabo told me so. I reckon if anyone has the answer to anything, it's Granny. After all, the woman is pert near nine years older than God. And if Granny says so, it's the last word."

"The same way you know that a horse with white feet brings good luck to its owner?"

She smiled. "And like gettin' a rainstorm after seein' the back sides of the leaves on a silver-leaf maple."

Pondering that thought, Jack quietly removed the ribbon from his arm and tucked it into his pocket for safekeeping.

Chapter 13

❦❦❦

"Mail's here!" Clell's voice rang through the settlement as his wagon rolled to a stop in front of the dining hall.

Accustomed to the daily ritual of the afternoon mail call in Rugby, Coralee paid little mind to Clell's announcement. As a number of colonists flocked around the mail wagon, she continued with her work, folding an assortment of clothes that she and Rachel had laundered earlier in the day.

A few moments later, Daniel was rattling off the names of various colonists and distributing an assortment of parcels and letters from the mail pouch. Each time a whoop of glee erupted from the crowd, Coralee assumed that another colonist had just received his monthly remittance from his family in England. Most of the men made no secret of the fact that their wealthy British families were supporting them until they could establish a source of income for themselves in Rugby.

Coralee had just placed a neatly folded shirt atop a stack of other garments, absently listening to the sound of Daniel's voice, when one particular name seized her attention.

"And the next item is addressed to Lord John Winslow," Daniel announced.

Coralee whirled, her eyes searching the crowd. In the next instant, she saw a tall, dark-haired gentleman emerging from the throng of colonists and stepping up to the wagon.

"I believe you've been expecting this letter for several weeks, Winslow." Daniel handed a thick envelope to Jack.

Jack stared down at the paper in his hand, inhaling a deep breath before ripping into the envelope. As he hastily scanned the document, a smile crept onto his lips. "Apparently, I'm purchasing a piece of property in Rugby this afternoon, Daniel. And the transaction will become official just as soon as this document contains two more signatures—yours and mine."

"It's as good as done, then. I'll sign the paper as soon as I've handed out the rest of the mail," Daniel assured him.

Jack wheeled and threaded his way through the crowd. Coralee's heart skipped a beat as he headed in her direction. Pleased that he'd finally received the long-awaited paperwork from England, she smiled warmly when he stepped up beside her. "Sounds like you got some good news from England today, Jack."

"It's good to know I can finally start working on the livery now." He returned her smile with a disarming one of his own. "Thankfully, someone was

vise enough to advise me that I could save a great
deal of time by clearing the trees from the property
before the legal paperwork arrived."

A heated blush rose to her cheeks. "That musta
been a right smart person who gave you that advice," Coralee teased, noticing that his eyes were
glowing with a warmth that she'd never detected
before. "Somethin' tells me you're pert-near to
bein' the happiest man in all of Tennessee today."

"And I'll be the happiest tomorrow," he insisted.
"In the morning, I intend to become the first occupant of the new inn."

Coralee's brows rose in surprise. "The inn is
openin' up tomorrow?"

Jack nodded. "And to celebrate the opening, the
colony is hosting an English tea during the afternoon."

"That sounds like a right peculiar time to be
havin' a tea party. I never heard tell of such a thing
happenin' smack-dab in the middle of the day."

Jack chuckled. "It happens every day in England.
Afternoon tea time is a common practice there."

She shook her head in disbelief. "Well, I never
would have reckoned anything like that would be
happenin' in this neck of the woods."

"It's not as strange as it sounds, I can assure
you." He moved closer to her, and his voice grew
husky and low. "You've introduced me to a lot of
mountain traditions, Coralee. Now let me have the
chance to introduce you to one of mine. Come with
me to the tea tomorrow afternoon. Let me acquaint
you with an English tradition that has been part of

my life for as long as I can remember. And let's celebrate my good fortune . . . together."

"I reckon I can't let you be celebratin' all by your lonesome, Jack." Unable to suppress her delight, Coralee grinned. "I'd be mighty pleased to go to that fancy tea party with you, come tomorrow afternoon."

An hour later, Jack was sitting at a table in the men's barracks waiting for Daniel to place his signature on the document that had arrived from England earlier in the day.

"Congratulations, Winslow." With a flourishing sweep of the pen in his hand, the colony manager placed his name on the paper. "As of this moment, you are now the official owner of one of the finest parcels of land in the colony of Rugby, Tennessee."

"To be honest, I was beginning to think it would never happen." Jack glanced over the document once again, suddenly seized by a curious thought. "Obviously, the colony board purchased thousands of acres here in Morgan County with the express purpose of reselling tracts of property to colonists like myself."

"Precisely." Daniel's brows narrowed. "Do you have a problem with that?"

"Not at all," Jack said. "But I haven't heard any mention of the property owners who sold the acreage to the board in the first place. I would assume the original owners are local residents who sold part—or all—of their land holdings to the colony."

"Actually, the board purchased most of the prop-

rty from a company in Boston," Daniel explained.
From my understanding, a group of Bostonian financiers intended to build a colony here about a decade or so ago, hoping to relieve an industrial depression in the northeastern part of the country. But before their plans materialized, the depression came to end and they lost interest in the project altogether."

"I see." Jack nodded absently. "That would explain why the mountaineers in this region are still languishing in poverty. They probably sold off their holdings for a pittance. And if they pocketed a tidy sum, I'm certain the money disappeared long ago."

"Probably so," Daniel agreed. "Actually, I suppose few people even remember much about the Boston company or their purchases in the area."

"At the moment, everyone is thinking in terms of the future," Jack pointed out. "I know my thoughts are focused in that direction. In fact, I'm quite anxious to establish my livery business." He leaned back in the chair and rubbed a hand along the line of his jaw. "I just wish I could find an experienced carpenter who had the time to construct the stables for me."

"Proffitt can't spare any of his crew at the moment," Daniel advised. "We were fortunate that he agreed to spare a few workers long enough to repair the leak here in the barracks."

"Then I suppose I'll have to find some other means for getting the work done." Jack stretched out his palms, chuckling. "Until then, it appears that the only available resources are my own two hands."

"Still, I'm glad to see you're determined to carry out your plans. We're in dire need of a livery around here."

Mindful that his endeavors in Rugby would determine the course of his future, Jack clenched his jaw with stubborn resolve. "And I'm willing to do whatever it takes to make a success of the venture," he vowed.

"Come noontime, we'll be closin' up for the day, Rachel," Coralee announced the next morning, gliding a hot iron over the sleeve of a white shirt. "I'm goin' to a party with Jack at the new inn this afternoon."

Rachel's eyes widened in surprise. "How wonderful, Coralee! Aren't you excited?"

"I'm pert near happier than a pig in slop," she admitted, "but my belly has been flutterin' like crazy all mornin'. Before the party gets started, I'm intendin' to run back to the cabin for a spell and get all fancied up. I've never been to an English tea party before, but I reckon it'll be fancy enough for me to wear my Sunday dress."

"Ma and I wore our Sunday dresses when we went to a fancy tea in Boston one time," Rachel remembered. "As I recall, the ladies were all dressed up and very, very polite. And all of them were careful to hold out their pinkies when they sipped on their tea."

"I didn't know you were supposed to do that."

Coralee frowned. "But, then, I reckon there's a bushel of things I don't know about goin' to a tea party."

"I'm sure you'll do just fine," Rachel assured her.

Coralee nodded in agreement. But by the time she'd donned her Sunday dress and headed back to the settlement, she was still trying to steady the fluttering sensation in her stomach. And when she strolled into the colony, the sight of Jack caused her heart to lurch in her chest.

He was standing in front of his newly acquired property wearing a tailored frock coat and dark trousers with a snowy-white shirt that she had laundered and pressed for him. Though his handsome appearance had always disconcerted her, his bold, arresting good looks were particularly unsettling to her today. As Coralee stepped up beside him, she found herself struggling to catch her breath.

Breathing became even more difficult as his eyes leisurely traveled over the length of her Sunday dress, studying the line of tiny pearl buttons that trailed down the center of her bodice, then sweeping over the gathers of the skirt that emphasized the gentle flare of her hips and the indentation of her tiny waist. Judging from his blatant scrutiny, Coralee suspected he'd noticed that the deep green color of her gown matched the hue of her eyes.

But the glimmer of approval in his gaze and the upward tilt of his lips told Coralee that he liked what he saw. "You've never looked lovelier, Coralee," he insisted.

"Thanks," she murmured, her voice strangled and hoarse from the lack of sufficient air in her lungs.

He nodded toward the inn. "Are you ready for some tea?"

"I reckon I'm as ready as I'll ever be," she replied, praying she sounded more confident than she felt.

He extended his arm to her. Coralee inhaled a deep, steadying breath and looped her hand around the sleeve of his jacket. The feel of his strong muscles beneath the fabric had the scorching effect of a heated iron on her skin, blistering her fingers and sending a rush of fiery sensations through her arm.

Making a valiant attempt to ignore her body's troubling reactions, Coralee lifted her chin and focused her gaze on the new inn.

For months, she'd been fascinated by the building, watching in amazement as the structure had taken form and shape and blossomed to life in the midst of the forested terrain. But now, studying the completed formation, Coralee found herself gawking, mesmerized by the sight of the imposing building.

From Coralee's point of view, the stately inn was as magnificent as the castles and palaces of her dreams. Wide verandas, supported by slender posts and trimmed with elaborate trills, encircled the first two floors of the building. Atop the structure, the third level had the effect of a peaked crown, adorned with a majestic arched window and dormers that overlooked the surrounding mountain vistas.

She was still perusing the ornamental trim as Jack guided her onto the veranda. "Welcome to the Tabard Inn, Coralee."

"The Tabard Inn?" She wrinkled her nose. "I was figurin' you'd be callin' this place the Rugby Inn. After all, it's sittin' here in Rugby, not in some place by the name of Tabard."

He chuckled. "Actually, Daniel suggested the inn should be named after a famous hostelry in Southwark, England, the Tabard Inn that Chaucer described in *Canterbury Tales*. In fact, the staircase here contains a baluster from the original Tabard Inn of Shakespeare's day."

Jack ushered Coralee through the wide wooden doors and led her over to the staircase. "Here's the original baluster," he said, pointing out the carved piece of wood.

"How fascinatin'," Coralee cooed, disguising her ignorance of the names and places that he'd described with an overly bright smile.

But she made no effort to conceal her astonishment as they explored the interior of the new building. Feeling as though she'd been transported into another world, Coralee gaped at the elegant furnishings that filled each of the chambers. Never in her life had she envisioned such a wondrous display of finery.

She was mesmerized by the huge oil paintings in gilded frames that adorned the walls of the rooms, impressed with the luxurious, soft rugs that covered the wooden floors, enchanted by the fine weave of the white linens that covered the tables.

Captivated by her surroundings, Coralee scarcely noticed the other guests who were enjoying the new facility. Though several colonists were playing cards, most of the gentlemen were simply wandering from room to room, sipping on tea and sharing good-natured laughs with their companions.

She was still gawking at the fine furnishings when Jack presented her with a dainty cup and saucer filled with hot tea. "Why don't we enjoy our tea on the veranda?" he suggested.

Coralee nodded in agreement and fell into step beside him. Within a few moments, they were seated on the veranda, enjoying the scenic view of the surrounding mountains.

Coralee grasped the handle of her teacup, praying that the delicate china would not crumble beneath the pressure of her fingers. Remembering to hold out her pinky, she lifted the dainty cup to her lips.

"This tea is right tasty," she remarked just as the swell of music filled the air. Coralee cocked her head to one side, listening intently, acutely aware that the sweeping refrains were far different from the toe-tapping melodies rendered by mountain fiddlers. "I never heard the like," she murmured.

"Several of the colonists have decided to band together and form their own musical group here in Rugby," Jack explained. "Judging from the waltz that I'm hearing now, I suspect most of the gentlemen must have received formal training in music."

"They sure know how to play them fiddles and horns," Coralee agreed, "but that English music doesn't sound anything like the music that comes out of the fiddles 'round here." Suddenly overwhelmed by the newness of all that she'd seen and heard, she nibbled on her lower lip. "Is everything like this in England, Jack?"

"Musical performances vary widely, depending on the experience of the conductor and the instrumentalists," he offered. "Symphony orchestras are—"

"I'm not just talkin' about music," Coralee tried to explain. "I'm talkin' about fancy dishes and pretty paintin's and fine chairs and everything else I'm seein' here in this place. Is everything like this back in England?"

"Not everything," Jack revealed. "Some aspects of life in Britain are rather plain in comparison to what you've seen here at the Tabard Inn. On the other hand, there are certain facets of life that are much more elaborate than this."

"But what about your life back in England?" she probed, genuinely curious. "Did you live in a big, fancy place somethin' like this one when you was a shirttail boy?"

A distant look clouded the blue of his eyes. "I grew up in a magnificent house that has belonged to my family for hundreds of years. It's a huge stone manor with twenty-four rooms, surrounded by hundreds of acres of land."

Her eyes widened in stunned disbelief. "If your granddaddies built a house that big, you must have

an awful big family. It would take a heap of kinfolks to fill up all them rooms."

"Actually, my immediate family are the only oc-
cupants of Havenshire Manor. My sister, Sabrina,
still resides with our parents at the estate, along
with my brother, Alexander, and his new wife."

Coralee tallied the number of residents on her
fingers. "For heaven's sake, Jack! There's only five
folks livin' in that big place!"

Jack bit back a smile. "The manor provides accommodations for a few servants as well. Not all
of the space is wasted, I suppose."

At that moment, Adam stepped onto the veranda. "Grant and I thought we should inspect
your new living quarters, Winslow."

Grant followed closely at Adam's heels. "We
want to see what kind of accommodations you
have here," he added with a grin.

Jack turned to Coralee with an apologetic smile.
"Pardon me for just a moment, Coralee."

"You go on ahead," she insisted with a wave of
her hand. "I'll still be sittin' right here when you
get back."

Jack disappeared into the building with Adam
and Grant, leaving Coralee alone with her
thoughts. She absently fingered the rim of her teacup, mindful of the sharp contrast between the
fragile, white china and the tin plates and mugs
that filled her cupboards at home.

How different, she thought. Jack had been surrounded by fine things all of his life, things like
delicate teacups and beautiful music that sounded

like none other that she'd ever heard. Coralee couldn't imagine living in a house that contained twenty-four rooms. At the moment, the mere challenge of envisioning a home that large was beyond the realm of her imagination.

Coralee leaned back in the chair and closed her eyes. Adjusting to life in Rugby must have been far more difficult for Jack than she could have ever fathomed, she realized. Waves of admiration for his resilience and fortitude swept through her.

She tightened her fingers around the dainty handle of her teacup, heaving a troubled sigh. Their lives were as disparate as china from tin, she feared, and their worlds were separated by far more than a stretch of ocean between two foreign lands.

"Miss Pearl's turnip greens taste mighty good," Coralee remarked over lunch the next day.

Seated across from Coralee in the dining hall, Rachel nodded in agreement. "I don't see how she cooks up all this food every day for so many people."

Coralee peered around the room. "Judging from the number of folks chawin' down in here today, I'm thinkin' a lot of new faces have been comin' 'round of late."

"That's because more and more people are arriving in Rugby every week," Rachel explained. "Pa said an English lady should be arriving soon, a lady who has been hired to cook for the restaurant in the Tabard Inn. And the colony has hired a gardener from England, too."

"I reckon we're gonna be livin' in the middle of an English village in a spell or two."

"You haven't said anything about the English tea you attended with Jack yesterday." Rachel's brows narrowed with concern. "Were you disappointed?"

"Not perzactly." Coralee shoved aside her empty plate and planted her elbows on the table. "It was a mighty fine party, the finest party I ever done seen. But everything was so . . . *different*."

"I suppose all of us will have to find ways to blend our traditions in Rugby." Rachel took a sip of water from her mug just as Jack stepped up to the table with a plate of turnip greens in one hand and a mug of coffee in the other.

"Good day, ladies. May I join you?"

Rachel smiled, springing to her feet. "I'd love your company, Jack, but I'm just getting ready to leave." She turned to Coralee, adding, "I'll take care of any customers until you can get back to work."

As Rachel scurried from the dining hall, Jack joined Coralee at the table. He peered down at the food on his plate and laughed. "I never thought I would be laughing about the prospect of eating turnip greens for lunch, but I haven't the slightest inclination to turn up my nose at them. Sleeping through an entire night on a bed for the first time in weeks has improved my attitude toward life in a most remarkable way, it appears."

Coralee grinned. "I'm glad you like your new livin' arrangements."

"The rest of my life has taken a turn for the better, as well. All of the lumber for building the stables was delivered from the sawmill this morning, and Adam and Grant have agreed to help me construct the building. We have plenty of volunteers who are finishing up the bridle path, and—"

"Comin' to the hoedown, Coralee?" A husky young man with a bright thatch of red hair bolted up to the table.

Coralee glanced up, a playful grin sprouting on her lips. "Have you ever known me to miss a hoedown, Simon?"

"Can't rightly recall that you have." A boyish grin lit up his freckled face. "You're gonna save me a dance, aren't you?"

"As long as you promise not to be steppin' on my toes." She peered down at Simon's shoes, wrinkling her nose in dismay. "Those big clodhoppers of yours could be a real danger to my little dancin' feet, you know."

A second man stepped up behind Simon. "I thought you were gonna promise me the first dance at this hoedown, Coralee."

Coralee laughed. "I haven't promised my first dance to anyone yet, Zach."

"But you're gonna save a dance for Simon and me, aren't you?" Zach asked.

"Of course I will," Coralee promised.

As the men turned and walked away, the smile on Coralee's lips disappeared when she noticed the troubled expression on Jack's face. "Is somethin' wrong, Jack?"

He shook his head. "It's just that I've never heard anyone mention a hoedown before now. I'm not familiar with the term."

"A hoedown is a big party in a barn with music and food," Coralee explained. "The men bring out their banjos and fiddles, and the women bring their favorite dishes for everyone to eat. Once that music gets to playin', we're like fat ponies cavortin' in high oats."

He shifted uneasily on the bench. "I assume guests must receive a proper invitation to a hoedown before they're permitted to attend."

Coralee bit her cheek to keep from laughing aloud. "We don't send out any written invitations, if that's what you're askin'. Considerin' most folks 'round these parts don't know how to read or write, it's not hardly necessary." She paused. "You wouldn't be interested in goin' to a hoedown . . . would you?"

"That all depends." Jack's eyes were teasing and warm. "Would you care if I tagged along with you?"

"I wouldn't care at all, Jack. In fact, I'd be right proud if you'd go along with me to the hoedown."

"It's settled, then." Jack grinned. "And I promise I won't step on your little dancing feet."

Chapter 14

~~~⌒⌒⌒~~~

The golden glow of lanterns was spilling from the open doors of the weathered barn when Jack arrived at the hoedown with Coralee the next evening. And as soon as he stepped into the building, he knew he'd entered a world like none other he'd ever seen.

The area was filled with all ages of people. Numerous children were scampering about the barn, waving and shouting to their small friends who were peering down at the crowd from the loft. Stoop-shouldered men accompanied spry, silver-haired women, while middle-aged couples chatted amiably with each other.

Jack recognized many faces of the young men who worked at the colony, though he'd never bothered to learn the names of most of the mountaineers. But he also noticed several people he could identify by name, including Coralee's brothers.

He swept his gaze across the room. Long tables along the walls were brimming with an assortment of cobblers and pies and shortbreads, and mugs of apple cider were flowing freely among the crowd.

But it was the music and atmosphere that fascinated him more than anything else. The rafters of the barn were practically shaking from the beat of the resounding music. Feet were tapping and boots were stomping in time to the lively tunes of fiddles and banjos.

And everywhere people were laughing, greeting friends and neighbors with back slaps and smiles. It appeared as if no man were better than another, Jack observed, just as a young man edged his way through the throng.

The man offered a shy smile as he stepped up to Coralee. "Miss Coralee, I'd be honored if you'd dance with me."

The man's voice was slow, his speech faltering and hesitant. With one glance at the man, Jack knew he was painfully timid. And judging from the cloudy look in his eyes, Jack suspected he was sorely lacking in mental abilities.

The man peered down at the floor. "I know I ain't very good at dancin', but—"

"Nonsense, Walter," Coralee insisted, looping her hand around his arm. "You can dance just as good as anyone here."

Within the next instant, Coralee was swirling across the barn floor, arm in arm with the faltering young man. But no sooner had she returned to Jack's side when a second man approached her.

Jack shuddered at the sight of the man's scarred face. Half of one eyebrow was missing, and his nose was pointed and long. Undoubtedly, the poor soul bore the ugliest features Jack had ever seen.

Yet, Coralee greeted the homely creature with a warm smile. "Homer Cates, I hadn't seen you in a month o' Sundays!" she exclaimed.

"Well, seein' as how you been missin' me so much, how 'bout if I take you on a little spin across the floor?" Homer cajoled.

Coralee nodded. "Let's get a move on, Homer."

Observing it all, Jack shook his head in disbelief. The refined ladies of London would have been repulsed by the notion of dancing with either of Coralee's partners. They would have turned up their elegant noses, ignoring the poor chaps as if they didn't exist or demanding that they be removed from their presence. And they would have never dared to risk the chance of being associated with such common creatures.

Yet, Coralee Hayes accepted Walter and Homer just as they were, without regard to their looks or intelligence.

But as the evening wore on, Jack noticed one disturbing similarity between the formality of London's society and the boot-stomping atmosphere of the mountain hoedown, a similarity he couldn't ignore, no matter how hard he tried.

As happened at most of the formal dances in England, there was one woman in attendance who stood out from the rest. And here, at this gathering of mountaineers, Coralee was the belle of the ball.

No other woman could come close to exuding the charm, the wholesomeness, or the beauty that she possessed. Jack had been around her long enough to know that she was naturally optimistic, as cheerful and bright as the glow of a candle on a dark winter's night. But it seemed as if everyone else in attendance at the hoedown was aware of that special glow about her, too, Jack noticed with a grimace. Especially Simon, Zach, and two other men who had been dancing with Coralee for most of the night.

A hot surge of jealousy shot through his veins just as Coralee came up beside him. "Aren't you goin' to dance with me tonight?"

"I'm not familiar with the steps," he insisted.

"And I wasn't familiar with your game of tennis, either," she reminded him with a grin, grasping his arm and pulling him onto the dance floor.

In the next breath, he was standing in the middle of the barn, concentrating on the intricate movements, trying to imitate Coralee's steps. Though he bumped elbows and backsides with other dancers, no one seemed to care. Laughter was the order of the day, it appeared. And Jack had to admit he was having a wonderful time . . . until Simon pulled Coralee into his arms and whisked her from sight.

Fuming, Jack stomped to the side of the barn, unable to control the hot flashes of jealousy roaring through him like a steaming train. And he was still seething with anger when Coralee stepped up beside him a few moments later.

"I'm ready to leave, Coralee," he announced stiffly.

"Is somethin' wrong?"

"Not a bloody thing," he snapped.

A shadow of concern crossed her face. She hastily bid good-bye to several people, then quietly slipped out of the barn with Jack.

"I was hopin' you'd like the hoedown, Jack," she said.

He glared at her. "You seemed to be enjoying yourself, I noticed. Especially with every damn man in the place chasing after you."

She pursed her lips together. "If you're talkin' about Walter and Homer, you should be ashamed of yourself, Jack Winslow. Those two men can't help bein' poor or ugly or slow no more than you can help bein' rich and handsome and smart. They got feelin's, just like everyone does."

"But what about Zach and Simon and the rest of your doting admirers?" Jack demanded, stalking over the trail that led to Coralee's cabin. "What about them?"

"What about them?" she shot back, scurrying to catch up with him. "They were just wantin' to kick up their heels and have a good time, just like everybody else attendin' the hoedown."

"Those brawny mountain boys weren't merely interested in dancing with you, Coralee. They wanted more—much more—than a chance to swing you around the barn a time or two."

She tossed back her head. "I don't know why you're gettin' so techious about this, Jack. Those homeboys weren't doin' anything wrong, and I wasn't, neither. I was just havin' me a good time, just like I always have myself when all that good toe-tappin' music is ringin' through the barn on hoedown nights."

"I'm delighted to hear that you had a wonderful time this evening, Coralee," he scoffed. "As for me, I was bloody miserable at your little boot-stomping affair."

He ripped over the trail like a madman, too infuriated to realize that the glow of a full moon was lighting his way along the winding path. Coralee sprinted alongside him, arms flinging wildly, maintaining an even pace with his long, hurried strides.

Jack was still fuming when they arrived at the cabin. He stomped across the porch and halted abruptly at the door. "Now that I've escorted you home from the hoedown, I believe I've completed my obligations for the evening."

With a curt nod, he turned to leave. But he'd taken only one step across the porch when Coralee reached out and grasped his arm.

"You aren't goin' anywhere, Jack." Her voice was steady and low. "At least not until you tell me what's goin' on in that head of yours."

"All right, then, I'll tell you." He jerked his arm away from her grasp. "Your willingness to accept a person—without regard for his shortcomings and flaws—is nothing short of astounding to me. In fact, it's an admirable trait that I admire and respect. But your acceptance of every bloody male at the hoedown tonight was like a slap in the face. I'm not accustomed to vying for a woman's attention— or waiting in line for the opportunity to dance with her."

"We never agreed that I wouldn't dance with anyone else tonight. Why, you never even said anything about it!" Coralee bristled with defensiveness. "Besides, I thought you were just taggin' along with me for the fun of it."

"But I didn't expect to be ignored for most of the evening. For someone who has been treated with the dignity and respect reserved for members of the British aristocracy all of his life, I'm realizing that it's highly insulting to be regarded as just another man."

"You're not just another man, Jack. Why, all the homeboys 'round here—"

"All those homeboys couldn't take their eyes off you tonight, Coralee," he cut in. "And I didn't like the way they were looking at you. I knew what they were thinking, knew what they were wanting."

"So you're claimin' to be some kind of mind reader?" she scoffed.

Annoyance seared through him. He reached out and grasped her shoulders, forcing her to meet his angry gaze. "I'm no mind reader," he grated. "But I have no doubts about the thoughts and desires of all those men who were gawking at you tonight . . . because I was wanting and thinking the very same things."

She regarded him, wary. "Then I reckon you'd best tell me what it is that you're wantin'."

"I don't have the bloody patience to tell you," he snapped, tightening his grip on her shoulders and pulling her against him.

He ground his mouth on hers with a kiss that was hot and hungry, fueled by a raw, primitive need he could no longer deny. And with one taste of her, all of his frustrations and anger, all the weeks of suppressed longing, exploded into a fiery rush of passion.

He pressed his body into hers, pushing her against the cabin, trapping her between the log wall and the length of his hard frame. Consumed by the flames of desire sizzling through him, he deepened the pressure of his mouth, searing her lips with his hot, openmouthed kiss.

She clamped her hands around his forearms, clinging to him as if she were trying to hold on to her last vestiges of control. "I know what you're wantin', Jack," Coralee rasped, her breathing short and ragged.

"I don't think you do," he warned. "I don't think you could possibly know just how much I want you."

"Oh, I know," she murmured, gliding her hands up the length of his arms. "'Cuz I'm wantin' you in the very same way."

That was all Jack needed to hear. With one swift thrust of his boot, he kicked open the cabin door. As he stumbled inside the log dwelling, he tightened his hold on Coralee's narrow shoulders, clawing at her dress with such frantic desperation that the material ripped beneath his hands.

Jack knew he was moving too fast, too hard, but he couldn't seem to stop himself. He tore into the gown and split the seams, shredding some of the material. Then, with one hard tug, he jerked the fabric down over her arms to expose the bare curve of her neck and the creamy sweep of her shoulders.

A gasp escaped from her throat. "My dress, Jack," she choked out. "My dress . . ."

"I'll buy you another one," he assured her. "I'll buy you hundreds of them. . . ."

He clamped his mouth down on hers again, claiming possession of her lips with a fierce hunger, determined to seize possession of far more. He thrust his hips forward, shoving the lower half of his body into the folds of her skirt.

"Feel what you're doing to me, Coralee," he murmured into her mouth as he kissed her.

Coralee trembled, staggering against him, when he placed her hand over the hard, throbbing bulge in his trousers. "You're so hard, Jack. So hard, so hot. . . ."

Fire burned his loins. Sinking to his knees, Jack dragged Coralee down to the floor with him. In the next moment, they were rolling across the braided rug, hands grasping and clutching, legs tangled and trembling.

Jack pressed Coralee's back against the rug, then dropped to his knees and straddled her body. Losing all control, he grasped the tattered pieces of her bodice and ripped the remaining fabric down to her waist. Then he hastily tugged at the thin ribbon that held her chemise in place.

But as he pushed the fabric aside, Jack's breath snared in his throat. Her breasts were huge and full, begging to be fondled and caressed and suckled. Cupping the generous mounds in his hands, he lowered his mouth to one breast, then the other, swirling his tongue across the hardened peak of each rosy nipple.

Coralee writhed beneath him, moaning with desire. "Oh, Jack," she whispered in a strangled voice.

He dragged his mouth away from her breasts, anxious to tear the rest of her clothes from her body, eager to be rid of his own restricting garments.

In the next moment, clothes were sailing across the room. Naked, Jack eased his weight over the length of Coralee's bare, trembling body, unable to contain the passion surging through him.

Coralee parted her legs and arched against him. "Take me, Jack," she urged. "Take me fast . . . and hard . . ."

He plunged inside her, stunned by the soul-jarring contact. She was hot and wet and pliant, ready and eager for each thrust of his hips.

He took her, hard and fast, just as she'd wanted, driving into her sweet inner core. She rocked beneath him, taking him inside her, dragging her hands over his back and begging for more. "Yes, Jack. Yes . . ."

His vision blurred, his body quaked. With one final plunge, he spilled his seed into her and cried out her name. "I never knew, Coralee. I never knew anything could be like this. . . ."

Exhausted and spent, he collapsed beside her. She brushed her fingers through his hair and snuggled the length of her body against his.

After a long moment of silence, Coralee heaved a contented sigh. "Somethin' tells me you Englishmen don't do anything like Americans do," she murmured lazily.

He lifted his eyes to her face. "What do you mean?"

A beguiling smile curved on her lips. "Don't you ever be thinkin' you're just another man to me, Jack Winslow. There isn't another man in this world who's ever made me feel the way you make me feel. And no other man has ever made love to me the way you just did."

"I could have been more patient." He winced. "I didn't give you any pleasure—"

"If you'd given me any more pleasure, I would've been clawin' at you like a mountain cat in heat." Her voice was soft and warm. "Besides, we always got next time."

"Ah, next time." He closed his eyes, smiling at the thought.

Within a few moments, Jack had drifted off to sleep, one arm draped over Coralee's bare midriff. She gently eased away from his hold, careful not to awaken him, and got up from the floor.

Shivering from the chill of the evening air that caressed her bare skin, Coralee quietly crossed the room and slipped into a white cotton gown and wrapper. After placing a quilt over the length of Jack's naked body and tucking a pillow beneath his head, she struck a match on the fire board and ignited the logs in the fireplace.

As the fire roared to life, she stared into the flames for a long moment, thinking about the heated blazes of passion that had burned within her only a few moments before. She sighed, supposing she should feel ashamed about what had transpired, about giving herself so freely to Jack.

But shame was not the emotion that Coralee was feeling. Still giddy and exhilarated from the furor of the evening, she only hoped she would have no regrets in the future for her reckless, wanton behavior.

Coralee turned and glided across the room, gathering up the garments Jack had recklessly tossed aside in that frantic, groping moment before he'd claimed her as his own. She had just retrieved a tattered remnant of her gown from the floor when a low moan rumbled from Jack's direction.

"Your dress . . ." Jack moaned again, propping himself up on his elbows. "I'm dreadfully sorry, Coralee."

"Don't you be frettin' about it none, Jack. It was my second-best dress, anyhow, not my Sunday one."

A shadow of guilt flickered across his face. "I'll buy you a new gown, I promise you, just as soon as I can."

She scooped up his white shirt from the rug. "Come fall, when I'm goin' to Cincinnati with one of my brothers, I'll just buy myself two new dresses. I haven't been workin' on my quilt much of late, but I'm makin' enough pocket money from doin' laundry to treat myself to somethin' extra."

Dismissing the matter, Coralee placed his clothes on the floor beside him. "I reckon I can be makin' us some coffee while you're gettin' yourself dressed."

She whirled, making a conscious effort to refrain from ogling him as he shrugged into his shirt and trousers. Fully aware that the sight of that beautifully sculpted physique of his would wreak havoc on what little common sense she had left, Coralee scurried to retrieve a coffee grinder from the cupboard.

By the time she'd summoned up the courage to steal a glimpse of him, Jack was fully dressed, sprawled out on the braided rug in front of the fire. As Coralee waited for the coffee to finish brewing, she placed a set of mugs on the hearth and settled down beside him.

"Tell me somethin', Jack." She arranged the folds of her nightgown over her legs, hugging her knees to her chest. "Did you really have such an awful time at the hoedown?"

Laughter rumbled deep within his chest. "To be honest, it was one of the most entertaining events I've ever attended. I've never experienced anything quite like it."

"Then, English dances must be a heap different than our hoedowns," Coralee surmised.

"Formality is the rule at an English ball," he explained. "Throughout the evening, ladies are flaunting their jewels and displaying their newest gowns. Most of the unmarried ladies—like my sister, Sabrina—are constantly attending balls, hoping to catch the eye of an eligible suitor."

"So they're tryin' to find 'em a man?" Coralee edged forward and removed the tin pot of coffee from the fire.

"That's one way of describing their intentions, I suppose." Jack's smile faded away as Coralee handed a mug of hot coffee to him. "During the hoedown last night, I suspected your motives were very much the same. And the thought of you with another man . . ." He shuddered. "I couldn't bear the notion, Coralee. I wanted the belle of the ball all to myself."

Though Coralee suspected she was not the first belle who had fallen prey to Jack's charms, the seductive remark both pleased and flattered her. "I reckon you musta gone to a heap of them fancy balls," she managed to say.

"I've attended my share of them," he admitted.

She took a sip of her coffee, suddenly curious about other aspects of Jack's life in his native land. "What other kinds of things did you do when you was livin' in England? What were you doin' with yourself all day long after you got up in the mornin'?"

He gazed into the fire, his eyes clouding with distant memories. "Normally, I started off the day with a morning ride through my family's estate. After breakfast, I played lawn tennis or golf for a few hours. Then, in the afternoons, I would attend a horse race or meet a friend at a tavern for a lager of ale."

"And all those servants at your daddy's house took care of warshin' your clothes and the like," Coralee speculated.

"Actually, a valet attended to all my personal needs. George maintained my wardrobe and monitored my social calender," Jack explained.

Puzzled, she frowned. "But if you were playin' tennis and golf all day long while that valet of yours was launderin' your clothes, when did you have time to be earnin' your keep?"

The hint of a smile appeared on his lips. "I didn't have to earn my keep, Coralee. My family's wealth provided everything I could possibly want or need. I didn't have to work for a living."

"You never worked a lick at all? Not one single day in your whole entire life?"

"Not until I moved to Rugby," he revealed. "And now I'm hacking down trees and constructing entire buildings by the sweat of my brow." Chuckling, he set aside his coffee mug. "I suppose I should be heading back to the inn now. I've got lots of work ahead of me tomorrow, and I want to get an early start in the morning."

Hours later, Coralee's lips were still burning from the heat of Jack's departing kiss, her mind spinning with thoughts about the events of the evening.

She'd never known anyone who could afford the luxuries of leisurely pastimes, never known anyone who devoted most of his time to the frivolities of life. Yet, Jack's revelations about his past had given her new insight into his penchants for indulging in games and idle distractions. Since work had not been required to sustain his life of privilege in England, he'd simply focused his attention on pleasurable diversions.

Coralee sighed as she gazed into the fire. There was so much about Jack that she didn't understand. And so much more she wanted to know.

Chapter 15

Next time, it would be different.

Jack sat on the edge of the bed and yanked off his boots, his mind filled with thoughts of Coralee and the passion that had sizzled so intensely between them throughout the evening.

Never had a woman given herself to him with such eagerness, such willingness, such uninhibited fervor. Jack had no doubts that she'd wanted him as badly as he'd wanted her. She'd made no attempt to disguise her desire for him, and her unbridled restraint had titillated his own throbbing needs even more.

And the fiery passion that had erupted between them had been unlike anything Jack had ever known.

But next time, it would be different, Jack silently vowed again. He would leisurely explore every inch of her in a slow, exacting way. He would taste and sample and savor every generous swell and enticing curve. Next time, he would . . .

Next time.

255

Jack's boot slipped from his hand and hit the floor with a thud. Holy Mother, what was he thinking?

He lunged to his feet, appalled by the realization that he was flagrantly ignoring his cardinal rule in the game of seduction, the rule that prohibited his return to a woman's bedchamber once he had claimed victory over her.

He paced across the pine flooring. If he played by his own rules, there could never be a "next time" with Coralee. As of this evening, the game of seduction had come to an end, culminating in one passion-drenched moment of triumph.

Jack curled his fists into tight balls as he stalked across the length of the room. Adherence to the rules of the game had never been a problem for him until now. In the past, he'd easily resisted the temptations of participating in a second round of seduction with the same partner.

But, then, no woman had ever stirred the depths of his desires before. Jack had never been obsessed with the taste and touch and feel of a woman like he was obsessed with Coralee. And never had he been consumed by the driving need that was surging through him, the overwhelming urge to claim Coralee over and over again as his own.

Jack shuffled across the room, considering his options. If he played by the rules, he would have to withdraw from further rounds of play with Coralee. And if he participated in a second game with her, he would be violating his own rules of conduct.

"To hell with the rules," Jack muttered.

He stripped off his clothes and crawled into bed for the evening, no longer willing to fight against the powerful force of desire raging within the depths of his soul.

"Have you ever seen the like of dirty clothes in all your born days?" Coralee glanced around the laundry shack the next morning, astounded by the number of garments that were waiting to be scrubbed and pressed. "Everybody in Rugby must be droppin' off their dirty clothes today."

"It seems like it." Rachel hoisted another bundle of soiled garments into the shack. "We've had a constant stream of customers in the last two hours."

"If we keep up this pace, we're gonna be plumb wore out by the end of the day," Coralee predicted. "Maybe both of us should get away from all this and take a break for ourselves every few hours or so."

"Sounds like a good idea to me," Rachel agreed. "I'm not very tired at the moment, though. Since you've been here since the crack of dawn, why don't you go first? I'll stay here and keep an eye on things until you get back."

Coralee nodded in agreement. "I won't be gone too long."

Within a few moments, she was sauntering along a tree-lined trail that led to a scenic overlook, hoping she would cross paths with Jack along the way. Though she hadn't seen him all morning, she suspected he had been working on the bridle path beside the Clear Fork. Now that the noon hour was rapidly approaching, he would probably be heading back to the settlement for lunch within a short time.

Coralee had just reached the stone ledge that overlooked a magnificent view of the mountains when she noticed a large figure of a man sitting beneath a shady oak tree. His long legs were stretched out in front of him, and his eyes were focused on the book in his hand.

Coralee edged closer, surprised that Grant seemed oblivious to her presence. In her few brief exchanges with him, he had always been friendly and congenial. But at the moment, it appeared as though he were too engrossed in his book to notice anything else around him.

"That must be a mighty good book that you're readin'," Coralee observed as she stepped up beside him. "You didn't even notice me walkin' over here to you!"

Grant glanced up and smiled. "Sorry, Coralee. I have the tendency to lose myself in a book when I'm reading."

She eased down beside him, curious. "Do you read a lot?"

"Every chance I get. As far as I'm concerned, books are one of life's greatest pleasures."

"You must love books 'bout as much as I love these mountains." Coralee gazed down at the bound leather volume in Grant's hand. "That's a nice-lookin' book, too. We don't have many books round these parts that look as fine as that one. Truth is, we don't have many books at all. A family Bible is 'bout the only book you ever see 'round here."

"But the Bible has lots of good stories," Grant insisted. "When I worked in the church, the children were—"

"You worked in a church?" Coralee echoed, somewhat surprised by the revelation.

Grant gave a sheepish smile. "I was a minister in England until a few months ago. I thought I might discover a new direction for my life by living here in Rugby, but I still don't know in what direction I'm heading. All I know for certain is that I'll always love books and reading, no matter what the future holds."

"I sure would like to know how to read better," Coralee admitted. "We've never had a schoolhouse or a teacher in Morgan County, but my ma learned me enough so I can read some verses from the Bible and sign my own name. But I haven't read a whole book before."

"Maybe you'll have more opportunities to read in the future. One of the founders of Rugby—a man who still lives in England—hopes to establish a library for the colony. Already, he has received several hundred volumes of English literature from generous donors to start the library's collection. And once the library is open, you'll be able to read all the books you like."

"How wonderful!" Coralee gazed longingly at

Grant's book. "Tell me about this story you're readin' now."

"It's called *Canterbury Tales*," he explained. "It was written by—"

"I've heard about that book!" Excitement danced in Coralee's eyes. "It tells all about the Tabard Inn!"

Grant laughed. "And it's a wonderful story, too. It's all about . . ."

Unbeknownst to Grant and Coralee, Jack stood a few feet away, his throat tightening with emotion at the scene unfolding in front of him.

He'd always known Coralee was a bright, intelligent woman. But he'd failed to detect how much she was starving to learn more about the world outside of these mountains . . . until now.

At the moment, she was enthralled with Grant's retelling of Chaucer's tale. Her face was awash with curiosity and delight, and her eyes were glimmering with a sense of longing that revealed she was yearning to experience the pleasures and joys of reading the story for herself.

A knot formed in Jack's throat. Coralee had been denied so much in life, he thought. He'd always taken books and reading for granted. Yet Coralee had lived her life without them, denied the opportunity for no other reasons than the circumstances of her birth and the isolated environment in which she'd been raised.

Jack swallowed thickly. Coralee's understanding of his own lot in life had been nothing short of astounding to him. Could he not render some understanding of his own now? She couldn't be blamed for her lack of formal education any more than he could assume responsibility for the order of his birth.

Still, Coralee possessed the intelligence and eagerness to learn anything. She embraced life with a genuine curiosity and a keen mind that absorbed knowledge with little effort. And if someone were willing to teach her . . .

Something tight and restricting gripped Jack's chest. God help him, he wanted to be the one to expose her to all the wonders of life. He wanted to teach her how to read, to show her all the things she'd never had the chance to see, to watch the delight glimmering from her eyes each time she discovered something new.

And somehow, some way, he knew that he would.

Four days later, Coralee darted across the lawn tennis court, hurled back her arm, and slammed her racket into an oncoming ball. As the round object sailed over the net and landed on the opposite side of the court, she squealed in delight.

Jack returned the serve across the net with a powerful backhand stroke. To Coralee's horror, the ball whizzed straight past her and hit the ground twice before she had the chance to swing the racket.

"That's the game." With a gleeful grin, Jack sprinted toward the net.

"And I lost again," Coralee moaned playfully. "But I'm gettin' better all the time, aren't I?"

"You're improving every day," Jack assured her.

She beamed at him. "I think my teacher deserves some of the credit. 'Course, I don't reckon I could ever beat you, considerin' I've already given you my secret for winnin'."

He laughed. "I had my doubts about that red ribbon of yours, but there must be something special about it. Adam and Grant haven't won a single match of lawn tennis since you gave it to me."

"Let's just hope it's still workin' its magic when we're playin' that croquet game this afternoon," she replied.

A few moments later, Coralee was strolling toward the settlement with Jack, heading to the Tabard Inn for an afternoon of croquet on the lawn. As she sauntered over the forested trail, she couldn't remember another time in her life when she'd felt so blissfully happy.

Since the evening of the hoedown, Jack had been extremely attentive to her. Tennis lessons had become a daily event between them, and Jack had even introduced her to the game of croquet.

Though Coralee was longing to initiate a discussion about the possibilities of their future together, she forced herself to refrain from doing so. After all, it would be highly inappropriate for her to bring up the subject. It was Jack's place—and not hers—to approach the topic of marriage.

And even if he should ask for her hand, Coralee wasn't certain what she would say. With each passing day, she sensed she was falling deeper in love with the Englishman, but she couldn't deny that the differences in their backgrounds and cultures were

sources of concern for her at times. How could two
people who were so different successfully blend
their lives into one?

Yet, in spite of her lingering doubts and fears,
Coralee had enjoyed Jack's company in the last
week. And the happiness swelling in her heart had
spilled over into other areas of her life, too. She
took great pride in the success of her laundry business, and she was pleased and impressed with
Jack's steady progress on the construction of the
livery stables.

The town site of Rugby was progressing nicely,
as well, Coralee noticed as she entered the colony
with Jack. Roads had been graded and cleared in
recent weeks, christened with English-sounding
names like Harrow, Reading, and Uffington.

Central Avenue, the main thoroughfare in
Rugby, stretched through the length of the village.
Approaching the dirt-covered road, Coralee motioned toward a planked walkway running along
the side of the avenue. "Looks like Uncle Paul and
his men have got this boardwalk all done now,"
she observed, stepping onto the wooden platform.

Jack fell into step beside her. "And now we don't
have to traipse through the mud after a hard rain,"
he added. "We can take the boardwalk from one
end of Rugby to the other."

Continuing along the boardwalk, Coralee admired the English-style cottages under construction
in the settlement. Though built of native materials,
the dwellings bore little resemblance to the log cabins that were scattered along the valleys and coves

in the mountain region. Gingerbread trim and dormer windows adorned the houses, which had been designed with sloping roofs and wide overhangs to provide shade for the summer months.

Coralee was perusing a particularly enchanting cottage when Jack slowed his pace to a halt. "I've been thinking about purchasing one of the lots along this street to build a cottage of my own," he revealed. He motioned to a nearby parcel of land that was filled with an abundance of trees and wild, flowering shrubs. "I'm particularly attracted to this tract over here."

"That's a right nice piece of land," Coralee assessed, somewhat surprised to learn that he was considering the purchase.

"The Tabard Inn provides much nicer accommodations than the men's barracks," he continued, "but I suspect I should be thinking about more permanent living arrangements."

Coralee's heart thundered in her chest. "You'd probably feel more settled in Rugby if you had a little place to call your own," she managed to say.

He nodded in agreement. "I might as well have a nice place to live while I'm here. All the work involved in building and establishing my livery business is taking much longer than I had anticipated, and it appears as though I won't be returning to England for quite some time."

As they continued on their way to the Tabard Inn, a myriad of emotions assailed Coralee. Part of her was elated by the knowledge that Jack would be living in Rugby on an indefinite basis. Yet, another part of her ached with sadness, knowing he had no intention of remaining here permanently.

By the time they arrived at the Tabard Inn, Adam and Grant were hauling the croquet equipment out onto the lawn. "Ready for a game of croquet?" Adam asked.

"I reckon I'm as ready as I'll ever be," Coralee replied with a grin. "I've been practicin' mighty hard at this game of late."

"And she's becoming rather proficient at whacking balls across the lawn with her mallet," Jack added. "In fact, I think we have the makings for a challenging game against the two of you."

The men had just finished setting up the stakes across the lawn when Vernon Sturgis appeared on the veranda of the inn. "I haven't played a game of croquet since I left England," Vernon remarked. "Would you mind if I played a round or two with you?"

Jack held out a long-handled mallet. "We've got plenty of equipment," he offered.

Vernon retreated from the veranda and stalked across the lawn. "It's about time we had some decent pastimes like this around here," he grumbled. "Of course, with the pitiful condition of this grass, I doubt we could ever hope to match the playing conditions of the lawns in England."

"At least we have access to some croquet equipment," Grant noted in a strained tone.

"Still, nothing is the same here as in England," Vernon said.

Jack distributed the remaining mallets, and the

game got under way. But as the players whacked their balls across the field, Vernon continued to expound upon the horrors of living in the colony, acting as though he were obligated to inform everyone about the atrocities of life in Rugby.

"We can't expect to receive word from our families on a frequent basis, either," Vernon continued. "The post is slower than a maimed tortoise around here."

Though Coralee had become accustomed to Vernon's grim outlook on life, listening to his stream of grievances began to grate on her nerves.

"I've lived here for five months, and I still can't adjust to the food in this place," he rattled on, adjusting his ball on the grass. "In fact, I—"

Vernon jerked his fingers away from the ball. Yelping like a wounded puppy, he furiously scratched his hand. "Something just *bit* me!"

Coralee darted across the lawn. "Let me see, Vernon."

He held out his hand, still scratching and clawing. With one glance at the red welts that were already forming along the surface of his skin, Coralee immediately recognized the familiar markings. "I do believe you got yourself some chigger bites, Vernon."

Vernon paled. "Chiggers?"

"Chiggers can't kill you," she assured him. "Those nasty little things are nothin' to be afraid of. They just spend their time bitin' your skin and makin' you itch like the devil. My granny always makes up a batch of parsley tea to take away that

itchin' feelin' from chigger bites. I'd bet Miss Pearl
would whip you up some of that parsley tea right
now if you got yourself on over to the dining hall
and asked her real nice and polite-like."

"Bloody hell," Vernon growled. "Living in this
place couldn't be any worse than living in the wilds
of a jungle."

"It's just chigger bites, Vernon!" Coralee shook
her head in disbelief. "It's not like you got bit by a
rattlesnake or nothin'."

He shuddered at the thought. "God help me, I
don't know why I've stayed here for so long.
There's nothing appealing about living in the midst
of a primitive wilderness."

"Then why are you stayin' here?" Coralee asked
bluntly.

An expression of bewilderment crossed his face.
"I have not the faintest idea," he admitted. "I've
felt like I've been exiled to hell ever since I set foot
in this place. I miss the bookstores and shops in
London, all the operas and parties and balls. And
I don't want any more grits and hog jowls for
breakfast. I want crumpets and jam and tea."

Coralee stole a quick glance at Jack, and an ache
swelled in her chest. The distant, clouded look in
his eyes and the hard set of his jaw told her far
more than words could say. Every instinct she possessed warned her that he was identifying with
Vernon's stab of longing for the things they'd left
behind in their native land.

At that moment, Vernon dropped his mallet to
the ground. "I've had all of this wilderness that I

can stomach," he announced. "I'm not going to spend another day here. I'm going to get out of this place before it eats me alive."

Vernon wheeled and stormed away. Watching him leave, Coralee couldn't ignore the beats of fear that were pounding away in her heart.

Jack leaned back in the rocker and breathed a sigh of contentment as a cool evening breeze wafted across the porch of Coralee's cabin. The twinkle of stars glimmered from the dark sky, and the air was fragrant with the scent of pine.

But as he turned his head and saw the furrows of worry that lined Coralee's brow, his sense of serenity vanished. "You've been rather quiet this evening, Coralee. Is something on your mind?"

She expelled a troubled sigh. "I reckon I can't hide my troubles from you any longer, Jack. I can't forget all those things that Vernon said about livin' in Rugby right before he packed up his go-poke and left on the train. And I've been thinkin' you might be missin' all those things you left behind in England, too. And I've been wonderin' if you were gettin' bone-tired of strugglin' to make your way around here."

Jack offered a smile. "I can't deny that I miss lots of things about my life in England, Coralee. But you don't have to worry about me leaving Rugby anytime soon," he assured her. "I've got too much at stake here. I have no intention of turning my back on everything I've worked to achieve in the last few months. And besides, I couldn't bear the thought of leaving . . . you."

Coralee held her breath as Jack pulled her up from the chair and swept her into his arms. And as he cupped her face in his hands and tilted her face to meet his, she trembled from the intensity of his gaze.

"I want you, Coralee," he whispered in an agonizingly tender voice. "And this time, we're going to take everything slow and easy."

He kissed her then, kissed her with such sweet seduction that she could feel herself melting in his embrace. His lips lingered over hers for something akin to an eternity, provoking a slow, simmering heat deep within her.

Between the enticing movement of his mouth against hers and the gentle touch of his fingers in her hair, Coralee became acutely aware of Jack's determination to savor the fullest measure of each moment. And she could sense from the tenderness of his caresses that he was desperately wanting to give her pleasure, too.

He was holding his mouth so thoroughly over hers that she wasn't certain when one kiss ended and another began. And when his lips broke from hers and began a steamy trail of hot, openmouthed kisses along her neck and throat, she shuddered from the burning sensations searing through her.

"Let me make love to you all night," he rasped. "Let me show you—"

"Then let's go inside, Jack," she urged. Without

waiting for a response, she grasped his hand and led him into the cabin.

As they sank down to the rug in front of the fire, Jack drew in a deep, shuddering breath. "This is perfect, Coralee. With the light of the fire, I can see everything about you." His eyes darkened with passion as he swept his gaze across her face. "And I want to look at you all night. I want to look at every part of you. . . ."

His hands trembled as he reached out and released the top button of her dress. He brushed his lips across her bare skin, inch by inch, until the last button fell free. Then he pulled back and gently tugged her chemise away from her breasts. "God, you're beautiful, Coralee. So beautiful . . ."

Coralee closed her eyes and groaned. Nothing could have prepared her for the sweet agony that Jack was arousing within her. Where he had once plundered, he now caressed. Where he had once groped, he now teased and brushed and stroked with such tender longing that she ached inside.

Sensations burst to life at every spot he touched and fondled. By the time he eased himself on top of her trembling body, Coralee thought she would die from the intense heat searing through her. And as soon as he buried himself deep inside her, an explosion of ecstasy roared through her, an explosion like none other she'd ever known.

Chapter 16

It was going to be a masterpiece.

Jack wiped the sweat from his brow with the back of his hand as he paused to view the progress on his livery stable. Only a few more days of work, he assessed, and the building would be completed.

Pride flooded through him, along with an overwhelming sense of satisfaction and accomplishment that he'd never known until now. Never in his wildest dreams would he have imagined that he could build such a creation with his bare hands.

Progress, at last. With the completion of the livery, he was taking the first step toward his future. He was moving closer to fulfilling his plan of returning to England as a wealthy man. And he was well on his way toward proving to the Duke of Havenshire that his second-born son possessed the stamina and skills to triumph at his endeavors.

His simple wooden livery could not compare to the extravagant stone stables at Havenshire Manor. But, then, Jack had no intentions of comparing the two facilities. After all, this was the only livery in the mountains. And within a few weeks, it was going to be the best livery that anyone had ever seen.

Jack suspected that his friends from England would laugh aloud if they could see his modest enterprise in the midst of the Cumberland Plateau. They would probably chide him about the venture, claiming he'd resorted to becoming a groomsman or a stable hand.

But when Jack returned to England, he would be the one who was laughing, he vowed, triumphant and wealthy from the success of his endeavors.

He retrieved a crumpled letter from his pocket, a letter from his father that had arrived earlier in the day.

My dearest son,

Your brief letters have been far too few to satisfy my curiosity about your new life in America. Although frequent newspaper reports are keeping us abreast of the developments in Rugby, I find myself constantly wondering how you are adjusting to the climate and conditions there.

Your mother, sister, and I are quite anxious to see, firsthand, how you and the colony are faring. We shall be setting sail for America in mid-September, arriving in Rugby in time for the colony's official opening.

Alexander will not be accompanying us on this journey—but for very pleasant reasons. His lovely marchioness is expecting the new heir to the Havenshire clan, and he does not wish to subject her to such an arduous journey at this time.

Needless to say, all of us are looking forward to visiting with you. Sabrina sends her fondest wishes, and your mother, her love.

> *With my sincerest regards,*
> *Your father*

Jack returned the letter to his pocket, thinking about all that needed to be done before his family's arrival.

Obtaining thoroughbreds for breeding was not his most pressing priority at the moment. He needed saddle horses and carriage horses for the influx of visitors who would be arriving for the colony's official opening and for the daily use of the increasing number of newcomers who were streaming into Rugby each week.

Jack was still thinking about the situation the next morning in the dining hall when he noticed that Clell seemed unusually exuberant. "I got me a new foal last night," the mountain man was telling a group of fellow residents. "It's the purtiest little creature you ever did see."

"I may be interested in taking a look at that new foal of yours, Clell," Jack remarked in a casual tone. "Have you considered selling it?"

Clell's brows narrowed. "All depends. Who's interested in buyin'?"

"I might be," Jack admitted. "I'm looking to build up my stock for the livery."

"I reckon you can take a look-see, then," Clell

offered, somewhat reluctantly. "We can run on up to my place after breakfast, if you'd like."

An hour later, Jack was standing in Clell's weathered barn, examining the foal with a critical eye. The horse seemed healthy and alert, with strong, limber legs and well-defined markings.

"What kind of price would you place on this foal, Clell?" Jack asked.

After Clell named a reasonable figure, Jack made his decision without a moment of hesitation. "As far as I'm concerned, you've just sold this little beauty, Clell. I'm expecting some funds from England next week, and I'll have the payment to you as soon as the post arrives."

Jack reached for the rope that was tied around the foal's neck, but Clell's voice stopped him cold. "Hold on a minute here, young fella," Clell warned. "I don't rightly recall that I've agreed to sell this little foal to you just yet."

Jack's eyes narrowed in confusion. "But you named a price, and I agreed to it. Are you holding out for a higher offer?"

"Nope, I ain't doin' that," Clell clarified. "But to be honest, I don't rightly know if you're good for the money. After all, I don't know nothin' about you, 'ceptin' that you come from England and you're livin' here in Rugby now."

Jack gaped at the little man in disbelief. Didn't Clell realize that he was contending with Lord John Winslow, the son of the Duke of Havenshire?

Apparently not, he conceded grimly. Yet, in England, an impoverished commoner would not dare to question the ability of a titled lord to pay his debts on a timely basis. Only a foolish chap would have the audacity to deny the request of a member of the British aristocracy.

Stunned that Clell was having doubts about selling the foal to him, Jack clenched his jaw tightly. Undoubtedly, his family's wealth was beyond the realm of Clell's understanding. And yet, the stubborn old fool had the nerve to hedge on selling a bloody horse to him!

Jack didn't know whether to laugh aloud at the man's lack of judgment or ram a knotted fist into Clell's weathered face. Fuming, he glared at the mountaineer.

Clell must have sensed the anger searing through him. "You know, some men who's growed up in these hills are honest as the day is long," he said. "Others, I couldn't trust as far as I could spit. But it don't matter who their family is or how much they got or don't got. You jest learn, over time, which men ain't worth a lick of salt and which men always do what they say they're a-goin' to do."

"So a man is only as good as his word . . . and you don't take the word of a man that you don't know?" Jack challenged.

"That's just about the way I see it, young fella," Clell said.

Frustrated and seething, Jack wheeled and stormed away. Jack was still fuming by the time he returned to the settlement. Deciding to vent his frustrations by focusing on his work, he picked up a hammer and scooped up some nails into his hand.

He had just nailed another plank of wood onto the building when he heard the sound of muffled laughter coming up behind him. He whipped around, startled to see that a pair of mountaineers had paused beside the edge of his property. As they studied the new building, their faces held expressions of mock wonder.

"Well, if it ain't the English lord," one of the men jeered.

"Good afternoon, gentlemen," Jack said tersely, recognizing the pair as Simon and Zach, the men who had been adamant about dancing with Coralee at the recent hoedown. "Is there something I can do for you?"

"I reckon not," Simon said. "We're just checkin' out your new stables."

Jack made an attempt to strike up a friendly conversation. "It shouldn't be too much longer until the project is finished," he explained. "And once I complete the livery, I suspect I'll be building a cottage for myself here in the colony."

"No cabin for you, I reckon," Zach predicted. "Of course, I can't see someone like you a-livin' in a log cabin."

"Unless he's shackin' up with someone that's caught his fancy," Simon added.

The men chuckled, but Jack found nothing humorous about their remarks. "I believe you should be watching what you say, gentlemen. Obviously, you're making some rather rude inferences about

Coralee Hayes. But from what I know of the woman, she would never agree to living with any man who wasn't her husband."

"I wouldn't be so sure about that," Zach argued. "She ain't had no man since Reuben died. She won't give none of us the time of day, but now you come along, wearin' your fancy clothes, talkin' your fancy English talk, and turnin' that purty head of hers—"

"Let it be, Zach," Simon cut in. "If Coralee's got a fancy for this fella, us hasslin' him ain't gonna change nothin' 'bout it."

Simon gave Zach a shove, and the two men shuffled away from the site. Jack whipped around and hammered a nail into a plank of wood in a vain attempt to restrain his temper. Obviously, the men resented him for invading their mountain domain and catching the eye of a local woman.

"Bloody hell." Jack slammed the hammer into the wood with all the force he could muster. "Maybe Vernon was right," he muttered. "Maybe none of this is worth leaving England for."

"What are you grumbling about now?"

As Grant's voice split the air, Jack turned and scowled. "I've got plenty to be grumbling about, I can assure you."

Adam stepped up to join them. "Maybe Grant and I can help you out, Jack. But we can't do anything unless we know what's troubling you."

"It's these blasted mountaineers around here. For some unknown reason, half the population of Morgan County has decided to vent their frustrations on me today," Jack muttered. "Quite frankly, I'm so disgusted with the local folks around here that I have no desire to talk about my dealings with them. I don't want to discuss anything that concerns Rugby, Tennessee. I don't even want to think about this colony anymore. At the moment, I'd like nothing better than to jump on the next train headed for Cincinnati and get away from this blasted place for a while."

Adam took a step forward. "Would you like some company?"

Grant followed Adam's lead. "We can leave anytime you're ready."

Jack stared at his friends in stunned disbelief. "Are you serious?"

"Why not?" Adam grinned. "We don't have anything better to do with our time. I, for one, would certainly enjoy a change of scenery for a few days."

"I wouldn't mind taking another look at Cincinnati myself," Grant remarked. "We didn't get to see much of the place the last time we were there."

"That's because we were in a hurry to get to Rugby," Jack recalled. "If we'd known what was waiting for us here, I suspect we wouldn't have been so eager to leave."

"But we can take our time exploring the city over the next day or two," Adam said. "And if you're willing to leave within the hour, I suspect we can hitch a ride with Clell when he heads down to Sedgemoor Station for the daily mail run."

"Then let's get moving." Jack dropped his hammer to the ground. "We don't have a minute to waste."

"I can't imagine where Jack has been all day," Coralee remarked to Rachel as they finished with their lunch. "I haven't seen him since early this mornin' when he was leavin' the dinin' hall right after breakfast. He said he was gonna take a look-see at a little filly over at Clell's place."

"Maybe he's down by the Clear Fork, working on the bridle path," Rachel suggested.

Coralee dismissed the possibility with a shake of her head. "There's not much need for anyone to be workin' down there anymore. Last I heard, the bridle path is pert near done."

"Perhaps he's been working so hard on his new livery stables that he forgot about the time. Maybe he simply forgot to take a break for lunch."

"I've walked over yonder a couple of times, but I didn't see hide nor hair of him." Coralee shrugged. "Maybe I'll take a look-see again in a spell."

"I'm certain there must be a good reason why you haven't seen him." Rachel's dark eyes glimmered with concern. "You really care a lot about Jack, don't you?"

Coralee managed a weak smile. "I just can't help myself, I reckon. He's pert near the best thing that's ever happened to me. I like bein' with him so much that I don't want to let the man out of my sight! And I know that's not good for either of us. It's not like we're hitched or anything like that."

"But would you like to be married to Jack?"

Coralee pondered the question for a long moment. She hadn't dared to ask herself that question of late. But as Rachel waited for a reply, Coralee knew instinctively what her answer would be.

She couldn't name an exact moment or time or place when she'd fallen in love with Jack Winslow. All she knew for certain was that she could no longer deny that she loved the Englishman with all of her heart and soul.

"I'd like nothin' better, Rachel," Coralee finally said. "In fact, I'd like nothin' more in this whole wide world than to be Jack Winslow's bride."

"Look at this, will you?" Jack peered down at his feet as he stood in the middle of a city street that was lined with rows of shops and businesses. "No dirt trails here, my friends. Cincinnati has cobblestone streets!"

Grant chuckled. "I'd almost forgotten real streets existed."

"And I'd almost forgotten how wonderful a real meal can taste," Adam added. "At dinner this evening, the restaurant at our hotel served the best food I've eaten in months."

"The wine wasn't bad, either." Jack massaged his temples and moaned. "But it's been so long since I've had the chance to indulge myself, I'm afraid all that wine has gone straight to my head."

"Then maybe we should be heading back to the hotel now," Grant suggested. "We've had a long

day, and we'll have plenty of time for enjoying ourselves tomorrow."

"I'm game for that," Adam said. "In fact, I'm
looking forward to sleeping in a real bed instead of
a hammock for a change."

"I think I'll turn in for the night, too." Jack
turned and fell into step beside the two men. "I'd
like to get an early start in the morning."

Beneath the soft glow of gas lanterns shining
over the venue, the men idly perused the window
displays of several shops as they worked their way
down the street. Just as the hotel came into view, a
particularly intriguing display of merchandise in
one window seized Jack's attention.

"Some of these shops appear to have a nice selection of goods," he remarked. "I think I'd like to
browse at a few more of these displays. If the two
of you want to go on ahead, I'll catch up with you
at the hotel a little later."

Agreeable to the request, Adam and Grant continued on their way. Jack edged closer to the exhibit
of merchandise in the shop window, mesmerized
by what he saw.

Behind the glass panes was a stunning gown in
a rich, deep shade of green, accented with rows of
tiny tucks along the bodice and narrow pleats along
the hem. Jet braid trimmed the scoop neckline and
the full overskirt of the gown, while black onyx
buttons held the cuffs of the wide sleeves in place.

From Jack's point of view, the dress was unde-
niably elegant, yet not frilly or overstated. All in

all, the gown looked as though it had been de-signed especially for . . . Coralee.

Coralee.

Jack's heart gave a crazy lurch as the error of his ways hit him, swift and hard. God help him, he'd departed Rugby in such haste that he'd said not a word to the woman about his impetuous journey.

Jack wanted to kick himself. He wanted to ram a clenched fist through the window, pound his head into a brick wall—anything to relieve the stabs of guilt ripping through him. Caught up in the frustrations of the morning and the hasty trip to Cincinnati throughout the day, he'd never once paused to think of telling Coralee about his plans. How could he have been so thoughtless, so incon-siderate of her feelings?

He stared through the glass panes, his gaze lock-ing on a pair of dainty slippers displayed beside the regal green gown. The slippers were a perfect match for the dress, he noticed, bearing the same hue of green and the same black onyx ornamenta-tion.

Jack stilled, seized by the memory of his vow to replace a dress that he'd ripped apart in the heat of passion, gripped by the haunting echoes of a mountain woman's fondest desire. *I'm hopin' to get me a new store-bought dress. And maybe some fancy new slippers, too, if I have enough money left. . . .*

Jack stepped back and peered up at the wooden sign that displayed the name of the dress shop. Making a mental note of the store's location in re-lation to the hotel, he turned to leave.

When the shop opened for business in the morning, he intended to be the first customer through the door. By purchasing the beautiful green gown in the window, he could fulfill his promise to Coralee . . . and perhaps make amends for his inconsiderate departure.

Lines of concern marred Coralee's brow as she surveyed the crowd that had gathered around Clell's wagon for the afternoon mail call. Where on earth was Jack?

Her gaze skittered over the throng once again. Adam and Grant were absent as well, she noticed.

"No tellin' what those fellas are up to," she mused, silently reminding herself that she had no reason to be worried. More than likely, the three Englishmen were roaming through the surrounding mountains on horseback or afoot, losing all track of time as they ventured over the winding trails.

Throughout the remainder of the afternoon, Coralee repeatedly told herself that Jack's whereabouts should be none of her concern. But the lack of his presence for the evening meal had renewed her anxieties by the time she closed up the laundry shack and headed to the cabin for the night.

And his continued absence the next morning intensified her worries even more until Coralee caught sight of Clell shuffling through the colony at midday. Seized by the hope that the keen-eyed mountaineer might have seen Jack and his friends somewhere along the mountain trails during the last twenty-four hours, Coralee called out to him.

"I heard tell you got yourself a pretty new filly, Clell," Coralee remarked as casually as she could. "Jack Winslow told me he was intendin' to take a look-see at it yesterday mornin'."

Clell nodded. "And he offered to buy her from me, too. I turned him down, seein' as how I reckoned I oughta hold on to her for a spell. But that Winslow fella got right testy about me rejectin' his offer." Clell chuckled. "But he'd done forgot all about our little spiff by the time I got him and his friends down to Sedgemoor Station."

Coralee's heart stilled. "Sedgemoor . . . Station?"

"I took the three of them to meet the train when I was makin' my mail run. But those fellas was so riled up about goin' to Cincinnati, talkin' about what they were gonna see and do, that I never heard another word about my little filly. And when that Winslow fella found out his monthly remittance from his folks back in England had come in the day's mail, he jumped on that train and never looked back when it startin' chuggin' down the tracks."

"I see." Coralee offered a brave smile. "Well, maybe you'll eventually find a good home for your new little filly."

She quietly returned to her work, stunned and dismayed to discover that Jack had departed Rugby without saying anything to her before he'd left. He'd given no hint, no warning, no explanation for his hasty departure . . . just like Reuben used to do.

She squeezed her eyes shut, his heartless disregard for her feelings wounding her to the core. She thought he'd care more about her than to leave without saying a word.

And his unknown motives for leaving disturbed her even more. Had the rigors of mountain life finally taken a toll on Jack and his friends? Had he left Rugby with the intention to return? Or was he running away . . . from her?

A lump swelled in her throat. In spite of Jack's recent assurances that he had no intention of leaving Rugby, his actions told her far more than words could say. And she refused to condone the man's reckless, inconsiderate behavior toward her, regardless of the depths of her feelings for him.

She pulled back her shoulders and lifted her chin, determined to find a way to ease the ache in her heart.

Jack arose early the next morning, eager to explore the city by the light of the day. His late arrival and the encroaching darkness had prohibited him from venturing too far from the hotel during the previous evening, and he was anxious to sample all that Cincinnati had to offer.

For his first stop of the day, he entered the dress shop near the hotel and boldly announced his desire to purchase the gown and matching slippers displayed in the window.

"I'm afraid we can't help you, sir," the clerk explained. "All of our gowns are customized for the wearer. If your wife could drop by the shop for a fitting, I'm certain we could—"

"But I want this gown to be a surprise for her." Jack swiftly estimated the clerk's height. "She's an inch or two taller than you, and—"

"Let's see what we have to offer," the clerk said.

An hour later, Jack emerged from the shop laden with an assortment of parcels. Pleased with his purchases, he ventured into a bookstore and bought several primers designed for beginning readers. Then he dropped off his bundles at the hotel and ventured back into the city streets once again.

But as the day wore on, Jack found himself becoming increasingly restless. The sense of excitement that had filled the morning hours had given way to a gnawing sense of discontentment by afternoon. And images of Coralee invaded his thoughts throughout the day.

When he sampled the fare of a restaurant, he wondered what Coralee would think about the meal. When he explored the offerings of a quaint shop, he wished she were exploring the shop with him, too. When he strolled through the streets, he wanted her walking alongside him. And when he watched the parade of people passing by, he wondered what she would say about them.

Late in the afternoon, Jack stood on the banks of the Ohio River, observing the vessels on the water. A ferryboat full of passengers was chugging across the river to Kentucky, while a paddleboat and several barges were making their way through the water. But in spite of the lovely setting, Jack was too consumed with the absence of one special person to appreciate the beauty of his surroundings.

How ironic, he thought. He'd leaped at the chance to spend a few days indulging in the pleasures of city life. But now that he was here, he was discovering that the city couldn't offer the one thing he wanted more than anything else in the world . . . *Coralee.*

An ache swelled in his chest. The woman had seeped her way into his blood, wedged her way into his heart. And every instinct Jack possessed told him that she would always be a part of him, no matter where he lived or what he did in the future.

God help him, he'd fallen in love with her. Coralee Hayes had defeated him in his own game. He'd fallen prey to the wiles of a woman's charms.

And never had he felt so deliriously happy. By acknowledging his feelings toward Coralee, Jack felt as if he could conquer the world. He could scarcely wait to get back to Rugby.

With his energy and spirits restored, Jack devoted the remainder of the afternoon to finding suitable breeding stock for launching his business in Rugby. After locating two fine specimens and arranging for the animals to be shipped to Sedgemoor Station on the morning train, he returned to the hotel to meet Adam and Grant for dinner.

"We noticed all the purchases that you'd dropped off in the room during the day," Grant remarked during the meal. "Tell us, Jack. Did you buy something from every shop in town?"

Jack grinned sheepishly. "I picked up a few things for Coralee while I was here."

"Ah, Coralee." Adam shook his head. "When are you going to admit you're smitten with the woman, Jack?"

"I admitted it to myself today." Jack chuckled. "So I suppose I can admit it to everyone else, too."

"You're not telling us anything that we don't already know," Grant returned with a smile.

"Take my advice, Jack." Adam adjusted the glove on his left hand, and his voice took on a serious tone. "The love of a good woman is the rarest of gifts. And once you find her, you'd be a foolish man to let her go."

"I'm just beginning to realize that," Jack admitted, silently vowing to remember Adam's words.

"I reckon my Sunday dress is gonna have to make do for me tonight, considerin' I don't have a second-best dress anymore," Coralee mumbled to herself as she dressed for the Saturday night singing.

She had just slipped the gown over her head when a knock sounded at the cabin door. Startled, she turned and scurried to welcome the uninvited guest. But as she opened the door, she froze in stunned disbelief.

Jack was standing on the porch with a smile on his lips and a sparkle in his eyes. "Aren't you going to invite me inside?"

"I didn't realize you were comin' back from Cin-

cinnati today." Coralee opened the door with reluctance. "But, then, I didn't know you were goin'
to Cincinnati in the first place."

"I can explain, Coralee." Jack stepped into the
cabin. "I didn't have any plans to make the trip—"

"But didn't you think I would be worried about
you?" she blurted out, unable to contain her emotions. "You're about the most thoughtless, incon-
siderate man I've ever done seen!"

"I know. What I did to you was unspeakable. Do
you think you can find it in your heart to forgive
me?"

Disconcerted by the unexpected apology, Coralee
stilled. "That all depends," she finally managed to
say. "How come you left in such a hurry?"

"It was an impulsive decision. That morning,
Clell refused to sell his filly to me, then your
friends—Simon and Zach—decided to badger me
about catching your eye. Frustrated, I threatened to
leave the colony for a few days and get away from
it all. The next thing I knew, I was boarding the
train to Cincinnati with Adam and Grant."

"So you were tryin' to get away from everything
in Rugby?"

"For a few days, nothing more."

"Then I reckon you were tryin' to get away from
me, too."

"Not deliberately." Jack reached out and tucked
a stray strand of hair behind her ear. "But I have
to admit I thought it would be easy to forget you.
I thought I could leave all thoughts of you behind

in Rugby when I left. But what I thought was wrong."

"What do you mean?"

"I was miserable without you, Coralee. Damn miserable." The sincerity in his eyes and the huskiness in his voice echoed his sentiments. "I wanted you there beside me. I wondered what you were doing here. I couldn't stop thinking about you. And I missed you. God, how I missed you."

"I'm glad you missed me. I was too busy frettin' and worryin' to miss you," she teased.

The hint of a smile curled on his lips. "I figured as much. I thought you might be more apt to forgive my unannounced departure if I brought back a peace offering with me."

He stepped outside and retrieved a large parcel from the porch. "This is for you, Coralee."

"Oh, my." Coralee sank into the rocker beside the fire, taken aback by Jack's thoughtfulness. Gifts were rare treats in her life, especially a store-bought gift like this one appeared to be. She gingerly fingered the parcel for a long moment, overcome with emotion.

Her heart leaped into her throat when she ripped into the paper and peeled back the wrappings. "Oh, Jack," she whispered, her voice raw and strained. "I've never seen a more beautiful dress in all my born days!"

"I was hoping you'd like it." His smile was warm and tender. "But if you'll look beneath the gown, I think you'll find something else hidden there."

An ache swelled in her chest when she retrieved the dainty green slippers from the box. "My slippers," she whispered in awe. "It's the fancy slippers I've been dreamin' about for so long. And they match my new dress. . . ."

She blinked back the moisture forming in her eyes. "I don't know what to say, Jack. These are the most wonderful and beautiful presents anyone has ever given me in my whole, entire life."

"I'm certain you'll think of something to say very soon. I've never known you to be short on words for very long." Jack swiftly retrieved two more parcels from the porch and handed both of them to Coralee. "Now let's see if these gifts render you speechless."

Coralee's eyes widened in shock. "They already have," she insisted. A few moments later, she was admiring two more beautiful gowns that Jack had purchased for her.

"I thought you might like to have a choice between wearing the royal blue or the deep burgundy during the official opening of the colony in a few weeks," Jack explained. "Lots of guests will be attending the ceremonies, and I knew you would be wanting a new dress to wear."

"But this is so much. . . ." Coralee's throat clogged with emotion. It was more than she had ever dreamed, far more than she could have ever imagined.

"I can scarcely wait to see you wearing your new gowns," Jack remarked in a blatantly suggestive tone. "And I can scarcely wait to take them off you, too."

"But what about my old Sunday dress?" she taunted, brushing her fingers across the bodice of her gown. "How do you feel about takin' it off me . . . now?"

His hand flew to the top button. "I'm working on it as fast as I can. . . ."

Hours later, exhausted and spent, Coralee snuggled her bare body against Jack's hard, lean frame. "I reckon you don't know that I missed my Saturday singin' tonight on account of you."

He feigned mock despair. "I'm dreadfully sorry, Coralee. I do hope you don't feel you've wasted your time this evening."

She flashed a beguiling smile. "What we were doin' was a heap more fun than singin' songs. I can't deny I missed seein' my family tonight, but I'll be seein' the whole lot of 'em at Sunday dinner tomorrow at Granny Clabo's cabin." She propped herself on an elbow in the bed. "You know, Granny said she'd invited you to Sunday dinner when you got ready to get yourself to preachin'. Seein' as how I missed out on my singin' tonight on account of you, I think you should do me a good turn and go to preachin'—and to Sunday dinner—with me tomorrow."

His eyes were teasing and warm as he gazed down at her. "One good turn deserves another, I suppose," he murmured, lowering his mouth over hers and pressing her back onto the bed.

Chapter 17

❦❦❦

"**G**ranny Clabo and Rachel and Maggie and all the other womenfolk at the meetin'house this mornin' will be havin' conniption fits when they see this new dress of mine." Coralee's hunter-green gown swished about her slender legs as she emerged from the cabin and joined Jack on the porch the next morning.

Jack took one look at her and froze. From the moment he'd caught sight of the gown in the shop window, he'd sensed the dress would look wonderful on Coralee. But nothing could have prepared him for the sight of her now.

The woman radiated with a beauty so mindboggling that he could scarcely catch his breath. Every tuck and fold of the gown flattered her slender figure, and the deep green hue highlighted the color of her eyes and the glorious mane of golden hair that tumbled over her shoulders.

"Something tells me all the menfolk will be having conniption fits, too," he finally managed to say. "They won't be able to take their eyes off you."

293

Coralee smiled and linked her arm around his. "I reckon we'd best be movin' on if we're gonna get to preachin' on time. Gettin' to the meet-in'house from here usually takes about ten minutes or so, but it might take us a spell longer to get there this mornin'. I'm not used to walkin' these trails in a pair of fancy slippers."

Jack laughed, reveling in the delight of her candid manner. "Then let's get moving."

When they arrived at the church fifteen minutes later, Jack was astounded by the number of mountaineers who were milling about the grounds. "I never realized so many people lived in these mountains," he remarked.

"We've got a heap of folks here this mornin' because we're havin' preachin' today," Coralee explained. "Our preacher man only preaches here one Sunday a month. The rest of the time, we have to share him with other churches 'round these parts. But he—"

"Coralee!" Maggie rushed up to join them, her eyes wide with wonder as she drank in the sight of Coralee's dress. "When did you get yourself that dress? I've never seen anything like it in my whole, entire life!"

Within a few moments, a circle of women had gathered around Coralee to admire her new gown. As the women gushed over the dress, Jack shifted his gaze toward the white frame building in front of him. How different from the magnificent cathedrals of London, he mused. Instead of stained glass, arched abbeys, or stone pillars, the rustic mountain building was adorned with nothing more than a narrow steeple. Yet, he couldn't deny that the stark simplicity of the mountain church held a beauty all of its own.

He was still gazing at the building when he felt the touch of a hand on his arm. "I reckon we'd best be gettin' us a seat now," Coralee suggested.

Jack had just settled into a wooden pew beside Coralee when one of the mountaineers stepped forward to lead the congregation in the opening hymn. Unfamiliar with the song, Jack glanced around for a hymnal so he could follow the words and music. But after a quick search of the pew, he discovered that no songbooks or prayer books were available.

Puzzled, he swept his gaze over the crowd. It seemed as though everyone in the church knew the song by memory. No one, it appeared, needed a songbook.

But, then, songbooks weren't necessary, Jack realized with a jolt. Most of the mountaineers couldn't read words or music. He didn't know whether to admire their astute memories or pity their lack of skills.

Throughout the next hour, Jack was taken aback by the informality of the service and the fiery emotionalism of the mountain minister's sermon. But he was just as astonished when he realized that the closing hymn sounded vaguely familiar to him.

"Something about that last song seemed very familiar to me," Jack admitted as he left the church with Coralee.

"I've been singin' it all my life," Coralee revealed, "ever since I was a little girl. Granny Clabo taught it to me. She learned lots of songs from her mama and daddy. She says they brought bunches of songs with 'em in their hearts when they came here from England and Scotland and the like."

"Perhaps that explains why the tune sounded so familiar," Jack said. "I'm certain it must be an old English melody."

"Could be." Coralee grinned. "If your great-granddaddy had been as adventurous as mine, you might have been born and raised in these hills, too, just like me."

Jack laughed. "Maybe we have more in common than we thought."

The enticing aroma of roasted pork was wafting through the air as Jack and Coralee approached Granny Clabo's cabin for Sunday dinner. "I hope you've got an empty belly," Coralee advised. "Harlan has been roastin' a pig since early this mornin', and we're gonna have the biggest pig-pickin' you ever seen."

Jack bit back a smile. Though he'd never attended a pig-picking, he felt quite certain the occasion would be a memorable one.

But as he accompanied Coralee to the gathering, Jack wasn't prepared for the size of the crowd assembled at the Clabo cabin. At least thirty adults were gathered at the log dwelling, he estimated, along with another dozen or so children. "I never realized you had so many relatives," he admitted candidly.

"With all the McCarters, Proffitts, and Bohanans 'round here, I reckon the Clabo clan accounts for half the population of Morgan County." Coralee grinned and held out her hand. "Come on, Jack. I want to introduce you to the folks you don't already know."

He slipped his hand over hers. "I'm not sure I'll remember all these names."

"Don't you be worryin' about that. It gets a tad confusin' for all of us sometimes. Everybody has different last names because Granny Clabo's three daughters—my ma, Rachel's ma, and Maggie's ma—took their husbands' names after they got married. Now, my branch of the family is the Bohanans, Rachel is on the Proffitt side, and Maggie is on the—"

Jack cut her off with a groan. "Don't tell me any more. I'm already getting confused."

Undaunted, Coralee guided him over to the McCarters. "This is Maggie's folks," she said, quickly rattling off the names of the four McCarter brothers and their parents.

Jack was still trying to commit the names to memory when Coralee dragged him away from the McCarters to introduce him to Crockett's wife and children. She had just finished with the introductions when Crockett came up to join them.

"Glad to see you've joined us for dinner today, Jack." Crockett stole a glance at Coralee and winked. "From the looks of things, it appears my little sister is mighty glad you're here today, too."

Coralee beamed. "I couldn't be happier."

Crockett shifted his gaze back to Jack. "You make sure she stays that way, you hear?"

"I'm trying," Jack said just as Granny Clabo's voice rang through the air.

"Soup's on!" Granny motioned for the group to gather around the long table that was laden with an assortment of foods. "It's time to eat up!"

Jack fell into line and filled his tin plate with generous helpings of roast pork and other dishes that the women had prepared for the meal. He had just put a slice of corn bread on his plate when Coralee came up behind him. "Let's sit down over yonder on that log," she suggested.

He nodded in agreement, mindful that no tables had been set up on the grounds for the meal. Some people were making places for themselves on the cabin steps, while others were seated in rockers or chairs on the porch.

What's more, no one seemed to care where they were sitting. As Jack settled down on the log beside Coralee, he became acutely aware of the relaxed, unassuming atmosphere and the chortles of laughter and snatches of good-natured teasing drifting around him.

Jack glanced over the setting, observing the mountain clan with interest. Obviously close-knit, the group seemed to cherish the notion that they were handing down family traditions from generation to generation during their weekly gatherings. And everyone appeared happy, content, at peace with themselves and the world around them.

He had just finished the last bite of food on his

plate when Harlan Bohanan walked over to him. "Welcome to the pig-pickin', Jack," he said with a grin. "You make sure you get yourself plenty to eat, now. We got a heap of pork just sittin' there waitin' for you."

"Thanks," Jack returned. "I may just take you up on that."

Harlan was a likable chap, Jack assessed, as the mountain man turned and joined his wife and children for the remainder of the meal. And like the others in the group, Harlan appeared to be happy with his lot in life.

Jack suspected that the man possessed nothing more than a small cabin and a pitiful excuse of a farm, even though he worked on construction projects in the settlement from dawn until dusk each day. If he were typical of most mountain men, Harlan bartered for what little he had. But, even so, the soles of his shoes were probably thin from wear.

Maybe Harlan was content because he'd never known anything better, Jack mused. But deep inside, Jack sensed that a man like Harlan Bohanan would never be happy in a place like London. Removed from his element, he would be like a fish out of water . . . just the way Jack had felt throughout most of his residence in Rugby.

Jack grimaced. He would always be the son of a British duke, a man born and bred to live the life of an English gentleman. He wasn't destined to be a backwoodsman without a pence to his name.

He stole a glance at Coralee, her beauty so overwhelming that it stole his breath away. Could she

fare in England? He'd grown so accustomed to her
winsome smile and saucy ways that he couldn't
imagine his life without her.

But would her smile radiate such happiness if
she were removed from these hills? Though three
new gowns had brought smiles to those gorgeous
lips of hers, Jack suspected that her bright spirit
would waver—perhaps even diminish completely—
if she were forced to wear those gowns in the rigid
structure of London society.

A sinking feeling suffused him. Jack couldn't
imagine a worse fate for Coralee Hayes than to be
snatched from everything and everyone that she
loved and be thrown into the restrictive world of
the British aristocracy. Her beloved mountains and
her family were as much a part of her as the delicate features of her face and hands and body. Without them, the very essence of the woman would no
longer exist.

He clenched his jaw, determined to set aside the
troubling thought.

"What a wonderful day." Coralee rested her
head on Jack's chest as they stood on the porch of
her cabin that evening. "Did you have a good time
at the pig-pickin', Jack?"

"It was the best pig-pickin' I've ever attended in
my life, Coralee."

She giggled. "You're just sayin' that 'cuz it's the
only pig-pickin' you've ever gone to."

"You know me too well, I suppose." Jack chuckled and draped an arm around her narrow shoul-

ders. "Truthfully, I had a very enjoyable day with your family. The food was delicious, and all of your relatives made me feel quite welcome."

"I'm glad you enjoyed yourself. I was hopin' you would, but I know you're not used to all these mountain ways of ours 'round here. I reckon it would take anyone a spell to get used to them."

"I learn something new every day here, it seems." He reached out and brushed his fingers through her hair. "But after an entire day of sharing you with all of your relatives, I'm looking forward to having you all to myself tonight. I have grand plans for both of us, you know."

She peered up at him, curious. "What kind of plans?"

His hand drifted from her hair to the creamy sweep of her neck, then glided over the bodice of her gown. "First, I'm going to remove this gorgeous dress from your body, and then . . ."

He pressed his lips along the curve of her jaw. "And then I'm going to make love to you until dawn," he warned, his voice just above a whisper. "All night long, we're going to—"

She eased back in the circle of his arms. "I don't know of nothin' that could sound any better than that, Jack, but I . . ."

Alarm raced through him. "What's wrong, Coralee?"

She gave her head a shake. "I can't explain it, but somethin' is tellin' me you don't need to be spendin' the night here at the cabin with me. Somethin' tells me you need to stay at the inn tonight."

He narrowed his eyes, suspicious. "What's the real reason, Coralee?" he demanded.

"There's no other reason than this feelin' I have," she tried to explain. "I reckon it's kinda like those feelin's that Granny Clabo gets sometimes. I just know that you shouldn't be stayin' here, but I can't tell you why."

Jack expelled a frustrated sigh. "I should trust your instincts, I suppose. But I don't want to trust them. I want to stay here all night . . . with you."

"I want you to stay, too, Jack. But I think it's best if you go back into Rugby tonight."

He pulled away from her with reluctance. "Just promise me you'll wear this dress again tomorrow night so I can take it off you then."

"I promise," she said, sealing her vow with a kiss.

Jack turned to leave, slightly unsettled by Coralee's intuitive feelings. But by the time he reached the Tabard Inn, he'd dismissed the thoughts from his mind. After a day of travel from Cincinnati, a passion-filled night with Coralee, and a second day of constant activity, Jack was too weary to think of anything else but sleep. Within a few moments after returning to his room, he promptly fell asleep for the night.

Hours later, something aroused him from a deep sleep. For some odd reason, he thought he'd heard someone shouting something about fire. . . .

Still groggy, Jack rolled over in the bed just as the pops and crackles of burning wood split the air.

He bolted upright, immediately sensing the stench of smoke drifting in the room.

Panic ripped through him. He leaped up from the bed and darted to the window, his heart thundering in his chest. *Not the livery*, he prayed.

But as he peered through the glass panes and saw the orangy-red flames, his worst fears came true. Fire was engulfing his livery. And all of his dreams and hopes for the future were vanishing in front of his eyes.

Jack shrugged into his clothes, raced down the stairs, and flew outside, hoping to save something, anything, from the fiery blaze. By the time he reached the livery, the conflagration had drawn dozens of men to the scene. "Water!" someone yelled. "We need buckets of water!"

Panic set in. Horses neighed. Men shouted. Smoke streamed from the building. And still the fire raged, crackling and burning, lighting up the dark sky with an orangy-red glow. Watching it all, Jack felt as if he had been plunged into the midst of a nightmare.

The men scrambled to locate buckets, then formed a human line to pass buckets of water from hand to hand between the creek and the livery. As the men set to work, Jack darted to the rear of the building and hurled open the double doors. Smoke billowed around him as he dashed inside the inferno and released the horses from their stalls. Within an instant, the horses had bolted through the open doors and galloped to safety in the open pasture behind the livery.

"Get out, Winslow!" someone shouted. "Get out now!"

Blinded by the thick smoke, Jack worked his way through the livery and dashed outside just as a portion of the building collapsed behind him with a thunderous roar.

Grant raced up to him, an expression of horror and concern etched into his face. "Are you all right?"

He managed to shake his head. "It was a close call. But as for the building . . ."

"The men are containing the blaze, Jack," Grant assured him. "They're getting it under control."

Jack stumbled to the side of the building, astonished to find that the men were limiting the spread of the fiery flames to one corner of the livery. Still, they maintained their frantic pace, passing buckets from hand to hand, until the flames began to waver.

Dawn was breaking over the horizon by the time the last flame had been extinguished. Jack shuffled through the ruins with Grant and inspected the demise of his dream.

"At least the rear portion was saved," Grant noted. "Your livery isn't a total loss, Jack."

"This isn't the time or place for your good cheer, Grant," Jack muttered. "Although I highly suspect a few people around here are glad to see that I've just lost every bloody thing I've worked to achieve since I've been here."

Grant frowned. "What do you mean?"

"I suspect a few people didn't want to see the

livery open." Jack narrowed his eyes with suspicion as he searched the crowd for a glimpse of Simon or Zach. "In fact, I suspect they might have done anything—even setting fire to the place—to keep it from opening."

"How could you suspect anyone of deliberately starting this fire?" Grant motioned toward the soot-stained faces in the crowd. "How could you accuse these men of setting fire to your livery when they worked all night to salvage it for you?"

Jack shrugged, too exhausted to argue. "Maybe someone who doesn't live in Rugby set fire to this place. Maybe someone—"

"Get a look-see at this, Winslow."

Jack turned, startled to hear Clell's voice. He hadn't realized the old mountaineer had been working alongside the colonists to extinguish the fire.

Clell lifted the charred remains of a lantern from the ruins. "Looks like we found the reason for this here fire," the mountaineer said. "Looks to me like a lantern tipped over and started the whole mess."

"I thought it was an accident," Grant said. "I didn't think anyone would—"

"It doesn't matter." Jack wearily dragged a hand through his hair. "Obviously, my suspicions were wrong. But accident or arson, the results are the same. Everything has gone up in smoke."

"But part of the livery is still standing, Jack!" Grant insisted. "You haven't lost everything. Just open your eyes and you'll see—"

"Drop it, Grant," Jack snapped. "What's the use of trying to salvage this mess?"

Coralee broke through the crowd at that moment, horrified to see the charred remains of Jack's livery. But it was the sight of Jack that broke her heart into pieces. Soot-blackened from head to toe, he bore the stance of a defeated man.

"What's the use?" Jack repeated. With a shake of his head, he wheeled and stalked toward the Tabard Inn.

Coralee lunged forward to catch up with Jack just as she felt the strong grip of a man's hand on her arm. She glanced up, startled to find that her brother Harlan was holding her at bay.

"Leave him be," Harlan warned. "The man needs some time to rest, time to collect his thoughts. He's too angry right now to listen to anyone." He released her arm, then turned to address the crowd. "Come on, men. We've got some work to do."

Jack stumbled into his room and ripped off his clothes, still reeling from the shock of watching the fiery blaze consume all of his dreams for the future. At the moment, he wanted nothing more than to escape from the horrors of this wretched place, to forget everything about the colony of Rugby.

He washed the soot from his skin and changed into a clean set of clothes, oblivious to the clatter outside the window. Then he left the room and worked his way down the stairs, hoping to steal a few moments to himself to sort out his chaotic thoughts.

He had just stepped onto the veranda of the inn when the sound of voices seized his attention. He glanced toward the livery and froze, amazed by what he saw.

At least a dozen men were clearing the charred remains of the fire from the site. A half dozen more were removing a load of freshly cut lumber from a wagon, and at least four men were sorting the lumber into piles. And moment by moment, more men were arriving on the scene.

Jack bolted across the grounds. "What's going on here?" he demanded.

Harlan picked up a plank from the wagon and grinned. "We've got to get you back in business, Winslow."

Daniel Yarby grabbed a handsaw from the bed of the wagon. "We need a livery, Jack."

"And we're not gonna let a little fire keep us from havin' it," Clell added, tossing a shovel of soot into a wheelbarrow.

The heaviness in Jack's heart suddenly lifted, replaced with an overwhelming sense of gratitude. With the support of men like these, how could he remain defeated?

He swept his gaze across the crowd, jolted by the sudden revelation that both Tennessee natives and British-born colonists were working together, side by side, to restore the livery. No man here considered himself better than another, he realized.

Everyone had banded together to lend a hand to one of their own.

A sense of pride surged through him. No matter if these men hailed from Tennessee or England, he felt privileged to belong to the group. And, amazingly, he felt a sense of pride for the colony of Rugby, the colony that had brought them together as one. "I never realized . . ."

At that moment, he felt the touch of a woman's hand along his arm. "We're gonna have your livery up and runnin' in no time, Jack," Coralee predicted with undisguised glee.

Jack peered down into Coralee's face and flashed a triumphant smile. "I know."

Chapter 18

Two weeks later, Coralee's heart swelled with joy as she wedged her way into the crowd of colonists and mountaineers who were admiring the newly restored livery. Jack stood in front of the building holding a hammer in one hand and a nail in the other.

"This is it, my friends," he announced to the throng. "It's the final nail."

As he drew back the hammer and drove the last nail into the wooden building, cheers and applause erupted from the crowd. Jack turned and faced the throng, his expression both startled and pleased. "I couldn't have possibly rebuilt all of this by myself," he insisted. "Congratulate yourselves on a job well done."

Clell nodded with approval as he raked his gaze over the structure. "I reckon Rugby has finally got itself a livery now."

"And just in time for the colony's opening ceremonies," Daniel added.

As the crowd broke apart, Coralee edged her

way toward the livery. Hoping to seize a moment alone with Jack, she paused at the corner of the building and waited as he finished his conversation with Daniel and Clell.

"I suspect you'll have more business than you can handle next week, Jack," Daniel said. "We're expecting dozens of visitors for the festivities. In fact, all of the rooms at the Tabard Inn have already been reserved for the week."

Jack set aside the hammer and frowned. "I hope I have enough stock and equipment to meet the demand."

Clell stroked his scraggly beard for a moment, as if he were contemplating a serious matter. "You know, I got me a pair of good workhorses I could loan you for a spell if you have the need for 'em. They're too old to make the trip down to Sedgemoor Station with me every day, but they've got a heap of strength left in 'em. I reckon they could give a nice, gentle ride to folks who might be wantin' to take a look-see at Rugby."

"That's generous of you, Clell." Jack grinned. "I'll certainly remember your offer if I need some extra horses next week."

"A pair of full-growed horses would be more useful to you than a little filly right now," Clell contended. "But seein' as how you might be needin' yourself some more stock in the by-and-by, I reckon I'll hold on to that filly of mine for a spell or two just in case you're interested in buyin' her later."

An expression of astonishment crossed Jack's

face. "What made you change your mind about selling her to me, Clell?"

"I've been watchin' you over the last few weeks, young fella, and I've taken a likin' to what I've seen. There ain't a man 'round these parts who's worked any harder than you have, gettin' this livery in shape for openin' day. Pert near as I can tell, you've been honest in your dealin's with folks, too. And I don't see no reason for refusin' to sell that little filly to you if you still got a hankerin' to buy her."

Jack extended his hand to the mountain man. "You've just sold yourself a filly, Clell."

After the two men sealed their agreement with a handshake, Clell and Daniel turned and walked away. Coralee picked up her skirts and headed toward Jack, grateful she could finally talk with him in private.

But she'd taken only two steps when Adam shuffled up to the livery and mumbled something to Jack in a low, quiet tone. Coralee paused again, waiting.

Though she couldn't hear this conversation, something about the hushed, strained timbre of Adam's voice warned her the discussion was a serious one. And there was something about Adam's demeanor that spoke volumes, as well. His shoulders were slumped, his gaze restless and uneasy. Several times during the exchange, he stared down at his outstretched hands with a pained expression on his face.

After a few moments, Jack reached out and

clapped Adam's shoulder, as if he were reassuring him about something. Adam nodded, then pivoted on his heel and walked away.

Jack was still standing there, his troubled gaze lingering on Adam, when Coralee stepped up beside him. "Are you givin' personal tours of your new livery today?"

He glanced down at her and grinned. "Only to one very special person."

As he swung open the wide double doors, Coralee reached out and grasped his arm. "I don't mean to be pokin' my nose into somethin' that's none of my concern, but I noticed Adam seemed upset about somethin' just now. If you feel like he's still needin' a friend to talk to, you don't have to show me the livery right now. I can wait until you and Adam have done some more talkin'."

"I believe Adam said all he needed to say." Jack sighed. "He told me the fire brought back a lot of painful memories for him, memories so vivid that the sight of the flames shooting up from the livery paralyzed him. While everyone else was pitching in and helping to put out the fire, he couldn't do anything but stand by and watch in horror."

"Poor Adam." Coralee's heart wrenched. "He must be feelin' something awful."

"I think the guilt has been eating away at him. He apologized profusely for not offering his help, and he wished me all the best for the future." Jack shook his head in dismay. "Oddly enough, I never even realized Adam wasn't among the men who were fighting the fire that night. The smoke was thick and blinding, and I scarcely noticed anything other than the flames. I didn't have the time to look around and figure out who was here and who wasn't."

"Somethin' mighty bad must have happened to Adam durin' another fire," Coralee guessed.

Jack nodded glumly. "Have you ever noticed that Adam wears gloves all the time?"

"Not really. Lots of men wear gloves, especially when they're workin' outdoors." Coralee paused. "But come to think of it, I've never seen Adam when he wasn't wearing gloves."

"That's because . . ." Jack winced. "One of his hands was terribly burned when he was trying to save his wife from a fire. Unfortunately, Adam's wife died in the blaze."

Coralee's hand flew to her mouth to stifle her gasp. "I can't imagine nothin' any worse. How awful that must have been for him."

"I suppose being so close to another fire stirred up lots of old memories that he was hoping to forget. And I suspect Adam doesn't care to discuss the matter any more for a while." Jack tugged at the doors of the livery. "So if you're ready for the grand tour of Rugby's largest, finest, and newest livery . . ."

"I'm ready." Coralee grinned. "You lead the way."

Jack hurled open the doors and Coralee stepped into the building. After one quick, appraising glance at the equipment and livestock, Coralee was amazed by all that Jack had accomplished in so

short a time. In the two weeks since the fire, he'd
fully stocked the livery with wagons, an assortment
of saddles and riding gear, a small carriage for two
people, and five horses that he'd acquired from the
local area.

"You should be very proud of yourself, Jack
Winslow." Coralee stretched up on her toes and
brushed her lips across his. "I know I'm proud of
what you've done. And I bet your family back in
England would be proud of you, too, if they could
see all this now."

His hands slipped around her waist. "It won't be
too much longer before they'll have the chance to
see the place for themselves. They should be arriving next week, a day or so before—"

"Your family is coming to . . . Rugby?" Coralee
leaned back in the circle of his arms and glanced
up at him in surprise.

"I thought you knew." Jack winced. "In the rush
to rebuild the livery over the last few weeks, I must
have forgotten to mention it to you."

"Well, I reckon I know now." She couldn't resist
reaching out and brushing her fingers through his
hair. "I'll be lookin' forward to meetin' your kinfolks when they get here."

"Everyone except my brother will be making the
trip," Jack explained. "Alexander will be staying
behind in England with his wife. She's expecting a
baby in a few months, and he thought they
shouldn't be venturing too far from home right
now."

"That's understandable," Coralee offered. "But

I'm sure you'll enjoy having your parents and sister here for a while."

A hint of a smile appeared on Jack's lips. "I suspect lots of surprises will be in store for them. Rugby, I'm certain, is unlike anything they've ever seen."

"And I reckon they're used to everyone actin' all proper-like, too." An uneasy feeling rolled through Coralee. "I sure hope I know what to say and how to act when I meet them."

"All you need to do is just be yourself, Coralee." He pulled her more tightly against him. "But if it will ease your mind, I can give you a quick course on the rules of etiquette."

"That would be nice, Jack." Coralee smiled. "And let's get movin' on it tonight. The sooner we get started, the better."

"I thought you weren't ever gonna get here!" Coralee opened the door and hastily ushered Jack into the cabin. "I've been waitin' all evenin' on you."

"It's only seven o'clock, Coralee." Jack slipped his hand around her waist. "We've got plenty of time to—"

"We don't have much time at all before your folks get here," she insisted. "And I got a heap of learnin' to do betwixt now and then."

Jack grinned, both amused by her impatience and gratified by her eagerness to please his family. "Then I suppose we'd better get started."

"But I'm not sure where to start," Coralee admitted with a worried frown. "All I know about actin' proper-like is that I'm supposed to hold out my pinky when I'm sippin' tea."

"Then maybe we should begin with table etiquette." Jack edged his way toward the cupboard. "I'm certain we'll be dining at the Tabard Inn's new restaurant with my family while they're here. From my understanding, the restaurant will have a distinctively British flair. I'll arrange a place setting on the table so you'll know which utensils to use during the meal."

He swiftly pulled an assortment of dishes and utensils from the cupboard. As he arranged each piece on the table, Coralee wrinkled her nose in disdain. "Why on earth are you puttin' out all those forks and knives and spoons?"

He bit back a smile. "Each utensil is used for a different purpose. You'll have a salad fork, a dinner fork, a butter knife, a teaspoon—"

"I don't understand, Jack." Coralee shook her head in dismay. "Why can't you just lick your fork clean after you eat your salad and then stab it into some taters on your dinner plate?"

Jack laughed. "Actually, I have no idea. Now that you mention it, it does seem rather senseless to have so many different utensils for one meal."

He stepped around the table and pulled her into his arms. "Coralee, I don't think you need any more etiquette lessons. You're absolutely charming, just the way you are."

His words failed to erase the furrows along her

brow. "But I want to act like a proper lady for your family," she insisted.

"You are a lady, Coralee Hayes." Desire simmered deep in his veins as he gazed down at her, and his smile faded away. "You're more of a lady than any woman I've ever known. . . ."

He bent his head and clamped his mouth over hers. Coralee had given him more pleasure than any other woman ever had, pleasure beyond his wildest dreams. But each time he'd claimed her as his own, his body and soul fulfilled, the driving need started all over again. It seemed as if he could never get enough of this woman, and he wanted her now more than ever.

He inched his hand up her back and under the fall of silky golden hair, gripping the back of her head with an open palm. Then he buried his face against her neck and shuddered. She smelled of fresh sweetness, natural and pure.

The sweet scent of her ignited a rush of desire within him. His mouth sought hers once more. As his tongue circled the moistness of her lips and plunged inside the sweet lushness of her mouth, his loins ached with need.

She clung to him, her hands stroking his shoulders, his back. He could feel her passion mounting, echoing the raw, throbbing ache that was pulsating through him. "God, Coralee . . ."

Coralee felt the wild, racing beat of his heart against her chest, heard the stark need in the tone of his voice. And she sensed the hungry touch of his hand as he reached between their bodies and tugged at the bodice of her gown.

"You don't know how badly I want you, Coralee," he rasped. "You don't know how much I want to be inside of you."

Coralee tried to speak, tried to tell him how much she wanted him, too, but words seemed unnecessary. She had no doubt he could see that her whole body was trembling, aching, with need as her dress slithered to the floor.

Jack swept her up into his arms and carried her to the bed. He shrugged out of his clothes, then eased down beside her. She glided her hands over his back, savoring the feel of him. The very touch of him intoxicated her, tantalized her, seduced her.

She writhed beneath him as he fondled her breasts and seared her skin with burning kisses. "I can't wait much longer, Jack," she choked out.

"You don't have to wait," he rasped, thrusting into her. "Come with me, Coralee. Come with me. . . ."

Unbearable pleasure spiraled through her, shaking her to the core of her being. She shuddered, clinging to him as he spilled his seed inside her and cried out her name.

Hours later, Coralee stole a glimpse of Jack as he slept beside her. She wished he would say something—anything—about his feelings for her. Never once had he mentioned anything of love or marriage or the future.

Yet, since his return from Cincinnati, something had been different about Jack. He'd seemed genuinely eager to spend time with her, to share the joys and disappointments of each new day. Things had been so good between them that Coralee was reluctant to spoil what they had with worries about his lack of commitment to her.

But the anticipation of the upcoming visit from his family only intensified Coralee's worries. Would his parents be pleased to know that he'd taken a liking to a mountain woman?

She closed her eyes, uncertain if she truly wanted an answer to her question.

A sense of frenzied anticipation prevailed in Rugby throughout the following week. Paul Proffitt's construction crew worked at a frantic pace to complete several building projects in time for opening day, while colonists pitched in to help Daniel with final preparations for the opening ceremonies.

By the end of the week, Jack was amazed by the amount of progress that had been made. As he stood in the heart of the settlement and swept his gaze over the new buildings, he smiled with satisfaction. Somewhere along the way of learning to live in the mountain wilderness, he'd developed a fondness for the place, he realized.

He sauntered over to the laundry shack, his heart skipping a beat when Coralee glanced up and smiled. "Tomorrow is the big day," she said. "Are you gettin' excited about seein' your family?"

Jack smiled. "Actually, my family is arriving today. I'm meeting them at Sedgemoor Station this

afternoon. Would you like to go with me and welcome them to Rugby?"

"I wish I could, Jack." Coralee motioned to the
mounds of clothes waiting to be pressed. "But
everyone wants their fancy clothes starched and
pressed for the big ceremony in the mornin'."

"I understand. But I can't deny that I'm disappointed."

She offered a smile. "Me, too."

"I'll see you tomorrow, then. You'll meet me at
the ceremonies?"

She nodded. "Just be lookin' for a woman wearing a blue dress that you bought for her in Cincinnati."

Jack laughed. "I'm sure I won't have any problems finding her."

Coralee maintained a bright smile on her lips as
Jack turned to leave, hoping her outward appearance masked the anxieties that were gripping her
heart.

The misty haze hovering over the scalloped
mountaintops was vanishing beneath the bright
rays of the sun just as Coralee arrived in the settlement for the opening ceremonies the next morning.

Though she had been aware that many people
were interested in the official opening of the colony,
she wasn't prepared for the size of the crowd milling about the place. It almost seemed as if the entire
world had arrived in Rugby overnight. Even her
own family had turned out for the celebration, she

noticed, catching sight of Rachel and Maggie with Granny Clabo.

She walked across the lawn of the Tabard Inn to join them. Just as she stepped up beside the women, Maggie pointed toward a well-dressed gentleman with a gray beard who was standing a few feet away. "I heard tell that man over yonder is the mayor of Chattanooga," she whispered.

Rachel nodded toward another gentleman, who was wearing a clerical collar. "And someone told me that man is the Episcopal bishop of Tennessee."

"I never seen the like of so many folks," Granny Clabo added. "Some of them musta been travelin' for days and days to get here."

Coralee nervously fingered the collar of her dress as she strained to catch sight of Jack and his family in the crowd. "Jack's family has traveled all the way from England to be here today," she mumbled.

Granny Clabo narrowed her eyes. "So that's why you're twitchin' at your collar."

Coralee sighed. "I can't help it, Granny. I feel like I got a bushel of butterflies flutterin' around in my stomach."

"Well, you just let loose of them butterflies," Granny advised. "You don't have no reason to be frettin' about meetin' Jack's kinfolks. You're a Clabo woman, aren't you?"

Coralee managed a weak smile. "I suppose so."

"Just because your birth name was Bohanan and your married name was Hayes don't mean you're not a Clabo," Granny admonished. "You got Clabo blood runnin' through your veins, child. And I don't want to see any Clabo woman actin' like she's ashamed of who she is."

"I'm not ashamed of who I am, Granny," Coralee hastily denied. "I just want Jack's folks to like me. And I want things to work out for Jack and me."

"Things will work out the way the good Lord intended, child, just as long as you don't mess up His plans."

The comforting touch of Granny's weathered hand around her own soothed Coralee's frazzled nerves. "Thanks, Granny. I needed to hear that."

At that moment, she heard the sound of a familiar voice behind her. "There you are, Coralee."

She whirled, her heartbeat quickening as she turned to face Jack. He looked gloriously handsome, she thought.

His eyes brightened as their gazes met and locked. "There are some people here I'd like you to meet." He extended his arm to Coralee as he flashed a winsome smile in Granny Clabo's direction. "I hope you don't mind me stealing your granddaughter for the day, Mrs. Clabo."

"You go right ahead, Jack." Granny chuckled. "Somethin' tells me she's in good hands."

Jack guided Coralee through the crowd and led her toward the rows of planked seats that had been set up for the ceremonies. Already dozens of people were assembled in the seating area, waiting for the ceremonies to begin.

He motioned toward an older couple seated beside an attractive young lady. "I thought you might ike to sit with my family," he explained just as the swell of music filled the air.

Coralee stole a glance at the band of musicians beside the podium. "I didn't realize we were gonna have music today, too."

"I think that means the ceremonies are about to begin." Jack winced. "I'm afraid the introductions will have to wait until the end of the program, Coralee."

"We've got plenty of time for me to meet your folks," she assured him, secretly breathing a sigh of relief. The temporary delay would give her a chance to gain her composure, she thought.

They had just slipped into their seats next to Jack's family when the Episcopal bishop approached the podium and offered an opening prayer. As the crowd reverently bowed their heads, Coralee seized the opportunity to steal a glimpse of the Winslow family, unnoticed.

With one glance at the Duke of Havenshire, Coralee immediately knew the man was Jack's father. The two men bore a striking resemblance to each other, possessing many of the same features.

She shifted her gaze to the Duchess of Havenshire, an exquisitely beautiful woman in a stunning violet gown. The Queen of England couldn't possibly possess any more elegance than Jack's mother, she thought. There was a regal air, a sense of refinement and grace, about the woman.

And then there was Sabrina. Coralee drank in the sight of the young woman's stylish dress and the sweep of dark hair that was swirled into fashionable mounds over her head. She was still perusing Sabrina's delicate features when the bishop closed the prayer with a thundering "Amen."

Not wanting to be caught gawking at Jack's family, Coralee hastily shifted her gaze to the podium. For the next hour, she listened attentively as several speakers expounded on the multitude of opportunities that Rugby would provide for the sons of England. After the ceremony concluded with the singing of "God Save the Queen," Jack reached over and grasped her hand. "Now I can introduce you to my family," he said.

Coralee inhaled a deep, steadying breath as she rose to greet the Winslows.

"I'd like you to meet someone who has become very special to me in recent months," Jack explained to his family. After making the round of introductions, he added, "Coralee has helped me through the many adjustments of learning to live in Rugby."

"I'm mighty glad to finally be meetin' y'all," Coralee offered. "Jack has told me a heap of things about you."

"Jack?" Sabrina echoed in bewilderment.

"Everybody 'round these parts knows him as Jack." Coralee laughed. "I plumb forgot his real name is Lord John! But I like 'Jack' a heap better. Until all these Englishmen got here, I never heard tell of nobody who uses 'Lord' for a name—unless it was the Lord God Almighty, of course."

A stunned silence swept through the group. The duchess paled. Sabrina looked as if she were gagging on a bad piece of meat. One corner of the duke's mouth twitched with amusement, and his face turned crimson, as if he were strangling on a suppressed gale of laughter.

"I do believe I'm feeling rather faint, Edward." The duchess placed an unsteady hand on her husband's arm.

"I'm not feeling well myself." Sabrina placed the back of her hand along her forehead and gave a helpless sigh.

"Perhaps we should return to the inn so both of you can sit down and rest before the reception gets under way," the duke suggested.

"I think that would be wise." The duchess gave a faint nod in Jack's direction. "Pardon us, dear."

As the threesome turned and walked away, a sinking feeling suffused Coralee. "Was it my imagination, or did they seem like they were in a hurry to end the conversation?"

Coralee thought she detected a flash of anger glinting from Jack's eyes just before he lifted one shoulder in a careless shrug. "They still haven't recovered from their long journey, I suppose. Perhaps they'll feel more like talking after they've had the chance to rest."

Though she accepted the explanation without argument, Coralee sensed that Jack was troubled by his family's unwillingness to continue the discussion. "Maybe we should be moseyin' on over to the inn now."

Jack nodded absently, as if he were lost in his thoughts. Coralee fell into step beside him as they headed in the direction of the Tabard Inn. They had just stepped onto the front lawn when Coralee caught sight of Granny Clabo. "I'll catch up with you in a moment, Jack. I want to talk to Granny Clabo for a moment."

"I'll meet you inside, then," he agreed.

As Jack turned and walked away, Coralee picked up her skirts and approached her grandmother. "I met Jack's folks, Granny." She sighed. "And they took off like a bunch of scared jackrabbits as soon as I opened my mouth."

"They may not be used to mountain talk, child," Granny reminded her. "They'll warm up to you in a spell just as long as you give 'em another chance to get to know you."

"I hope so. Are you comin' to the reception at the inn?"

Granny shook her head. "No, child. I've had enough festivities for one day. You run along and have yourself a good time."

"See you tomorrow, then," Coralee said, turning to cross the lawn.

She was threading her way through the crowd of guests on the veranda, heading for the front door of the inn, when she noticed that Jack was standing a few feet away, deep in conversation with his family. Not wanting to intrude, Coralee paused to wait for an appropriate moment to approach them. She came to a halt beside the door, unable to keep herself from listening to the conversation between Jack and the Winslows.

"I can't imagine how you've survived without

your taverns and gaming halls, John," Sabrina was saying. "What do you do for entertainment here?"

Jack smiled. "We manage rather nicely. Life in Rugby is not as dreary and boring as it may appear."

"Apparently, your brother hasn't had a great deal of time for indulging in idle pastimes of late, Sabrina." The duke turned to his son. "I'm impressed with your business endeavors, John. I'm not certain I could have done as well myself under the circumstances. But it appears as if your livery business—and your breeding stock—will provide you with a handsome source of income in the future."

"Everything has been working out quite nicely," Jack agreed, "and I have every intention of expanding my breeding stock soon. Still, I'm glad to hear that you approve of what I've done so far."

"You look healthy and strong, too. I do believe Rugby is agreeing with you, dear," the duchess remarked. "But I would like to hear more about this mountain woman who seems to have intrigued you—the woman we met at the conclusion of the ceremonies."

Sabrina rolled her eyes heavenward. "Surely she was just a touch of local color to amuse us."

"I do hope Sabrina is right, dear," the duchess continued on. "I would hate to think you've developed a fondness for this mountain woman."

A heated flush rose to Jack's face, and the line of his jaw hardened. Observing his reaction, Coralee felt a knot coil in the pit of her stomach. *He was embarrassed . . . ashamed . . . of her.*

The duchess's voice drifted across the veranda. "It's obvious she's hardly the type of woman who is suitable for a man of your—"

"But you've only just met her!" Jack countered. "How can you disapprove of her so quickly? How do you know what kind of woman she is?"

"I can tell by looking at her. She may be wearing a nice gown, but her clothing can't disguise that atrocious mountain twang of hers. For a gentleman with your education and background, you deserve someone with . . ." She paused, obviously struggling to find the words to express her thoughts in a tactful manner. "Someone with more refinement," she finished.

A sickening feeling rolled through Coralee. She leaned against the door, feeling as if she might become physically ill.

All along, she'd convinced herself that the depths of her love for Jack were strong enough to withstand any obstacles that might come her way. But how could she hope to compete against the traditions of a family, the customs of an entire country?

She wanted Jack to be proud of her for who she was. She didn't want him to be embarrassed by what she wasn't. And she couldn't be something other than herself. She could never hope to meet his family's standards. She was a mountain woman, a widow who could barely read. She wasn't part of their world. And she could never hope to be.

An ache swelled within her, an ache more painful than anything she'd ever known. Their two worlds had just collided, she realized. And the force of the impact had crushed all of Coralee's hopes for a future with Jack.

Not wanting to cause him any further embarrassment, Coralee blinked back the moisture from her eyes and whirled to leave. But she'd taken only one step across the veranda when she heard Jack call out to her.

"Don't leave, Coralee." In the next instant, he was beside her, his hand grasping and tugging at hers, his eyes troubled and pleading. "I have something to say to my family that I want you to hear."

"I don't think I need to hear anything more." Coralee's voice trembled. "I can see I've embarrassed you just by being here."

He grasped her arm and peered down into her face with so much emotion glistening from his eyes that Coralee's breath snagged in her throat. "You haven't embarrassed me at all, Coralee. It's my family—and the way they've treated you—that's the cause of my shame."

A flash of understanding gripped her. Anger—not shame—had provoked the heated flush in his face and the tight grip of his jaw. A ray of hope flickered in her heart. "I'll stay, Jack. I'll listen to what you have to say."

As Coralee stepped up beside the Winslows, she was acutely aware of Sabrina's disapproving glare and the duchess's pale face. And she was mindful that the duke's lips were still twitching as if he was rather amused by the entire matter.

"I do hope you realize that any association with your new friend would be highly inappropriate at a social function of this magnitude in England," Sabrina announced to her brother, completely disregarding Coralee's presence.

"We're not in England, Sabrina," Jack snapped. "We're in America. Life is different—much different—here."

"How well I can see that," Sabrina countered. "Obviously, titled gentlemen spend a great deal of time consorting with a lesser class of people."

"Titles—and wealth—have no meaning here." Jack's voice was strong and clear. "No one's worth is measured by the order of their birth or the amount of their land holdings. Do you know how to measure the value of a person's worth, Sabrina?"

Without waiting for a reply, Jack continued on. "You say you're going to do something—and you don't back away. You do what's right, and you're honest about what you do. You devote yourself to your family, and you're willing to lend a hand to a neighbor in distress—no matter where that person comes from or who he might be."

He sucked in a deep, shuddering breath. "The people here—especially Coralee and her family—have shown me the joys of living in a place where every man is equal. And I won't stand for anyone—especially a member of my own family—belittling her. She's been denied opportunities in life that most of us take for granted, but she's found the strength to rise above her lot in life. This woman might not be schooled in social graces or the art of English etiquette, but she knows about things you could never learn from a book. And she might not have a fancy title in front of her name, but Coralee Hayes is more of a lady than any titled aristocrat I've ever known in England."

Jack's eloquent defense of her character and her heritage overwhelmed Coralee with emotion. Teary-eyed and trembling, she reached out and squeezed his hand.

Jack's grip tightened around her fingers. "I do hope—for all of our sakes—that we can come to terms with this matter before you return to Havenshire Manor. I've voiced my viewpoint, and I hope you can accept it. Perhaps you'll be more receptive when Coralee and I join you for dinner this evening. But for the moment, you'll have to pardon me. I have a private matter to discuss with Coralee."

Chapter 19

A s Jack escorted Coralee onto the lawn of the Tabard Inn and through the settlement, she had no idea where he was taking her. But she couldn't have asked him where they were going even if she'd wanted to. Her throat was so clogged with emotion that she couldn't utter a sound.

A few moments later, they were ambling over a mountain trail that led to a scenic overlook. When the majestic view came into sight, Jack tugged at Coralee's hand. "Let's sit down over here and enjoy the view," he insisted, guiding her over to a smooth boulder that jutted from the mountain slope.

As soon as they were seated on the boulder, Jack draped an arm around Coralee's shoulders. His muscles were rigid with tension, she noticed, and the line of his jaw was hard and taut.

She remained silent, waiting for the aftermath of his fury to subside, hoping the glorious scenery of the mountains would ease the pain in his soul. After a long moment, he broke the silence between them with a troubled sigh.

"I've been determined to win at the game of making a success of my life in this place," he began, his voice strained and low. "And the prize for my success would be a triumphant return to England as a wealthy man in my own right. I wanted the British aristocracy to see that I had proven my own worth." His laugh was bitter and harsh. "Even today, I was anxious to prove my worth to my own father, to show him the livery and the breeding stock, to make him see that I wasn't an irresponsible rogue."

"There's nothing wrong with wanting your father's approval or acceptance, Jack," Coralee pointed out. "Besides, he seems extremely proud of you."

"I can't deny that I'm pleased with his praise over my endeavors," Jack admitted. "But all my efforts to prove my value and worth aren't necessary anymore. And I didn't even realize it until I heard myself telling my family that everyone is equal here, that the only measure of a man's worth lies in the value of his word."

"I know it hasn't been easy for you to come to terms with the ways of a new land, Jack." A lump rose in her throat. "But I think you've done a remarkable job."

"But something else happened when I told my family about the equality of people here in America, Coralee. As soon as I voiced the thought, I realized I don't belong in England anymore. And you well know, all along, I've said I intended to return to England as soon as I make my fortune here."

"You've always made it clear that you never intended to stay here in Rugby forever," Coralee agreed.

"But I don't have any desire to resume my old life in England now. I'm not Lord John Winslow any longer. I'm Jack Winslow, a man with a new life, a new homeland."

"A new . . . homeland?" she echoed. "Does this mean you're planning to stay in Rugby?"

The hint of a smile played on his lips. "That all depends on you, Coralee."

"On . . . me?" She blinked in confusion.

He reached out and traced the outline of her lips with the tip of his finger. "I can't continue to live in Rugby unless you marry me, Coralee. I can't spend the rest of my life here without you by my side. I love you, Coralee Hayes. I love you more than I ever realized I could love anyone. And I want you to be my bride. Will you marry me?"

Joy surged in her heart. "I've been wantin' you to ask me that question for a coon's age, Jack. There's nothin' I want more in this whole, entire world than to be your bride." She hurled her arms around his neck and kissed him thoroughly, unable to contain the exhilarating bliss within her. "I've been lovin' you since the day I dunked you in the laundry tub, and I'll be lovin' you till the day I die."

He chuckled. "So you wouldn't have any objections to getting married soon?"

"I'm ready to marry you anytime you want."

"Good." He pushed back a strand of golden hair

from her forehead. "Then I'd like for us to wed before my family returns to England."

She edged back, surprised. "But your family won't be likin' this at all, Jack."

"They'll come to their senses," he predicted, his tone confident and strong. "At the moment, they're still trying to absorb the shock of the differences between our cultures. But I have no doubts they'll accept our marriage, Coralee. They've always encouraged me to take a bride for myself."

A shadow of concern crossed her face. "But they want you to have an English bride, Jack. They don't want you to have a mountain bride."

"When they see how happy I am now that you've agreed to marry me, I'm sure they won't have any objections. And once they get to know you, how could they not love you? There's so much about you to love." His hands drifted across her abdomen. "I do hope you want to have a family of our own. I'd like for us to get started on a family right away."

"A family? Why, if I get in the family way, I won't be havin' no more monthlies." A dreamy expression crossed her face. "No more monthlies. . . ."

"I'd like to tell my family about our wedding plans over dinner this evening." Jack held tightly to Coralee's hand as they headed back to the Tabard Inn. "They haven't had the chance to see anything other than the livery, and I'm anxious to show the rest of the colony to them today. And once they've toured the settlement and spent some time with us, I'm certain they'll be much more receptive to the idea of our marriage."

A twinge of apprehension sliced through Coralee. "I wish I could share your confidence, Jack," she admitted uneasily. "But I don't rightly know how we can change their opinions about me in one day."

"Something tells me that we don't have to do anything." Jack grinned. "I noticed my father wasn't voicing any objections to anything this morning. In fact, he seemed rather amused at times. And if I know the Duke of Havenshire, I suspect he has already advised my mother and sister that they've been much too hasty in rendering judgment on you."

Jack's optimistic remarks boosted Coralee's spirits. And when they reached the Tabard Inn, she was astonished by the changes that had transpired in the duchess and her daughter. As Coralee stepped up to join them, they acknowledged her presence with cordial nods. Though both women maintained an air of guarded reserve about them, their caustic attitude had disappeared, it seemed.

Perhaps Jack was right, Coralee thought as she accompanied the Winslow family on their tour of Rugby. Perhaps the duke had persuaded his wife and Sabrina to take a second look at the colony— and at Coralee—before voicing any more opinions.

As the day progressed, Coralee noticed that the two women seemed increasingly interested in Jack's new homeland. With each passing hour, they

asked more and more questions about the colony
and the surrounding mountains. By the time they
returned to the Tabard Inn for dinner, Coralee was
hopeful that they might accept her forthcoming
marriage to Jack without objection.

As soon as they were seated in the restaurant,
Jack offered a warm smile to his family. "I hope
you liked what you saw today," he began. "And I
hope you have a better understanding of why I've
grown to love this place."

The duchess placed a napkin in her lap. "I must
admit that I never realized how different life could
be outside of England . . . until now." A hint of admiration sparkled from her eyes as she glanced
over at Coralee. "I don't know of many women
who would have the courage and strength to survive by themselves in a place like this."

"All my friends back home in England don't
have to worry about anything other than planning
their new wardrobes each season," Sabrina admitted uneasily. "None of us contends with the worries that you have here, Coralee."

The duke gazed fondly at his son. "I suspect
you've learned more about life since you've lived
in Rugby than you ever learned at Cambridge. I
know I've certainly come to a better understanding
of the differences between our cultures today. I had
no idea that all of the colonists and mountaineers
worked together to rebuild your livery after the
fire. But that willingness and spirit of cooperation
tell me a lot about the people here—and prove your

point that no man should consider himself better than another."

"But your son is the most remarkable man 'round these parts," Coralee offered. Her heart swelled with joy as she glanced over at Jack. "He's got more determination and courage than any man I've ever known. And he's the finest man I've ever met in my whole, entire life."

Jack beamed as he turned to his family. "Coralee has agreed to become my wife. And we'd like to wed before you return to England."

"I know I'm not perzactly what you had in mind for a daughter-in-law," Coralee said. "I haven't had much schoolin', and I don't know about all the proper ways of sayin' and doin' things like a real English lady would. But I'm gonna spend the rest of my life tryin' to make your son happy, Mr. Duke and Mrs. Duchess. I don't have much to offer, but I'm gonna give him everything I got. I'm gonna love him like he's never been loved before. And I'm gonna keep on lovin' him with all my heart and soul for the rest of my life."

The duke nodded his approval. "Something tells me you know what's important in life, dear. I don't know that my son could have chosen a finer lady in all the world to be his bride."

Tears of joy swelled in the duchess's eyes. "My son is a fortunate man to have the love of a lady like you, my dear," she said, grasping Coralee's hand in acceptance.

Sabrina gave a wistful sigh as she focused her gaze on Coralee and Jack. "I never realized just

how important love could be until now. I've just
been wanting to marry a man who could give me
a title and a place in society."

"Marry for love, Sabrina," Jack advised, never
once removing his gaze from Coralee's smiling
face. "Don't settle for anything less."

Coralee's smile broadened. "It'll make you happier than a pig in a pen full of slop," she insisted.
"Believe me, I know."

Two days later, showers of rice rained over the
newlyweds as they emerged from the simple white
church nestled in the Cumberland Plateau.

Coralee beamed as she drank in the sight of the
colonists and mountaineers who had attended the
wedding. "Looks like a heap of folks are wishin'
us well."

Jack slipped a hand around his wife's slender
waist and grinned. "Half of these people are our
relatives, Coralee."

Coralee swept her gaze across the crowd, pleased
to see the smiling faces of the people she loved . . .
Granny Clabo, Rachel, Maggie . . . and the Winslows.

At that moment, Adam emerged from the
throng. "Glad to see you've finally come to your
senses and married this woman, Winslow."

Grant stepped up beside the couple and smiled.
"And it's about time the two of you observed an
old English wedding tradition. Back in England,
the bride and groom always seal their vows of love
and commitment with a wedding kiss."

Coralee peered up at Jack and smiled. "That's a tradition here, too."

Love glowed from Jack's eyes as he pulled his wife into his arms. "Then we'll celebrate our traditions together . . . for a lifetime or two."

Epilogue

~~~⌒◯◯⌒~~~

May 1881

Jack stood on the deck of the steamer, one arm draped around Coralee's narrow shoulders. Cool Atlantic breezes whipped across his face as the vessel steamed toward Philadelphia.

"We're almost home now, Coralee," he mused. "In another day or two, we'll be back in Rugby."

She peered up at him, her face awash with radiance and joy. "I can't wait to be tellin' Granny all about our trip to England. She'll be havin' conniption fits when she hears about everything we saw and did!"

"I'd wager your granny will be ecstatic about all the presents you bought for her, as well."

"And she won't believe how many new dresses I got for myself," Coralee added. "You know, Sabrina and I got along real well when we were shoppin' together. In fact, I'm thinkin' we could become really good friends. She promised to be writin' me from time to time, you know. And I promised I'd write her back, seein' as how I can read and write so much better now since you got me those primers in Cincinnati."

Jack tightened his hold around his wife, his heart swelling with more pride and love than he'd ever dreamed possible.

Introducing Coralee to the sights and sounds of England, he'd never enjoyed himself more. But, oddly enough, the visit had given him a new appreciation for his adopted country and the life he'd established in Rugby with his mountain bride.

Jack had been astounded when he'd found himself longing for a glimpse of the mist hovering over the mountains of the Cumberland Plateau. And more than once, he found himself yearning to breathe the scent of pine that constantly lingered over the forested trails.

At that moment, the steamer lurched against the force of a crashing wave. Coralee paled, leaning against Jack and clutching the railing for support.

Alarm raced through Jack. "Perhaps we should find the ship's doctor, Coralee. If you're getting sick—"

"I'm just feelin' a little dizzy, that's all." A smile curled on her lips. "I'm not hurtin', and I don't need no corn likker to take away the pain."

Jack breathed a sigh of relief. "That's good to hear."

She snuggled closer to him. "In fact, I reckon I won't be needin' any more corn likker for quite a while, seein' as how I won't be havin' no more monthlies for a spell."

Jack's brows rose in surprise. "No more ... monthlies?"

"Not for six or seven more months, I'm figurin'."

Jack's heart thundered in his chest. "A ... baby?" he choked out.

Coralee nodded. "We're gonna have a heap of news for everybody when we get back to Rugby."

Jack swept his mouth down to hers, overwhelmed by the depths of his love for his mountain bride and the bright promises of their future together.

Author's Note

Dear Readers,

Coralee Hayes, Jack Winslow, and the rest of the characters in *Mountain Bride* are purely figments of my imagination—but the setting for this book is based on historical fact.

The colony of Rugby, Tennessee, opened in 1880 to provide the younger sons of English aristocrats with the opportunity to pursue their dreams in the New World—without fear of having to engage in trades or skills that might bring embarrassment to their families in England. Under British law, English aristocrats bequeathed family fortunes to their eldest sons, leaving "second sons" with no rightful claim to an inheritance.

Creating an outlet for the talents and skills of England's second sons became the mission of Thomas Hughes, a member of the British Parliament and the noted author of *Tom Brown's School Days*. Determined to develop a society for these young men based on wholesome living and the pursuit of hap-

piness—without the British stigmas of social caste—
Hughes located a tract of land in Morgan County,
Tennessee, for his "New Jerusalem." By 1879, in-
vestors had been secured, capital raised, and a col-
onization company, the Board of Aid to Land
Ownership, had been formed.

Second sons who arrived in Tennessee before the
official opening of the settlement in October 1880
encountered many of the problems faced by the fictional Jack Winslow. Delays in obtaining clear titles
to land tracts in the colony, for example, led a
group of bored colonists to create a lawn tennis
court and a bridle path along the banks of the Clear
Fork.

Rugby's Tabard Inn, the namesake of the hostelry
in Chaucer's *Canterbury Tales*, provided accommodations for numerous guests who visited the colony. Frequent reports about Rugby appeared in
British newspapers, luring both guests and new
residents to the settlement.

By 1884, Rugby's population was comprised of
more than four hundred residents. Not all Rugbi-
ans were Englishmen, however. Some native east
Tennessee mountaineers resided in the colony,
along with several British families and New England transplants.

Though an outbreak of typhoid and a lack of sufficient management skills contributed to the demise
of the colony in 1887, many of the colonists remained in the region, establishing permanent
homes in the Cumberland Plateau.

Today, reminders of the noble venture still exist

in Rugby, including numerous English cottages built by original colonists and a public library that holds more than seven thousand original volumes of Victorian literature.

For the purposes of storytelling, I've embellished and expanded my research findings to create a fictional glimpse of life in Rugby before the official opening of the British colony in 1880. The mountain vernacular, however, required little research on my part. As a sixth-generation Tennessean, I've long been acquainted with many of the quaint sayings scattered throughout the pages of *Mountain Bride* . . . and I hope you've enjoyed every word.

Susan Sawyer

Avon Romances—
the best in exceptional authors
and unforgettable novels!